She was the prettiest thing he'd ever seen . . .

He had to make a conscious effort to breathe. His stomach felt as if it had a pack of weevils skittering inside.

He knelt beside her, his eyes intent upon the oval face of delicate ivory, the full blush-colored lips, the well-formed cheekbones, and the hair the color of sunlit honey. Corby tenderly brushed a few strands of hair away from the woman's dust-streaked face, his touch lingering for a moment on her scratched cheek. Why on earth did his fingertips feel so tingly? And why did he have the uncontrollable urge to taste those sweet-looking lips? Without warning, the woman's eyelids fluttered open, revealing eyes like two pieces of shimmering jade, so large, so deep, so divine . . .

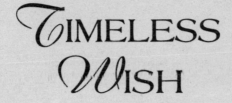

TIMELESS WISH

Barbara Sheridan

JOVE BOOKS, NEW YORK

TIME PASSAGES is a registered trademark
of Berkley Publishing Corporation.

TIMELESS WISH

A Jove Book / published by arrangement with
the author

PRINTING HISTORY
Jove edition / April 1999

The Penguin Putnam Inc. World Wide Web site address is
http://www.penguinputnam.com

ISBN: 0-515-12499-0

A JOVE BOOK®
Jove Books are published by The Berkley Publishing Group,
a member of Penguin Putnam Inc.,
375 Hudson Street, New York, New York 10014.
JOVE and the "J" design
are trademarks belonging to Jove Publications, Inc.

PRINTED IN THE UNITED STATES OF AMERICA

10 9 8 7 6 5 4 3 2 1

Heartfelt thanks to:

My editor, Jessica Faust, and my agent, Linda Kruger, for giving me a chance

Billy Wirth for inspiring the "God-awful" Hillhouse grin

Cheryl and Lenore of The Old Book Barn, and Gaye, Rosalie, Lisa, and the rest of my OIRW friends for assorted encouragement and helpful hints

The WHR gang for the virtual finger-crossing and best wishes

Rose and Rachel for being my friends for more years than I want to admit to

Bob, Butch, Dory, Bob Jr., Bruce, and Kim of the Renaissance Group

My family: Anthony, Jessica, and Victoria, for the laughter and the tears

And finally, to my friend, David Niall Wilson, Writer Extraordinaire, Master of Dark Domains . . .

Prologue

INDIAN TERRITORY
NEW YEAR'S EVE
1898

STARING OFF INTO the inky darkness, Sheriff Corby Hillhouse did not hear the door open behind him. When his cousin Jason touched his arm, he jumped.

"C'mon back inside, Corby. It's awfully cold and Star is worried about you being so downhearted tonight."

Corby flashed a false, casual smile, something he'd been doing for years. "I'm fine, Jace. It felt a bit close in there with all the people." *All the couples,* his lonely heart corrected. "You go back in. It's almost midnight, and if Star doesn't get a New Year's kiss from you, she'll whip out that Bowie she carries for protection and skin us both alive."

Jason laughed before giving his widowed cousin a sympathetic pat on the back. "My brother-in-law was just saying if you make a wish on the brightest star as the clock strikes midnight that wish will come true."

"Is that so?" Corby asked skeptically, his faith in wishes destroyed long ago.

Jason shrugged his broad shoulders. "That's what Trevor said, but who knows?"

Corby answered with a sly grin, glad to see he wasn't the only one not fond of the arrogant surgeon.

The voice of Jason's wife drifted through the partially open door behind them. "Has anyone seen my wayward husband?"

"You'd best get back inside," Corby said.

Jason put his hand on his cousin's shoulder. "Happy New Year, Corby."

"Same to you, Jace," Corby replied softly, knowing full well that the coming year might be every bit as miserable as the one just ending.

Heaving a weary sigh, Corby brushed the dusting of snow off the porch railing and leaned back, resting against the support column he'd helped his cousin cut from the surrounding stand of trees. That was how long ago now—close to six years?

Corby rolled a cigarette while trying to banish the twinge of jealousy that he invariably felt when he thought of Jason and Star's happy marriage. But, hell, they deserved it. He was glad his cousin wasn't cursed as he was.

The sound of the party guests inside counting down the final seconds of 1898 diverted Corby's attention. The tall case clock near the front door began to chime. Impulsively, Corby let his dark eyes search the sky for the brightest star and made a wish he felt would never be granted.

Please send me a woman my love won't kill . . .

Chapter 1

LAURA BENNETT CLICKED off the television, silencing the irritating, upbeat voice of Dick Clark and his fellow merrymakers. She was in no hurry to greet the new year.

Ignoring the tumbling stack of unopened mail and small packages on the coffee table in front of her, she got up from the antique sofa and went to the ebony mantel to stare at the two framed photographs that had been her sole companions for more than a month. On the left was a smiling, toothless baby; on the right, a dapper silver-haired man. Losing custody of Candace to the teenage mother who had abandoned her at birth had devastated Laura, but at least she'd had Grandpa Alex to lean on. Now, with him gone, she had no one to fill the void.

Her closest—and only—friend was far away and busy with her own life. The interior design business that Laura had been building since pulling off of the self-destructive fast lane four years ago wasn't enough to keep her happy anymore.

Laura touched the photographs with trembling fingers. "I miss you," she whispered.

Not wanting to cry again, she turned away and walked to the recessed bookcase, seeking solace in the only thing she had left, the collection of historical romances that she'd treasured since her college days. She took them out one by one, remembering the plots and characters as she studied the colorful covers. Why couldn't real life be like this? Why couldn't *she* find love and happiness in the strong arms of a tall, dark, handsome cowboy?

You almost did, Laura's heart reminded her.

"Almost," Laura said flatly, picturing herself on the cover of the paperback in her hand. She tried to imagine what the cover blurb on the story of her life would say.

He was the man of her dreams until he found the man of his own dreams . . .

Being dumped by Jake Hillhouse had crushed her, but it wasn't his fault. He'd told her at the start of the relationship that it was an experiment, that he needed to sort out who he really was.

With a sigh, Laura slid the book back into place. Not even reading would comfort her tonight. She drifted through the spacious condo, searching for something to occupy her time.

In the kitchen she found a bottle of champagne given to her by a client.

Think it over, Laurie, Grandpa Alex lectured from inside her head. *You haven't had a drink in years. You don't want one now.*

Laura studied the bottle, her fingers poised to remove the foil over the cork. She didn't want to step back on that road, but she didn't want to deal with this grief, either. Finally she set the bottle aside and picked up the TV remote control. Surely there was something other than Dick Clark on. She zapped past the New Year's Eve specials and anything with happy couples, settling on a lengthy commercial extolling the virtues of various cable services.

A wry smile lifted the corners of Laura's mouth when the Disney Channel began its pitch. "I'll do that. I'll wish upon a star and everything will be better—right?" She tilted her head back to peer through the kitchen skylight. If only it were that simple. If only wishes could come true.

Grabbing the champagne bottle, Laura tore off the foil and popped the cork. She tipped the bottle toward the television. "Hey, Jiminy, wish on this!"

Laura's gaze fell upon Grandpa Alex's red-checked chef's hat on the counter, exactly where he'd left it three hours before his death. She lowered the champagne bottle. She couldn't disgrace his memory by falling off the wagon. He'd spent too many long nights helping her stay sober. She dumped the contents of the bottle down the drain, then went to her room.

After undressing and climbing into bed, Laura glanced out the window to her left. "I'm wishing away, Jiminy, old boy, so don't fail me now. When I wake up, I expect to find a happy new life on the other side of that bedroom door."

Chapter 2

THE SOUND OF a child crying filtered into Laura's sleep-blanketed mind shortly before seven the following morning. Only half awake, she climbed out of bed and staggered across the wood-plank floor toward the sound, yelping when she stepped on a splinter.

The sharp pain cleared the sleepy cobwebs from her brain, and she felt plush carpet beneath her feet just as she did every morning.

"What on earth—" The question froze on Laura's lips at the sound of the telephone.

Laura answered on the third ring, reaching for the bedside lamp with her free hand.

"Happy New Year!"

"Galen?" Laura asked, wondering how she had gotten a splinter in her carpeted apartment.

"Of course it's me, ducks."

As always, Laura was amused by Galen Hillhouse's accent, an unusual combination of Cockney slang and Oklahoma drawl. "Hold on a minute."

"I'll hold all day, luv. I put this call on little brother Jake's card."

Laura laughed as she limped to the adjacent bathroom for

a Band-Aid. Cradling the cordless phone on her shoulder, she pulled the splinter free, then positioned the Band-Aid on her foot. "Galen, you guys are twins, Jake is a foot taller than you. Why do you call him your little brother?"

"Because I came out first."

Laura laughed again, putting the splinter incident out of her mind. "Happy New Year to you, too," she said, returning to the bedroom. "Where are you? London? Paris?"

"Nope. I'm back in the U.S. of A.—I think."

Laura plumped her pillows, then leaned back. "You're not sure? Did you tie one on last night?"

"Tie one on? Ha. I'm in Warburton, Oklahoma, where they're half stuck in the old Indian Territory days and alcohol is for all intents and purposes illegal—though not unheard of." Galen paused. "Laurie, did you—"

"Almost."

"Laurie . . ."

"I dumped it without even a sip. I'm through with that, so let's change the subject. How have you been?"

"Not bad. Actually, I've spent the last few days wondering if I should be a pain and bug you or if I should put the B&B on hold until you're up to it."

Laura's brow furrowed. "You lost me."

"Oh." Galen paused. "I sent the details with your Christmas present. Didn't you get the package? The FedEx people said it was delivered."

"I haven't opened my mail in a couple of weeks, not since the funeral. I'm sorry."

"I understand, luv. Anyway, I really need your help. Do you remember the house I inherited from my parents, the Victorian Gothic?"

"Queen Anne," Laura automatically corrected. "Victorian Queen Anne. Yes, I've seen pictures of it." She winced as the pain flared up in her foot.

Galen chuckled. "I don't know how you keep all those time periods straight. A house is a house to me." She paused. "Anyway, with me out of the country and Jake knee-deep in work out in L.A., we hired a caretaker to look after the place. What he 'cared to take' was our money."

"How's the house?" Laura asked quickly, a little surprised by her need to know.

"The house is structurally sound, but that bloody jackass let the outside deteriorate. He must have rented the place out for parties. You wouldn't believe the crap I had to clear out when I got here. What the old homestead needs is some serious TLC, and what Jake and I need is a helpful friend who just happens to know how to replicate antique interiors in her sleep, blindfolded, with both hands tied behind her back. Hint, hint."

Laura smiled—really smiled—for the first time in weeks, but the smile slowly faded. She needed this lifeline Galen was offering her, and yet . . . "Can I have a couple of days to think about it?" she asked, guilt prodding her when Galen's upbeat tone disappeared.

"Sure, luv. Take your time. The house has been standing here for over a hundred years. I think it can wait a few days for the big makeover to begin. Do me one favor. Open the package I sent you. There are a bunch of old pictures showing the house in its heyday. I thought they'd help you get a feel for what I want to do. Most of the original furniture is here, but we have to fill in the extras—period curtains, paintings, and what have you."

Laura forced the guilt away. "I'll decide soon, and if I don't come out there I'll give you a list of decorators. I have a friend in Oklahoma City who'll give you a good discount on anything you need."

There was a strained silence, then Galen spoke.

"I'm not trying to get a freebie, Laura. I want *you* to do it. You have a gift for this kind of thing. You and old houses go together like fish and chips."

"It's not the money, Galen. I just don't know if I can do the job."

"The change might do you good."

"Maybe," Laura said, knowing full well that seeing Jake Hillhouse would increase the sense of loneliness she'd been struggling with. "I'll let you know soon."

Laura showered and changed into clean jeans and a sweater, then ate a light breakfast before settling down to open

Galen's package. The accompanying letter explained about
the careless caretaker and Galen's plan to turn the historic
house into a bed-and-breakfast to take advantage of the
area's growing tourist trade.

> *I've had it with Fleet Street, investigative reporting,
> and two-timing boyfriends. I want to be my own boss,
> to deal with pleasant people for a change. . . .*
> *. . . To give you an idea of how I'd like the house to
> look, I've enclosed the oldest set of photos I could
> find. And, to get you in the mood for coming to
> Choctaw country and mingling with us "natives," I
> chose your Christmas present accordingly . . .*

Laura sifted through the plastic foam "popcorn" and removed an old family album and a gift-wrapped CD titled
Spirit Songs: A Collection of Native American Flute Music.
She closed her eyes, trying to recall the sound she'd heard
so often in her college days, but couldn't. It was too faint,
too fogged by the chaotic years that had followed.

After popping the CD into the player, Laura settled back
on the Duncan Phyfe sofa, letting out a wistful sigh as the
music filled the room, weaving its way through her murky
memory. How could she have forgotten such a beautiful
sound? It reminded her of a human voice in a way—a haunting, soothing, somewhat sad voice. She closed her eyes
again to picture Jake Hillhouse sitting on a lonely stretch of
beach at dawn, playing a song similar to this. The unique,
dreamy music seeped into her pores, just as it had done
twelve years ago, and she continued to imagine him—his
long black hair, his sexy smile, his trim, powerful body.

Laura's green eyes snapped open. This nonsense had to
stop. She hit the button on the remote control to lower the
music's volume, then opened the rust velvet cover of
Galen's family album. There was one photo to a page, each
approximately four by six inches, mellowed from their original tones to shades of muted brown and ivory.

The first picture showed the magnificent Queen
Anne–style house with the corner tower and wraparound

porch. Laura knew the family stories of how Galen and
Jake's great-grandfather, Jason Hillhouse, had built the
house himself back in 1893. With the lilting flute music
drifting through her head, Laura turned the page. The next
photo showed Jason and Star on their wedding day.

How happy they seemed, how much in love. Laura's
pleasant thoughts fragmented the instant she turned the page
to see the Hillhouses posed with their attendants.

She could not shift her gaze from the best man. For no ap-
parent reason the flute music playing behind her became
louder, swirling around her, insinuating itself into every part
of her body.

"Who are you?" Laura whispered, disappointed that she
couldn't step into the picture and ask him in person. She
touched the old photo, wanting to feel his dark hair, the
swarthy skin stretched across his well-formed jaw. But it
was his eyes that truly held her spellbound. She had never
seen such gorgeous eyes—they reminded her of the phrase
"windows to the soul." He seemed so alive, so *real*.

Laura's common sense reeled her imagination in. What
was wrong with her? She hadn't gone gaga over a guy in a
picture since she was a kid and blew her allowance on teen
idol magazines. She turned to the next page, making a conscious effort to focus on the background details and not on
the people in the photos.

It was a lovely home, decorated with figured wallpaper,
lots of varnished woodwork, and massive late-nineteenth-
century furniture.

Setting the album aside for a moment, Laura went to her
room for the reprint of an old Sears, Roebuck catalog and
skimmed through until she came to the furniture section.
Galen would flip when she learned that the heavy carved
dining table that had fed generations of Hillhouses had cost
less than twelve dollars new.

Laura's spirits continued to rise as she studied the house
photos and thought of restoring the woodwork's luster, re-
pairing and replacing the interior moldings that Galen said
were damaged. The job would require going on a treasure
hunt to scour area antique shops and garage sales for suit-

able bric-a-brac and framed prints to use as accent pieces, a part of the job that she loved. The project was just what she needed to take her mind off her grief and loneliness. Maybe this wouldn't be such a bad year after all.

The sight of the old album's last picture reined in Laura's good humor. The portrait shot featured Jason and Star Hillhouse's best man at his own wedding.

Laura placed her hand over the beaming bride's face and studied Galen's relative as she had before, disturbed by the sudden realization that reminded her of Jake.

What was she thinking? She couldn't go to Warburton. Taking on this project was supposed to help her get over her loneliness, but seeing Jake again might make it that much worse. Even though he lived in L.A., she knew he would eventually show up. Going there would be a mistake. She should stay here, spend some time alone, lose herself for a while.

Laura put the old photo album on the marble-topped coffee table, then got up and walked over to the sliding-glass balcony door. Peering down at the traffic thirty stories below, she debated the two evils— being miserable here or being miserable in Warburton.

Without warning, the antique photo album tumbled to the floor, landing on the remote control for the entertainment system. The CD player turned on again.

Laura snatched up the album and leafed through it to make certain that the priceless pictures hadn't been marred in any way. She stopped at a picture featuring Galen's handsome ancestor outside the Warburton jail, proudly showing off his badge and displaying a newspaper that proclaimed NEW COUNTY SHERIFF.

Laura took the album with her when she went to the phone. Looking at the picture of the anonymous man with the incredible dark eyes, she called Galen.

It's a machine, luv. You know what to do.

"It's Laurie. I'll come out to help you on Monday. I'll fly in at Oklahoma City and drive down after I see my friend who deals in wallpaper reproductions."

*   *   *

In Oklahoma City, Laura placed the wall-covering order, allowing her instincts to guide her, then went to lunch at a nearby diner.

"Can I get you something for dessert?" the waitress asked, clearing away Laura's empty dish. "We have fresh peach pie."

Laura looked at her watch. She had a pretty long drive to Warburton, but that dessert sounded awfully good. "Pie would be great."

When the waitress returned, Laura gestured toward the shop visible through the diner's front window. "Do you know when Photo Antiquities opens?"

The waitress nodded and refilled Laura's coffee cup. "Angel usually opens around nine-thirty, but recently she's been doing some work for the historical society in the mornings." She glanced at the large clock mounted on the wall behind her. "She'll probably be in around two."

Laura looked at the clock as she sipped her coffee. She really should hit the road, but . . . She looked down at the leather backpack resting on her lap. Galen's family album was inside, and as crazy as it was, Laura had the urge to copy the picture of the gorgeous sheriff. The idea had begun as a faint twinge while she waited to board her flight in New York. By the time the plane touched down in Oklahoma, the crazy idea had been nagging at her for a solid hour. She was determined to put the notion out of her mind, but seeing that shop made it come back with a vengeance.

Laura's attention shifted gears when the waitress called out to the redhead coming through the front door, "Hey, Angel, I have a customer for you."

I can't believe I'm doing this, Laura thought as she browsed through the small gallery that Angel Lazlo had set up in her photography studio.

"Here you go, Laura."

Laura went to the counter.

"Tell your friend that restorationists like myself are grateful for folks like her who retrofit these old albums with acid-free pages. You would not believe the mess I've been working with—a collection spanning ninety years that was stored in a damp basement for at least ten." She showed Laura the reverse side of Galen's original photo before replacing it in its protective acetate sleeve. "I found out the name of your mystery man. It's Corby Hillhouse."

Reaching for the photo's enlargement, Laura smiled to herself. That name had a nice ring to it. A very nice ring.

"He is a hunk and a half. Kind of makes you wish he was still around."

"He is."

"What?"

Laura looked up, scarcely aware of what she'd just said. "I mean, he's still around in the sense of the family genes. My friend Jake is a descendant of his, and they look a lot alike."

Angel Lazlo grinned. "Is this Jake spoken for?"

Laura took out her credit card. "Unfortunately, he is."

Jake was far from Laura's thoughts once she hit the open road. No wonder Galen wanted to give up the hustle and bustle of the big city to return to her roots. This part of the country was absolutely beautiful. Unbroken by the sharp edges of tall buildings, the sky stretched far and wide, its color like that of a cornflower in full bloom. The land bordering the highway was like a green lagoon supporting clumps of brown islands that she realized were groups of honest-to-goodness cows.

Laura opened the car window all the way, ignoring the bite of the wind, which whipped her honey-blond hair about her face. She switched on the portable CD player she'd brought from home and listened to the Indian flute music, stealing a glance at the framed photograph she'd left peeking out of her backpack.

"You are one handsome devil, Corby Hillhouse," Laura whispered, reaching down to touch his rugged jaw. This fascination was insane, but she couldn't help herself. She felt good having this picture near her. She felt safe . . .

The blare of an eighteen-wheeler's air horn destroyed the brief fantasy.

Laura jerked the steering wheel to the right. The car hit a slick spot, spinning like a top before it slid off the road.

The air bag ballooned in her face, its powdery residue blinding her eyes, burning her throat. She had to get out of here.

Chapter 3

"WHAT THE HELL?" Corby Hillhouse muttered as a figure appeared out of nowhere in the road up ahead. It seemed to be a boy or a slightly built man with long blond hair. He spurred his horse, but by the time he'd reached the spot, the person was gone. He decided that he'd seen an animal distorted somehow by the fading daylight.

Chapter 4

THE BURLY TRUCK driver reached out to steady Laura. "Whoa, ma'am. You stay put until the highway patrol gets here."

Rubbing her eyes, Laura looked at the asphalt under her feet. She could have sworn she was standing on a dirt road a minute ago. She blinked and stared at the trucker. "Where's your horse?"

"Ma'am?"

"Didn't you just ride up on a big white horse?"

He eyed her suspiciously. "You'd better sit. I think you hit your head."

"I guess I did," Laura said, looking past him, certain that she'd seen a mounted rider.

"Will you guys stop hovering?" Laura shouted, after her friends asked for the third time if she was injured. "I am fine. I was wearing my seat belt. I don't have a single scratch."

"But that highway patrol officer told us you hit your

head," Jake Hillhouse said, brushing his long fingers across her forehead.

Laura frowned, annoyed by the concern and by the physical contact that a week ago would have made her heart palpitate.

"I worry about you, Laurie."

"I don't need you to worry about me."

Jake's dark brows arched. He raised his hands in submission, then left the kitchen.

Laura turned to Galen, who was staring in disbelief. "Can we stop playing Twenty Questions and get down to business?" Laura asked, taking fabric swatches and wallpaper samples out of her backpack. Without thinking, she touched the photograph of Corby Hillhouse before closing the backpack flap.

Galen craned her neck. "What's that?"

Laura slid the backpack off the old oak table to her lap. "Nothing."

Surprising herself as well as Galen and Jake, Laura took control of the restoration project for the Hillhouse family's ancestral home.

Rising before dawn, not going to bed until midnight, she set a feverish pace to complete the downstairs rooms. She rarely left the house, going out only when she felt the need to check the local newspapers for notice of a garage sale or flea market in the area. While Galen found some of Laura's "finds" not to her liking, she had to admit that they seemed right at home in the old house, even the garish blue-and-yellow stoneware canister set.

As February became March, the bulk of the interior work was completed, but Laura found herself feeling out of sorts. She didn't want to return to New York when she was finished here, but there was no logical reason for her to stay. This little section of Oklahoma wasn't exactly a hub of interior decorating opportunity, and while she could certainly use it as "home base" and take her services throughout the state, she didn't want to. She wanted to be here, in this house. She needed to be in this house. Just breathing the air made her feel alive, like she'd almost found what she'd spent a lifetime searching for. If she could just find a way to make this security last . . .

The sound of Jake Hillhouse's voice drew her attention.

"Ah, Grasshopper. It is good to see you sit still for a change."

Laura smiled. "What can I say? I'm in a kick-back mood today." She pulled out the oak chair next to her and got up to bring another cup and the coffeepot to the table. "Did you finish your t'ai chi already?"

"Didn't start," Jake answered, spooning sugar into the cup of coffee Laura handed him. "I thought I'd see if you wanted to join me. It'll be like the old days."

Laura shrugged. "Another time, maybe. I kind of lost interest." She averted her eyes when Jake gave her a questioning look. At one time she'd been so interested in martial arts that she had earned a black belt in karate. She didn't want to explain herself to Jake.

"Humor me. It will relax you, and from the looks of those pretty little shoulders, I'd say you're tense as hell."

"I'll watch today," she said. "Maybe I'll join you tomorrow."

When they finished their coffee, Laura followed Jake out the back door. They walked around the porch to the east side of the house and watched the soft gray eastern light turn the sky to a gentle pink as the sun rose up above the distant hills, slowly bathing the white frame house in an ethereal glow.

Laura sat on the wide porch steps and watched Jake begin the exercises as Indian flute music drifted lightly on the morning breeze from the boom box he'd brought outside with them. Strange. She'd always gotten a neat little tingle deep down, watching Jake move, but now it was gone.

It wasn't long before the haunting music lured Laura from her seat to take her customary place at Jake's right. It felt good to do this again. She hadn't even been aware of the tension Jake mentioned until she felt it ease out of her body with each slow, practiced movement.

She joined Jake in the mornings that followed and felt as

carefree as she had back in college, until the afternoon she and Galen shared a pizza for lunch.

"I'm not one to pry, luv, but when I was putting clean sheets on the beds—" Galen paused as Laura's back went rigid. "Why do you have an eight-by-ten glossy of my great-grandfather's cousin tucked under your pillow?"

Laura nearly choked on her cola. "I meant to tell you about that," she said when she caught her breath. She began plucking a piece of pepperoni from the pizza on her plate. "I had it copied by a photographer in Oklahoma City. She didn't damage the original. In fact, she wanted me to compliment you for having the album retrofitted to preserve the pictures. She works with the Oklahoma Historical Society and . . ."

"Stop evading, Laurie. I'm a reporter. I have a built-in BS detector." Pausing, Galen put her hand over Laura's clammy one. "Is it Jake? The picture kind of looks like him without all the hair."

Laura looked up, then back to her pizza. It would be easy to say that she was still pining for Jake, but she didn't want to lie. Moving the cordless phone out of Galen's reach, Laura gave her friend a sheepish smile.

"I don't want you to call the men in white coats when you hear that I had the picture copied because I think your ancestor is sexy as sin."

"Why?"

"I don't know," Laura admitted, taking her dish to the old zinc-lined sink. She turned, suddenly feeling as though she'd done this before. Shaking off the déjà vu, she shrugged. "I guess it's his eyes." She stopped when Galen rushed out of the room. When Galen returned with the family album, Laura joined her at the kitchen table, again feeling as though she'd had this "girl talk" session—or one like it—before, in this same room.

Galen turned to the photo in question. "I don't get it, ducks, but maybe it's because he looks too much like my father and brother with that bloody cat-that-ate-the-canary grin. What is it that you see in his eyes?"

"A lot of things," Laura replied softly. "But mostly I see sadness, like there's something missing in his life."

Galen let out a sharp laugh. "Sadness? No way. Look at that smile."

Laura exhaled a soft sigh. "I know all about those kinds of smiles. See?"

When her friend looked up, Laura flashed the smile that said she was the happiest woman alive. It was gone as quickly as it had come, causing Galen to do a double take from Laura to the photo album.

"You look like him, and that's the way you looked—"

"All the time I was in L.A. with Slash Braddock and his wasted entourage," Laura finished. "I wore that smile at every photo op, at every concert, in every music video, at every party. I even used it in the bedroom, but all the while I was empty inside. I wanted something, but I didn't know what it was or how to get it, so I partied myself into intensive care . . ."

Laura's words drifted into silence as she remembered it all. She'd have gone from the hospital to another party if Grandpa Alex hadn't caught that tabloid report and tried to contact Laura's mother, his own estranged daughter.

In poor health herself, she had neither the resources nor the desire to help her only child get her life back in order. Alex had stepped in, filling the void, giving to his grandchild the love and support he'd been unable to show her mother.

Laura's thoughts returned to the present when Galen touched her hand.

"You should have told me, luv. I'd never have gone abroad if I'd known the breakup with Jake hurt you so bad. If you'd had me to talk to, you never would have gotten involved with those losers."

Laura shook her head. "It wasn't Jake. There's always been something missing, but it's way inside me. The thing with Jake made me face it, and I decided to fill my little void with all the wrong things."

She gave Galen a quick smile. "Don't get all guilt-ridden. I wouldn't have told you, anyway. I wouldn't have wanted anyone to feel sorry for me or fuss over me, and I have the strangest feeling that your ancestor was the same. Do you know anything about him?"

"Not really," Galen said, closing the family album's velvet cover. "I sort of remember our grandfather looking through this with me when I was young. He said I reminded him of his mother, Star, and he thought Jake would keep alive the 'man with the badge' tradition that Jason and Corby started." Galen got up and took a can of soda from the refrigerator. "I don't remember him saying much else about Corby, but I imagine he and his family are buried in the old churchyard. Do you want to swing by there and look?"

A wave of nausea swept through Laura, but she concealed it. It was as if Corby was alive somewhere as long as she thought of him that way. "Cemeteries aren't my thing." She looked at her watch. "Don't you have to pick Jake up? He should be getting back from that film shoot in Dallas. Why don't you leave now and I'll wait here and put the finishing touches on that big dresser in the master bedroom. I'll have it done by the time you guys get back from the airport."

"You call that an airport? It's just a dirt strip paved with cow chips—" Galen stopped short when Laura shivered. "Are you all right?"

"I'm fine," Laura insisted, rubbing the gooseflesh on her arms. "Get going. The way you drive, the thirty-minute trip will take three hours." She pasted on her old casual smile, despite the queasy feeling in her stomach. What was wrong with her today?

Galen touched the back of her bronzed hand to Laura's pale forehead. "If you get sick or anything you call me on the cell phone."

"I promise. Get going. I have work to do."

Laura walked Galen outside and then watched the red GMC Jimmy disappear behind a stand of pines at the end of the private road. She shivered again. *Maybe I'm losing it,* she thought. How else could she explain this feeling that her friends would soon be gone from her life?

Maybe she should follow, in case it was a weird premonition of some kind. She didn't have her rental car any longer, but Jake's motorcycle was in the old barn and she knew how to ride it.

"They're not going out of your life."

Laura stopped in midstride and spun around. There was no one around. Had that been her own voice? She *was* losing it. She was talking to herself and hadn't even realized it. Maybe she *should* call Galen back, or try to catch up. Maybe she'd inhaled too many fumes refinishing the old wood.

Turning back and forth between the house and the barn, Laura struggled with the choice, finally deciding to follow the stronger impulse, which told her to stay here, finish restoring the old dresser, and relax.

Chapter 5

"PERFECT," LAURA WHISPERED when she surveyed her handiwork. The large walnut bureau looked fabulous now that the broken molding was repaired, the deep gouge filled in, and the wooden drawer slides replaced so the drawers were all in place and even. The only thing left to do was rub in a final coat of oil and reattach the antique drawer knobs.

The last brass knob slipped out of Laura's oily fingers twice. The third time, it rolled two feet away, and she inadvertently kicked it further, sending it through the French doors she'd opened to ventilate the room and out onto the balcony. She bent to pick up the knob again, only to have it slip away when the telephone in the downstairs hall rang, startling her.

Cursing the timing, Laura hurried to get the phone. "I'm fine," she assured Galen. "Take your time, stop to eat if you want. I promise to call you if I feel sick."

Laura returned to the bedroom and began the hunt for the wayward brass knob. It had rolled between the slats in the sawn-wood balustrade and was now resting between the edge of the balcony and the railing. Laura tried to reach through the slats, but her hand wouldn't fit.

She tried to push the knob back toward her with a screw-driver but only managed to move it further to the left. Perhaps a different angle would help. Laura stood up and bent over the railing, but her fingers were a few inches short of the goal. She thought of pushing the knob off the edge of the balcony, but feared that with her luck it would roll down the small hill below and get lost in the brush.

If only such knobs could be bought new. She'd been lucky to scavenge these from a warped piece of furniture someone had set out with their trash. The knobs had a porcelain insert in the center with a tiny painted rosebud in the exact shade of yellow as the roses painted on the frosted-glass globes of the electrified gaslight suspended from the center of the bedroom ceiling.

Laura drummed her fingers on the balcony railing, her eyes drifting back to the knob tottering on the balcony's edge as if daring her to come get it. The sensible thing to do would be to wait until Jake got back. He was tall enough to reach it by leaning over the rail. Yes, that was what she'd do. She'd wait for Jake.

Laura went back inside and washed her hands, then went to her own room to listen to one of the Indian flute CDs she and Jake used for t'ai chi. But the more she tried not to think of the unique drawer knob on the balcony, the more it taunted her until retrieving it became an obsession.

"Come on. Come on, come on," Laura muttered, stretching as far as she could, only the toes of her left foot on the ground. Her muscles ached from the strain, as she tried to stretch just a little further. *Yes!* Her brain shouted in triumph when her fingertips brushed against the knob. She leaned her full weight forward on the rail to give herself the extra inch necessary.

Too late, she recognized the sound of splintering wood.

The railing snapped and she hurtled forward, instinctively closing her eyes. She felt herself falling for what seemed like forever. The impact of landing, when it came, was un-expectedly light.

Her eyes shot open and the world became a green-brown

blur as she tumbled down the hill. She rolled over and over
like a limp rag doll, not in pain but in a haze of prickly sen-
sations while a strange, multicolored light show bombarded
her with blinding flashes,

Suddenly the tumbling stopped and the light show turned
to blackness.

Chapter 6

"GOOD HIT, SON!"

"It's a good hit because you don't have to chase it down!" Corby shouted, as the baseball sailed past his outstretched arm and rolled down the hill twenty feet behind him.

"Stop your bellyaching," Corby's cousin Jason called from the pitcher's spot. "This game was your idea. We don't have another ball, so don't come back until you find it."

"Then help me look!"

Jason laughed. "You missed the catch. You chase it."

Humor danced in Corby's dark eyes. "You missed it, you chase it," he mimicked, trotting to the crest of the sloping ground. Corby smiled to himself when he realized that this had been the best day he'd had in a long time, though he didn't quite understand his own good spirits.

Lord knows, there wasn't much to be happy about, with his cousins getting ready to pack up and move to Kentucky. He wasn't sure who was going to take care of his motherless daughter. But he would work his way around that complication, confident that Cousin Jason would help him out.

Spying something poking through the tangle of dried undergrowth up ahead, Corby approached, expecting it to be the baseball. He reached for it, then jerked back. That bit of scuffed leather was no ball. That was a piece of a shoe, a shoe like none he'd ever seen.

With unnatural slowness, Corby's gaze slid up past the strange shoe to the shapely leg encased in snug, faded denim to the slim, gently rounded hips. Then further up, to the smallish breasts, accentuated by the close fit of the unusual white shirt with the painted decoration of a cowboy hat and a Plains Indian warbonnet above the word "Oklahoma." Before he could give the strange clothing much thought, his gaze fell upon the woman's face.

She was the prettiest thing he'd ever seen.

He had to make a conscious effort to breathe. His stomach felt like it had a pack of weevils skittering inside.

He knelt beside her, his eyes intent upon the oval face of delicate ivory, the full, blush-colored lips, the well-formed cheekbones, the hair the color of sunlit honey. Corby tenderly brushed a few strands of hair away from the woman's dust-streaked face, his touch lingering for a moment on her scratched cheek. His heart wished with all its might for the power to heal her scratches this instant.

Her cheek was so soft, so warm. Why on earth did his fingertips feel so tingly? And why did he have an uncontrollable urge to taste those sweet-looking lips? Without warning, the woman's eyelids fluttered open, revealing eyes like two pieces of shimmering jade, so large, so deep, so divine . . .

"Corby?"

She spoke in a sensuous whisper that prickled the skin on the back of his neck.

"Yes, little one. And who are you?" he heard himself ask, even as he wondered why it seemed so right for her to be here. With him.

Her answer was a smile that made Corby's blood roar through his ears and raised his temperature a good three degrees.

"Your eyes are so sad."

The softness of her voice transferred to her touch when

she lifted her hand, letting her fingers comb through the hair at the back of his head.

"Don't be sad . . ."

Completely vanquished by her odd words and delicate touch, Corby allowed her to coax him down for a kiss.

The gentle press of the blond woman's lips turned Corby's blood to liquid fire that scalded a path from his frantically beating heart to his aching groin. He'd never felt anything like this. Never wanted it to end . . .

"Corby, didn't you find that ball yet?" Jason Hillhouse barked from the top of the slope.

Corby's head shot up. He had to force his tingling lips to form the words. "I—I found a woman!"

"A little early, isn't it?" Jason teased. "I didn't think the women ripened until after the blackberries did."

"I'm serious, you damn fool. I think she's hurt. Send for the doctor!"

Corby turned his attention back to the woman as the rest of his family came down to investigate. A powerful urge to protect her from their prying eyes made him shift this way and that to block their view.

"Who is she?"

"Is she dead?"

"Where'd she get those clothes?"

"I thought Jace had the property fenced."

"How'd she get here? I don't see a horse or tracks."

Jason's wife, Star, arrived on the scene and took command. "You fool men get out of the way and give the girl some air!"

She pushed past her husband's brothers and nephews. She tried to shove Corby aside as well, but he refused to be moved, a fact that clearly surprised the onlookers.

"I don't think she has any broken bones," Corby said, finally taking a step back in deference to the knowledge that Star had gained from her physician father.

"I think you're right," Star replied, kneeling to check the woman's limbs. She felt for the pulse, then glanced up. "Was she awake at all? Was she able to speak or hear?"

Corby bent down on one knee, his eyes never leaving the

unconscious woman's face. "She said my name like she knew me and then . . . she kissed me."

The startled silence was broken by the sound of Cousin Jacob's boys snickering.

"Who is she?" Star asked.

"I don't know."

The teenage boys laughed again.

Corby's eyes raked over them. "It's true. I never saw her before. I don't know how she knew my name."

He peered down at the woman again. He was a lawman. He should be wondering the same things as his kin—who she was, where she'd come from. And yet it didn't seem to matter.

Star's rough poke in the ribs put an end to Corby's musings.

"You two lift her onto this and carry her into the house," she said, indicating the pine board her husband had brought down.

Corby helped get the mysterious woman onto the makeshift stretcher, feeling a rare flash of jealousy toward Jason, who inadvertently brushed against the woman's breast when he lifted her hand from the ground.

The family gathering broke up once Star's father, Dr. McNamara, arrived and went upstairs to examine his patient.

Corby stopped himself from following the doctor upstairs. Too nervous to sit, he paced the length of the large parlor, awaiting the doctor's return, his mind beginning to fill with questions, his body brimming with feelings he could not explain.

"Seeing as how you're so talkative, I think I'll go to the kitchen and see if I can unstick the keys on the typewriter Star brought from the office," Jason said when Corby failed to respond to his attempts at small talk.

"You do that," Corby mumbled, walking over to the upright piano situated near the curved bay window.

He picked up a little ceramic spice container filled with wilting wildflowers from the piano bench and studied it. Orange flowers in a blue-and-yellow holder was one crazy combination, almost as unusual as the clothing the blond woman had been wearing.

"Do you like 'em, Pa? I picked 'em for you!"

Corby stiffened at the sound of his four-year-old daughter's excited voice. He didn't want to face her, but he knew he had no choice. She was tugging on the back of his vest to get his attention.

He looked down into Sabrina's pretty dark eyes and tried to block the haunting image of her mother, Daisy. "They're real nice flowers, 'Brina. Why don't you take them into the kitchen?"

Corby tried to hand the little cinnamon-canister vase to her, but she refused it, her smile drooping into a frown and her eyes growing as sad as her mother's had been the last time Corby had seen her alive.

He held the vase in both hands, afraid to reach out to the daughter whose mother had died because of his lapse of judgment.

Sabrina's eyes misted just as Jason and Star's twin girls ran into the room looking for her. They tugged on her calico skirt.

"C'mon! Mama says we hafta play outside."

The look Sabrina gave him as she left the parlor was like a knife to Corby's heart, but he told himself it was for the best. He couldn't let her come to depend on him. If she did, he would fail her the way he'd failed her mother and the woman he'd loved before that.

They'd trusted him. They'd needed him, but he hadn't been there when it mattered most. He'd been afraid the first time, selfish the second, but the end result was the same—two women had died.

He loved his daughter too much to put her in danger. The arrangements he'd made for her were for the best. His relatives were better equipped to look after her than he was. He'd known that the moment he'd seen Quinn McNamara deliver her from her dying mother's body.

The best thing he could do for Sabrina was to leave things as they were. Let her depend on people who were worthy of the affection she had to share.

Chapter 7

CORBY'S CONCERN FOR his own shortcomings fell by the wayside when he heard footsteps descending the oak staircase. He darted to the parlor door just as his cousin Jason came from the kitchen through the swinging door. Corby stepped closer to the foot of the maroon-carpeted staircase, questioning Dr. McNamara as he descended.

"How is she?"

"She has bruising around her ribs, some superficial cuts and contusions, but nothing serious that I can detect. She doesn't seem to remember much of her identity or original whereabouts. She does know all of us by name, though. Do any of you recognize her?"

Star shook her head as she slipped past her father.

"I can't place her at all, Quinn," Jason told his father-in-law.

"Me either," Corby answered, despite the nagging feeling that he had seen the woman somewhere before.

"She's resting now," Quinn McNamara said. "Perhaps in the morning she'll remember more." He paused, then looked at Corby. "Star tells me the young lady kissed you?"

Corby cleared his throat, trying not to let Jason's annoying grin get to him. "She did, but I don't know who she is."

"She sure knows you," Jason teased.

"And you," Star added. She folded her arms in front of her and gave both her husband and Corby a disparaging look. "We're all adults here. If she's one of your old friends from some Chippy Hill bordello, you can both admit it. I assure you I won't be too terribly shocked."

Jason playfully chucked his wife under the chin. "I haven't had any of those kinds of friends since before we were married, sweetheart, and you know it." He turned to his cousin. "Corby?"

Angered by the implications, Corby clenched his fists at his sides. "She is not from Chippy Hill." His tone defied argument or question.

He took his hat from the mirrored stand near the door. "I'd best round up Sabrina and get her back to Libby and Peter's."

Star stepped forward. "She's welcome to spend the night. If you'll come into the parlor, I'd like to talk to you. Libby tells me you've been avoiding the issue of their move—"

"Can't this wait?" Corby interrupted. "I have to get into town and relieve my deputy. I'll be back this evening to check on . . ."

"On who?" Star prodded.

"On that woman," Corby said, glad he'd been able to stop short of saying "*my* woman."

Outside, as he took his gelding from the barn, Corby glanced up at the back-bedroom window, where a dim light glowed behind the lacy curtains.

Who are you, little one? And why do you make me feel like a schoolboy kissed for the very first time?

Laura waited a few moments after the bedroom door closed before she opened her eyes again. She sat up and took a long look at her surroundings.

This was weird. Really weird. She was in her room in Galen's house, only it wasn't Galen's house.

The wallpaper sprinkled with sprigs of violets was intact, the background a crisp white instead of the aged ivory she was used to. The furniture smelled of fresh lemon oil and gleamed in the diffused light of the brass-based hurricane lamp on the bureau near the door. The windows were covered with a white lace panel and heavy purple velvet draperies pulled back with tasseled cords. Galen had purchased ruffled priscillas.

An unfamiliar woman's voice filtered beneath the door, along with the quick padding of small feet and the ringing of childish laughter.

"Hush, now, or you won't get your bedtime snack. Hush. There's a sick lady in that room. James, don't run. Nita May, stop pulling your sister's hair, or your mama will whup your bottom."

A bittersweet smile came to Laura as she thought of Candace. Her foster child had such a sweet laugh and pretty blue eyes. Before finding Candace, Laura had often dreamed of a house filled with happy, laughing children. There was a time when she dreamed of what children fathered by Jake Hillhouse would look like. Would their coloring show their Choctaw heritage, with the dark eyes, rich complexion, and brown/black hair that he and Galen shared, or would it mirror her own European ancestors, with light hair and green eyes?

Laura chewed on her dry bottom lip and began to trace the scroll pattern on the quilt coverlet draped across her middle. There were more important things to worry about than her biological clock—namely, what the hell had happened to her and where on earth was she?

Even the idea that she'd traveled back through time was out of the question. Of course, the other possibilities weren't any easier to swallow. She could be lying beneath the balcony in a coma, having some weird virtual dream while her brain cells short-circuited by the millions. Or she could be dead. This might be heaven.

That one was a distinct possibility, especially as the memory of kissing Corby Hillhouse came back to her. That had been good, if entirely too brief. His hair had been so silky between her fingers, his eyes sadder and sexier than in the pictures, and the feel of his lips touching hers had actually made her faint.

Oh, yeah, this was heaven.

It could be hell, Laura's cynical side chimed in. *Remember the wedding picture?*

The dreamy grin fell off Laura's face like the cartoon anvil she'd seen dropped on the hapless coyote countless times. Like old Wile E., she was pulverized.

True, she hadn't led the most moral life between the ages of nineteen and twenty-five, but she'd been walking the straight and narrow for four years now and she definitely deserved some slack.

The sound of footsteps on the landing cut into Laura's thoughts and she lay back, closing her eyes and listening to the voices.

"Jason Hillhouse, you stop that. I thought you came up to use the bathroom."

"I'll get there."

Laura heard Star's sharp intake of breath and her muffled moan. "What do you think you're doing?"

Jason's bawdy laugh followed. "After six years of marriage you have to ask?"

"Put those hands back down at your sides and do the business you have to do." Star paused and cleared her throat. "Daddy told me to check on the woman Corby found twice an hour."

"Well, then, you have time for a kiss . . ."

Laura bit her thumbnail. This was way too weird!

But it *had* to be real. These people couldn't be the product of some bizarre brain screwup, could they?

Hearing the door latch spring, Laura shut her eyes and tried to regulate her breathing to make it appear she was sleeping. A gentle hand touched her shoulder.

"Hello, can you hear me?"

"Mmmm," Laura murmured as she slowly opened her eyes to look into the face of Star McNamara Hillhouse, Galen's great-grandmother.

"Don't be afraid," Star said. "You're safe here." She turned up the oil lamp she'd brought over from the bureau. She looked into Laura's eyes, shielding them, then removing her hand to check the reaction of the pupils. She set the lamp aside. "Do you remember your name?"

What do I do now?

"Laura." The word came out on its own. "My name is Laura Bennett."

Star smiled a smile Laura knew well. It was the same comforting grin Galen had always given her.

"That's a good sign. You go back to sleep. I'll be by to check on you again. I have to wake you periodically during the night."

Laura nodded and closed her eyes, opening them after she heard the bedroom door shut.

What was happening to her? Had she really traveled back to the late 1800s?

The faraway screech of an owl broke the stillness, and Laura closed her eyes again. Her head was beginning to throb, and she suddenly felt like a spokeswoman for "Jet Lag International."

Just go to sleep, her practical side said. *This is all some weird dream. You've obviously been spending too much time looking through that old photo album. It will be better when you wake up.*

Laura pulled the quilted coverlet up over her shoulders. She hoped so. She really hoped so.

Chapter 8

CORBY FINGERED THE broad brim of his black felt hat. "Your brother's moving east puts me in something of a bind, Jace, and I was wondering . . . if it's not too much trouble . . . would you and Star give me a hand with Sabrina?"

"Of course—"

"We won't do any such thing," Star broke in as she came into the parlor. Ignoring her husband's displeasure, she stood before his cousin, who was seated on a high-backed velvet chair. "We are not the girl's parents, Corby. You are, and it's high time you acted like it."

Corby's stomach twisted. "You know I'll pay you for keeping her. I can't have her living at the boardinghouse with a bunch of rowdy men. Who's going to watch over her when I'm on duty?"

"He's right, Star," Jason said firmly.

Star stood her ground, dismissing the comments with a wave of her hand. "You didn't have to sell your house. You could have moved into a different one. Sabrina needs to have a real home. She needs to sleep in her own bed."

Corby sprang out of the wing chair. "Fine. I'll get my daughter and relieve you of the burden."

Star blocked his path. "I won't let you terrify that child by pulling her out of bed at this hour."

"Make up your damned mind, woman! Either you want Sabrina here or not!"

Jason stepped between his wife and cousin. "I'll appreciate you not cursing at my wife," he said to Corby, then turned to Star. "I think you owe Corby an apology. You talk like he up and left her with strangers and never looked back. He provides for her and spends time with her."

Corby looked down at the hat in his hands, not wanting to face the truth. He was glad when Star's tone softened.

"I know you love Sabrina, but I also know what it's like to be a little girl without a mother. Sabrina is younger than I was when my own mother died, but she's lonely just the same. I see it in her eyes when she watches Jason with our children and sees how close Peter and his daughter are. I wouldn't mind having her here part-time, but she needs to be with you more, and I think you need it, too." Star paused. "It's not her fault Daisy died."

"I know that—" Corby stopped, looked down at his hat again. "I have to go. I told Clay I'd take his shift tonight." He looked at Jason, avoiding Star. "I'll be by to pick up 'Brina tomorrow afternoon, if that's all right with you."

"That's fine, Corb. We'll keep her anytime you want. For as long as you want," Jason said with a ring of finality in his voice. Star's intake of breath intensified the knot in Corby's stomach, but he left the house without further comment, troubled by the strained atmosphere he'd created.

"Oh, hell," he muttered, just before reaching the stand of tall pines that separated Jason's house from the junction with the main road. Corby turned in his saddle to look back at the house, regretting that he hadn't had the chance to look in on his mystery woman, his pretty little one.

A wistful smile curved his wide mouth as an image of her flooded his mind and warmed the coldness in his bones. It was pure fancy to think she'd miraculously been sent to comfort and please him, but wouldn't it be fine if it was true, if he could be given another chance?

The brisk evening breeze stoked a steadily growing fire in

Corby's blood as he imagined how good it would feel to cradle that dainty white body next to his at night, to taste the intoxicating sweetness of those lips anytime he chose, to wake up and greet each day peering into that beautiful smiling face, those bewitching green eyes . . .

Why? Just so you can fail her too?

Dejected, Corby kicked his mount into a gallop, ordering himself to put his "pretty little one" out of his mind—for her own good.

Chapter 9

LIGHT WAS BEGINNING to fill the room. A door scraped open.

Laurie? Laurie, is that you?

Laura bolted upright. That was Jake peeking in the door. She was home!

She rubbed her eyes. The bedroom door was closed again. This wasn't Galen's house. It was nothing but a dream.

Still drowsy, Laura settled back and closed her eyes, not quite sure if she should be relieved or worried.

Some time later, she awakened again to the sound of the bedroom door opening. This time the sound was accompanied by the impatient whispers of children. Laura kept her eyes closed, struggling to keep a straight face.

"See, 'Brina? We told you she was real."

"Yep."

"'Cause your daddy found her, you get to keep her."

"Yep. Cousin Johnny said so. He got to keep the puppy *his* daddy found."

"Is she dead?"

"I dunno. Touch her, Martha Jane."

"*You* touch her, Nita."

"You touch her, 'Brina. She belongs to *you*."

A tiny shiver hit Laura's spine when the small fingers ran along the length of her arm and clasped her hand.

"She's pretty. Do you think I can make her be my ma?"

The quiet voice was so hopeful, so eager that Laura wanted to cry. She'd once said eerily similar words herself.

She was just there, Grandpa. I don't know who left her. She's so pretty. Do you think they'll let me keep her, be her mother?

Laura slowly opened her eyes, bringing a collective gasp from her three visitors.

"Don't be afraid," she said, as she sat up. When she smiled, the girls relaxed and took a step closer. The two taller girls were dressed alike, in lace-trimmed pink night-gowns, their long black hair done in braids secured with small pink bows. Their shining dark eyes were wide with awe, their rosy mouths hanging open. But it was the small-est girl, the one trying to hide behind the twin on the right, who captured Laura's heart.

She bore a close resemblance to her companions, but un-like them, she seemed a lost, frightened kitten and Laura wondered if this could be Corby's daughter. Her dark eyes had that same sad, haunted look she'd glimpsed in photos of Corby and again when she saw him in person.

This was the one who had touched her, the one who wished for a mother.

"My name is Laurie. Who are you?"

Noting that Laura's interest was focused on their shy cousin, the twins pushed her forward. "She's Sabrina. I'm Nita."

"I'm Martha Jane," the other twin added.

Nita nudged her cousin. "Look at her, 'Brina."

Laura held her hand out to the girl. "You can come closer. I won't bite." Peeking up, Sabrina took a tentative step for-ward. Laura leaned toward her. "I only bite little girls with pink hair ribbons. They taste good for breakfast. Do you know where I can find some?"

The girl's giggle warmed Laura all over. When she pointed, Laura turned her attention to the twins. "Mmmm."

The twins looked at each other, then broke for the door, running straight into their mother.

"Nita May, Martha Jane," Star said. "Didn't I tell you not to disturb our guest?"

"Yes, ma'am," they answered in unison. They looked back to Laura. "Sorry."

Laura smiled. "It's all right, I wasn't really sleeping when you came in."

Star kissed her daughters' foreheads. "Take yourselves down to breakfast, then get dressed and tidy up your room. You too, Sabrina."

Sabrina shared a smile with Laura and ran after her cousins.

Star watched them go before she shut the door.

"You have beautiful children," Laura said.

"Thank you. The twins are mine. Sabrina is Corby's daughter."

"I know. I mean, she looks like him."

Star cleared her throat as she pulled a dainty side chair close to the bed. "How do you feel this morning?"

"Not too bad," Laura lied. "My head aches and I feel sore all over, but I'll live."

"Daddy will be stopping by. He'll give you something for the pain."

"No," Laura blurted. "I mean, it's not that bad." She ran her hand through her hair. "Thank you for helping me yesterday."

"You're welcome, though I don't need to be thanked for doing what's right." Star paused and checked the small enameled watch pinned to the bodice of her gray silk dress.

She said nothing, but Laura knew the bombshell was going to hit any minute, and she prayed she could deflect it. She did a quick mental countdown. *Five, four, three, two . . .*

"Do you remember what happened to you, how you came to be on our property? You appear to know us, yet we have no idea as to who you might be."

Laura opened her mouth but said nothing. She could try the old amnesia ploy— she'd read enough books with that plot to get her through for a time— but somehow she doubted that Galen's great-grandmother would buy it. Like her descendant, she was a reporter and undoubtedly had her own inbred BS detector.

"I'm not sure how I got here. I came to vis—"

Taking a quick glance at Star's face, Laura panicked.

"Ah, I have no family living. I was traveling, to get my mind off some things. I'm really not sure what made me come here," she said, crossing her fingers in the folds of the cotton coverlet.

Star gave her a long, hard look. "I can't force you to tell me, of course. However, if you've come to avenge any arrests or punishments made by my husband or Corby, I assure you you'll regret it."

Shocked, Laura made a slight gesture with her hands. "No, never—I mean, I love . . . I mean . . . I'm sorry I can't give you a better explanation, but I swear that I would never harm your family."

Star studied her for a moment but said nothing. She stood up when the doorbell chimed downstairs. "That will be Daddy. Please come down to the kitchen for something to eat after he examines you. I put a change of clothing for you in the wardrobe."

Dr. McNamara's examination confirmed what Laura already suspected—that she had no major injuries. Although she did seem to be suffering from what the doctor called a "moderate congestion of the brain." It took great effort for Laura to contain her amusement at the antiquated term, which she guessed was akin to having a mild concussion.

She promised to do as he said: "Abstain from severe mental labors" and get plenty of fresh air and subdued exercise.

"No mental labors, huh?" Laura mumbled to herself when the doctor left. "I guess that could mean racking my brain to figure out what happened and how to get back to Galen's."

Surely one day couldn't matter. Besides, she was dying to get a load of this house in all its Victorian splendor. It would be a kick to live the historical-heroine life instead of only reading about it.

In fact, looking at the flowered porcelain pitcher and basin that Star had sent up with her father, Laura was reminded of one of her favorite books. This was like the scene in *Montana*

Angel, when Skye Corbin woke up in the big ranch house after being rescued from the burning orphan train.

Like the fictional character, Laura took her time with the sponge bath, savoring the sweet smell of the lavender soap, watching the play of sunlight on the fine Austrian porcelain.

Wrapping a towel around herself, she went to the wardrobe cabinet across the room. There she found what she'd worn yesterday hanging alongside a "Gibson girl" outfit: a black woolen skirt and a black-and-white-striped shirtwaist. The unmentionables were there, too, and Laura was quickly put off by the sight of the harder-than-a-board corset, which was tied in the back and had half a dozen or so fasteners going down the front.

"Another time, maybe," Laura said, pushing the corset aside to reach the other things: the knee-length drawers, camisole, and flounced petticoat. The drawers weren't too bad. Of white ribbed cotton, softened from many washings, they felt a little like leggings, and the camisole, of the same fabric, reminded Laura of a tank top, except that it had crocheted lace and ribbon trim around the neck and armholes.

The stockings Star had left were of smooth black silk, and although Laura had to take off the drawers, pull up the thigh-high stockings and stretchy garters, then don the drawers again, she had to admit that it was worth the effort. The stockings felt very nice against the skin, very sexy.

Laura let out a wistful sigh as the face of Corby Hillhouse swam before her mind's eye. That man was sexy incarnate.

Her green eyes opened wide as his daughter's words came back.

Do you think I can make her be my ma?

Where was the girl's mother? Had she died? Run off with another man?

Another little girl swam up through the depths of Laura's memory, and she swallowed hard as she remembered the look in her foster daughter's eyes when the social worker took her. She was only a few months old, but she'd known what was happening.

I can't go through that again, Laura thought, taking the high lace-up shoes over to the bed.

Chapter 10

L AURA LEFT THE bedroom pondering one of Grandpa Alex's favorite sayings, about things happening for a reason whether or not the reason made sense.

Had she been zapped back here to see the house in what Galen called its heyday? Maybe there was some secret treasure hidden somewhere. Had she been brought back to see Corby, to put an end to this crazy infatuation she'd developed? What a disappointment it would be to find out that he was just your average male-chauvinist jerk.

The unspoken questions stopped forming in Laura's mind when she turned on the landing and descended the final flight of stairs, bringing the parlor into view. *Yes!* She'd been right about the piano. Jake had cursed her like a longshoreman that first night she arrived. He'd just moved the piano earlier that day, against the east wall where Galen wanted it, but she had insisted that it belonged in the alcove formed by the bay window.

Laura walked around the parlor. This was super. This was just the way she wanted it to look. She'd racked her brain trying to decide what parts of the room not seen in the old pictures looked like and she was pleased to see she'd guessed correctly.

The half-round table with the stereoscope and the box of slides was next to the door—not in the study as Galen had suggested.

The smell of lemon oil wafted through the room and Laura drifted with it back into the hall. There was the dining room across the way, with the same dark-patterned wallpaper. The seats of the high-backed walnut chairs were flatter in Galen's dining room. Of course, they hadn't yet been worn down by a few generations' worth of Hillhouse butts.

Next, Laura took a peek into Star's study at the end of the long, narrow hall. She hadn't needed to do a lot of restoration in here, except for conditioning the leather of the tufted sofa and chairs. That big rosewood desk looked the same, and Laura guessed that Star might feel honored to know her great-granddaughter had hung a portrait of her on the wall behind the desk alongside a framed edition of the newspaper that Star founded, the *Choctaw Sentinel,* and the bone-handled Bowie knife she'd worn strapped to her thigh for protection during the days when she'd traversed the Indian Territory on horseback in search of the news.

Galen's great-grandmother was a woman ahead of her time, and Laura hoped they might become friends. It would certainly make this journey into the Twilight Zone easier to deal with.

However, Laura's thoughts of bonding vanished as she approached the kitchen door.

Chapter 11

CORBY GRITTED HIS teeth as his landlady and sometime lover, Mariah Nitakechi, straddled his lap when he
pushed away from the table in the spacious boardinghouse
dining room.

"I missed you last night," she cooed, kissing his ear, flick-
ing her tongue over the lobe.

Corby pulled back and unwound her arms from his neck.
"Get up. Someone might come in."

"We're all alone," she whispered, unpinning her black
hair. She undid the top buttons of Corby's shirt, slid her
hands inside it to tease his small, hard nipples.

"I can't, Mariah. I have to get over to the jail. Adam's not
due in until four," he lied, inexplicably disinterested in having sex with her. He'd felt this way since early January,
though he didn't know why.

Mariah wiggled her lush bottom on Corby's lap, frowning
when he failed to respond. "You never want to anymore,"
she grumbled, getting up. "Do you have a woman someplace?" she demanded, pointing one of her hairpins at his
head.

Don't I wish, Corby mused.

He stood, refastening his shirt buttons. "No, Mariah, I do

not 'have a woman someplace,' but if I get one, you'll be the first to know."

"At least your mouth has life left in it," Mariah remarked, casting a cold look toward the fly of Corby's twill trousers.

"You'd be surprised at the life left in these old bones," Corby quipped. "Sometimes it just takes an expert to ignite that spark."

Mariah's black eyes flashed and she crossed her arms in front of her, accentuating her ample bosom. "You never had any complaints before. Why now?"

Corby left the dining room, his boot heels scraping on the wooden floor. He took his hat off the rack near the front door, hating the feel of Mariah's angry stare on his back. Knowing that she would follow him outside and make a scene, if only to draw attention to herself, Corby decided to face her now. "I'm sorry for what I said. I've got a lot on my mind, that's all. I need to get someone to look after Sabrina, I have to help Peter and Libby move their belongings to Kentucky soon, and today I have to go all the way to Fort Smith to file a report for Jason. He was called down to Tuskahoma to act as an official escort for those senators from Washington."

The lines around Mariah's mouth softened. She approached Corby, caressing his rugged face with the tips of her fingers. "Well, then, when you get all your running done I'll make it a point to take extra-special care of you. You always were my favorite boarder."

Corby let her kiss him, though he barely returned the kiss. He lifted her arms from his shoulders. "I have to go." He turned back when Mariah called his name in that throaty voice that had once made him hornier than a billy goat every time he heard it. "What?"

"Do you really think I'm beautiful?"

"Of course I do," he said quickly, tipping his hat, slipping out the door. *But you're not the pale beauty who kept me awake all last night.* He closed his eyes for a moment, picturing the woman he had found. *What are you doing now, little one? Are you thinking of me?*

* * *

Laura's thoughts were far from Corby as she eavesdropped on the conversation Star Hillhouse was having.

"She's obviously hiding something. We just have to find out what that something is—preferably before Jason gets back and tells me to keep my nose in my own yard."

"Where could she possibly be from?" another woman asked. "That shirtwaist of hers was so unladylike, so form-fitting. Decent women don't dress like that."

"Let's not go to any name-calling," Star said. "At least not until we know who she is and where she's from."

Laura entered the kitchen. "I told you who I am, and I'm from New York City. I believe I mentioned that."

"I believe you didn't," Star countered. "Still, it's a start." She stood up and indicated her companion. "Laura Bennett, I'd like you to meet Libby Hillhouse. She's married to one of my husband's brothers."

Laura nodded to the woman. She wasn't quite sure what to say to Star. And to think she'd once accused Galen of holding the patent on the Choctaw version of chutzpah.

"I promised you a meal," Star said, pulling out one of the pressed-back chairs at the table. "Would you like eggs and sausage?"

"I could really go for a cheeseburger with onions," Laura thought aloud. *Way to go, Einstein,* she added silently when the other women's eyes widened.

"What on earth is a cheeseburger?" Libby asked.

"It's—"

"I believe it's a meat patty of some sort served like a sand-wich," Star offered.

"Exactly," Laura answered. Shifting her gaze to the win-dows to watch the children playing out back, she had an idea. "If you have a piece of beef handy, I could show you how to make some. Your kids would love them for lunch."

Laura crossed her fingers behind her back and looked at the women. Star's sister-in-law was obviously against the idea, giving a subtle shake of her head, but Star looked Laura directly in the eye before indicating the enormous ice-box/refrigerator near the sink and the hand-operated meat grinder attached to a butcher-block table.

"Be my guest. I'm always looking for new recipes."

Soon, Laura was especially thankful for the hours spent at Grandpa Alex's side in the restaurant he owned in the Village. Pizza had been his specialty, but he could mix a mean burger, and fortunately she remembered his instructions now. She didn't want to make any foolish mistakes under the watchful eyes of her female companions. Luckily, the monstrous iron range was fired up and ready to go, although it took a bit of time for the heavy iron skillet to heat. But once it did, Laura was in her glory. She felt just like another of her fictional heroines—Bree Sommerfield, who charmed the socks off a crusty old neighbor with her cooking skills in *Caldwell's Woman.*

As Laura predicted, the assembled Hillhouse children dug in to their burgers with gusto. Even Galen and Jake's grandfather-to-be, the toddler Matthew, got into the act, albeit with his fingers. She'd always wondered how Jake had come by his hearty appetite.

Leaving her own burger only half eaten, Laura went out to the back porch. She was beginning to be unnerved by the way Corby's daughter kept staring at her. She moved off the porch and sat down cross-legged in the yard, her back resting against a young maple tree that in her time had grown to more than seventy feet tall. She closed her eyes and tried to meditate—maybe she could go as deep as Jake. He'd always said that when the vibes were good he was in another world.

"Ma'am?"

Laura groaned inwardly and slowly opened her eyes. As she feared, Corby's sad-eyed daughter was standing before her. "Could you help me with my shoe? I can'ts tie yet."

Those eyes did Laura in, and she reached for the girl's shoelaces, stopping when she took the lace ends in her hands. She patted the pocket formed by the folds of her long skirt. "Sit here with me. I'll show you how I learned to tie."

Sabrina hesitated, then sat, and Laura felt her heart constrict the same way it had this morning when the girl held her hand. Pushing the feeling away, she took Sabrina's shoelaces and made two loops. "See, you have two little bunnies. But these are mean little bunnies and they like to fight." She wound one loop over the other. "And when they fight they get all tangled up and their mothers come and try to tug them apart." She made a knot, then another. "But the more they tug, the tighter the bunnies get."

Sabrina giggled and fingered the little bow Laura's fighting bunnies made. "Can I try?"

Laura untied the shoe. "Just take your time, and don't be mad if it doesn't work at first," she said, unaware that she and Sabrina had an audience back in the house.

"You don't think she's trying to poison us, do you, Star?" Libby whispered.

"Don't be silly. I watched her the entire time she ground the meat for those patties and made them." She tapped her index finger on the windowpane. "Look," she said, her brown eyes intent on the giggling Sabrina.

Libby looked out the window. "Isn't that sweet?"

"That gives me an idea," Star said.

"What?"

Before Star could answer, the front doorbell rang.

Chapter 12

CORBY TURNED AWAY from the door, hoping the delay in answering meant that Star was otherwise occupied. If she was, it would give him a few more hours of not having to think about what he was going to do with Sabrina. Oh, hell, he couldn't run off—he had to get those reports of Jason's and run them to the U.S. marshal's office in Fort Smith.

Reluctantly, he turned back just as Star opened the door. He recoiled, expecting her to badger him immediately, but instead she gave him a warm smile and gently took hold of his arm.

"Hello, Corby. Isn't this a pleasant surprise. Silly me— you've come for Jason's papers. Pull up a chair in the parlor and I'll get them. It may take a few minutes."

Star hurried to the kitchen and told Libby that Corby had arrived.

"I'll keep him company."

Star grabbed the back of her skirt to stop her from leaving. "No. I have a plan." She opened the back door and called to Laura, "Libby and I have our hands full with the children and their messy hands. Could you please go into my office across the hall and get the brown envelope on my desk? There's someone in the parlor waiting for it."

"Sure," Laura said, wondering how the women could have their hands so full if the kids were clearing and cleaning their own plates and glasses.

She retrieved the envelope, then walked the few feet to the parlor, feeling the hair on the nape of her neck rise.

Corby looked up at the sharp intake of breath, unwilling to believe that he was actually seeing the woman he'd been thinking of for countless hours. Lord, but she was even prettier than she'd been yesterday, although something had to be said for the close fit of the strange clothing she'd had on. Still, just knowing of the dainty curves below the layers of fabric she now wore got him hotter than a Fourth of July bonfire. He stood, holding his hat in front of him to hide the evidence of his impure thoughts.

"Hello," she said in a voice that dribbled over him like warm syrup. She stepped forward, an envelope in her hand. "This must be for you."

"I suppose," he answered, reaching, losing himself in the depths of her eyes. He breathed in and felt like he'd just gulped a glass of whiskey. She smelled of flowers with a hint of new-cut grass. He wanted her. Now. Right here.

Clearing his parched throat, Corby took a step back, though he couldn't take his eyes off her. "How are you feeling today? Do you remember anything of what happened to you?"

"I think I might owe you an apology," she said, lowering her gaze, her cheeks tinging pink. Corby's blood surged to all the wrong places.

He turned slightly, pretending to look out the window. "You want to apologize? For what?"

"You know." She paused. "For what I did. The kiss."

She whispered the last word and Corby turned back quickly, afraid that she had run off. She hadn't. She stood there bold as brass, a little embarrassed but not regretful. He knew all about regret, and it did not show in those eyes.

He grinned. "I can't say it was too unpleasant. By the

way, I'm Corby Hillhouse, but I suppose you know that. You said my name when I found you."

Think fast, girl, Laura's mind screamed. She thrust out her hand, catching him off guard. "I'm Laura Bennett from New York. I have some friends originally from the area. They showed me a newspaper once with your picture in it." She pointed to the badge pinned to the front of his black vest. "You were elected sheriff, as I recall."

"Been reelected, too," he said, his wide smile lighting the far reaches of his chocolate-brown eyes. He shook her hand, holding on to it for a very long time. "Did you come to visit these friends of yours? Maybe I know them."

Had to step right in the stuff again, didn't you? "Well," Laura hedged, "actually they relocated a long time ago. I've just been wanting to see this part of the country."

His smile wavered and Laura felt a chill. He was looking at her as a lawman, not as a mere man.

"You traveling alone? It ain't safe for a woman alone around these parts."

"I'm a big girl. I can handle myself." His eyes hardened further, and Laura pitied those who got on his bad side. She was glad when Star came in, with Libby a few steps behind, holding little Matthew.

"Sorry for taking so long. I take it you two have introduced yourselves?"

"We have," Laura said, turning her attention from Corby at the sound of excited children's voices in the hall. She watched intently when Sabrina ran into the room. Anyone could see how happy the little girl was to see her father. And everyone could see that Corby Hillhouse cringed at the sight of his daughter. Backing away from her outstretched arms Corby patted Sabrina on the head. Patted her like a puppy.

"I'm sorry, 'Brina. I have to get moving and deliver these papers for Uncle Jace. I'll be seeing you." He tipped his hat before putting it on. "Ladies,"

"I'll be seeing you?" Laura repeated to herself, watching him rush out as poor little Sabrina wilted before her like a dandelion picked at the height of summer. The nerve of that man. And she had thought her own father deserved to get the

Bastard of the Year award for the way he treated her when he was drinking. This guy was stone-cold sober. What was his excuse? It had better be *damned* good.

Hearing the slight sniffle, Laura took hold of Sabrina's trembling hand. "Come outside with me. We'll practice tying your shoes some more."

Sabrina brightened, if only a little, and clutched her hand. "Okay, Laurie."

"Laurie?" Star inquired.

Laura nodded. "I'm not used to being called ma'am. It makes me feel like an old lady."

Star smiled as they exited the parlor. She trailed behind, pulling Libby aside when they reached the rear porch. "About that plan I mentioned earlier . . ."

Chapter 13

THE TRAIN RIDE to Fort Smith, Arkansas, seemed especially long to Corby, who shifted this way and that in his seat, unable to get comfortable because of the lingering reaction of seeing his pretty little one, who now had a name. Laura Bennett. It was a fine name for a fine woman.

A strange woman, the lawman in him added. *A woman who travels alone wearing tight men's britches and shirts that show off things better left decently covered, except in private.*

Corby tempered his displeasure, reminding himself that she'd been properly clothed this morning. Maybe someone had taken her real clothes and she'd gotten the first things she could find.

But none of that really mattered. Laura Bennett's business was her own, unless she chose to cause trouble in or around Warburton. Somehow he doubted she would turn out to be a troublemaker. He settled back as best his manly parts would allow and remembered how nice it felt to hear her voice, see her pretty face, feel those soft lips . . .

Once his own business at the marshal's office had been tended to, and thoughts of Laura Bennett made clear thinking all but impossible, Corby decided to spend the time until the next train at one of Fort Smith's brothels. Afterward, sated from the little blonde he'd chosen, Corby ambled back to the train station to wait for his trip back home. Thoughts of Laura Bennett still would not leave him—until he ran into a bad memory from the past.

His dead first wife's father. Owen Webster.

They stared each other down, Corby taller, Webster larger by the force of his hatred.

"I ought to kill you, Indian. I should have done it a long time ago."

Corby held his hands out at his sides. "Here I am, Web."

The portly man drew his Remington revolver, his fleshy jowls growing a deeper shade of red. He held the gun on Corby for a long time, suddenly reholstering it after a crowd formed. "Too many witnesses," he muttered, pushing past Corby.

Corby exhaled a long breath and lowered his arms. Owen Webster's parting words, whispered so he alone could hear, rang in his ears. "Now that I know you're still alive, Indian, I'll make you pay. I'll make you pay for taking away my baby girl."

Corby shook his head and started toward the train station. Pay for Lorena's death? He'd been paying for twelve long years. His guilt saw to that on a regular basis.

Chapter 14

LAURA STOOD WITH her hands on her hips, shaking her head at Star McNamara Hillhouse, who was putting away the dinner dishes. "You did not just say what I think you said. You did not just ask me to set up housekeeping with Corby and Sabrina."

"I believe my exact words were, 'I'd like to hire you to be Corby's housekeeper if you have no immediate plans to leave town,' but I imagine 'set up housekeeping' fits the bill."

Laura shook her head, then let the water in the zinc-lined sink drain down into the large wooden tub in the enclosed space below. When the tub was full she carried it outside to dump it, as Star had done after lunch.

"I'm not a maid. I'm an interior designer," she reminded Star when she returned.

Star dismissed this with a curt wave. "Then redesign the interior of Libby's house. She's leaving behind the sofa and kitchen table and chairs. Sabrina already has a bed there, and my father has some old things in his attic. I'm sure that between me and my other two sisters-in-law we can get enough linens and dishware and such to tide you three over."

There was a cheap thrill attached to this little scheme of

Star's, but Laura didn't want to commit to anything, especially where Sabrina was involved. They would both be hurt in the end. "I don't know how long I can stay. I might have to leave on short notice. I can't give you any specifics because I don't know them myself. I'm sure you can find someone else for the job."

Star pushed in the kitchen chairs, then called out the back door for the children to go up to their rooms and get ready for bed. She took Matthew out of his high chair and gave Laura an appraising look. "I'm sure there are any number of young women from our congregation who would literally jump at the chance to get into Corby's good graces, but I want you to do it. I've seen you with Sabrina. She likes you—and she doesn't warm up easily, even to family. She needs a woman in her life. She needs to have a home of her own. I'm hoping that her thickheaded father will come around eventually. It would be a great help if you could stay in town until then."

Laura tried to protest, but the words refused to come out. She thought of her friend Jake's favorite phrase when he had been her sensei, teaching her the martial arts.

Go with the flow, Grasshopper. Let it lead you until you gain the strength and knowledge to take it where you want to go.

Chapter 15

JAKE HILLHOUSE INADVERTENTLY tore out a few strands of shoulder-length hair as he shoved it back from his face with agitated motions. "I saw her, Galen. I know I did. She was right here in this bed at dawn. I called her name and she sat up."

Galen tried to place a sympathetic hand on her twin's shoulder. He jerked away, glaring at her. "You were out all night looking for her. You were exhausted. You wanted to see her, so you did. That's why she disappeared before your eyes."

"No!" Jake paced the spot in front of Laura's white iron bed. "I saw what I saw. There's something weird here, Sis. I know it. Laurie would not leave without telling us. And if she hurt herself by falling through that busted railing, she would have turned up. The cops surely would have found her. I have a bad feeling."

Galen looked at her brother, convinced that his feeling stretched back further than he would ever admit. "Look, maybe she got a call from New York. Maybe there was a problem with Alex's estate or restaurant. She'll be in touch."

"If she can."

Chapter 16

SETTLING HIMSELF IN the train seat, Corby banished the ugly face of Owen Webster from his mind with the only alternative he could muster—the brief meeting he'd had with Laura Bennett. He tipped his hat down to shield his eyes from the setting sun and dozed, substituting her lovely face for that of the skillful woman with whom he'd whiled away the afternoon.

But this time, as he reached an imaginary climax, he felt the shattering explosion he had missed earlier. The pleasure shook him down to his toes and back up to the ends of his hair, and he wondered what it would really be like with her . . .

The erotic fantasy broke off abruptly when the train screeched to a halt, throwing Corby forward against the seat in front of him. The compartment filled with noise, crying babies, frightened women, as he struggled to regain the wind that had been knocked out of him.

"What do you men want?" the conductor shouted. "This ain't no money train. We don't even have any mail on board yet. Why don't you just leave and we'll for—"

A gunshot finished his sentence for him.

Corby remained crouched between the seats, taking stock of the situation. Three men, all armed, one with a rifle. They looked at the terrified passengers as if searching for someone in particular. They started forward, grabbing men at random, demanding valuables of some.

Cocking his Colt, Corby bided his time. They were three rows back.

"You have a badge—*do* something!" the woman across the aisle said loud enough for the bandits to hear.

Cursing under his breath, Corby slowly rose, revolver aimed between the leader's eyes. "There's too many innocent children here, and I'm not stupid enough to think I can take all three of you at once without one of them getting hurt."

He stepped into the aisle, still aiming. "You boys take what you want, and you an' me will settle this off the train." With his free hand he unhooked his own silver pocket watch from his vest, his eyes barely skimming the men in the back of the car who had drawn their own firearms and were edging closer. He hoped to hell they intended to help. He held the watch out. "Is it a deal?"

The lead gunman laughed and took aim.

Corby fired.

The train car filled with shouts and screams, but in the end the laughing bandit lay dead and his companions were subdued and tied.

"Settle down now, folks. The excitement's over," Corby said, checking the dead man's pockets. He found part of a crumpled pay voucher.

Heavily creased, dirty, and smeared, the printed *W* inside a double circle gave Corby the answer he needed. He knew that voucher mark well, having received and even written some in his tenure at the Webster ranch near Paris, Texas.

His gut feeling had been right. These men hadn't been after money—they were after him. Seizing one of the survivors by the collar, he jerked him to his feet, then spit in the man's face. "When your sorry ass gets out of jail, you give that to Web. Tell him I got the message."

Shoving the man back down to his knees, Corby turned to two other male passengers. "Get that body covered with something and take it to the baggage car while I see if the engineer is still alive."

One of the men sneered. "I don't take orders from no red-skin, even one with a tin star."

Corby said nothing, choosing instead to replace the bullet he'd spent. "I am not in the mood," he said, the meaning quite clear. He made his way to the engine, revived and untied the engineer and stoker, then returned to his compartment. The dead man had been moved.

Chapter 17

LAURA FELT A flash of maternal longing when Sabrina climbed up on her lap as she sat on the front porch steps of Star and Jason's house a few evenings after agreeing to Star's job offer. Sabrina was spending the night, along with her cousin, while Libby and Peter packed their belongings for their move to Kentucky.

"Will you tell me the story again, Laurie?"

"What story, sweetie?"

"The funny one 'bout the wascally wabbit and the little black duck."

Laura laughed. She'd been grasping at straws to entertain the child, whom she'd been going to visit every day, at Star's insistence. She was about to recount the plot of an old cartoon when she saw a rider approaching. Her pulse quickened. It was Corby. She hadn't seen him in almost a week, but then again, neither had Sabrina.

Laura's heart rate returned to normal.

"Tell you what, kiddo. We'll save the story, because here comes your daddy to see you."

"Oh," Sabrina said, giving her father only a cursory look as he dismounted some distance away and led his gelding to the water trough set up for visitors. "I hafta go pee now."

She scrambled off Laura's lap and hurried into the house.

Laura stood, dusted off the back of her long brown skirt, and met Corby at the bottom of the steps. "I hope you're happy with yourself."

"What?" he asked, removing his hat and running his fingers through his hair.

Anger prevented Laura from acknowledging how sexy the simple motions were. "What is your problem? Why do you avoid your daughter? Star thinks you blame her for your wife's death."

Taken aback by the candor, Corby took the defensive. "How I treat my child is none of your concern. Now, if you'll excuse me, I have something to talk over with my cousin Jason."

"Jerk," Laura grumbled. Boy, had she ever been wrong about him. That business about eyes being windows to the soul was a dud, but at least one old saw held true: A picture certainly was worth a thousand words. Unfortunately, in the case of Corby Hillhouse, most of them were of the four-letter variety.

"I will certainly get the word out," Jason said after hearing of Corby's encounter on the train. "If anyone starts asking too many questions about you, they'll be sent packing."

"I appreciate it," Corby said, leaning on the sofa armrest. He wouldn't have brought the matter up at all, but he wasn't the only one whose back needed watching.

"So what brought this on?" Jason asked. "You aren't exactly the type that people tend to hold grudges against. You and this outlaw go back a ways?"

Corby took his time answering, not wanting to raise more questions. He didn't want to bring up Web's name or explain how he'd kept his first marriage a secret because of the part he'd played in Lorena's death. Too little, too late—just like with Daisy.

"It goes back so far I don't even remember the half of it. After my pa died and I took off for those two years, I hooked up with an outfit in Texas, then caught the foreman fiddling with the books. Guess some men like holding grudges, especially if it's against an Indian. You know how that goes."

"Don't we all."

Needing to change the subject, Corby brought up the only other thing on his mind. "So, why is that woman I found still hanging around?"

Jason shrugged and sat on the corner of his wife's desk. "Star's taken a shine to her for some reason. She's been helping with the kids, giving old Rosa a rest. Lord knows, after raising Star, that poor woman should have gone into retirement a lifetime ago. Do you remember the time . . ."

Corby nodded, barely listening to his cousin's reminiscence.

"Well, I have to get back to town," Corby said, as Jason was about to launch into a third tale. He stood and stretched his back.

"Want me to walk you out?"

"I think I can find my way."

Smiling, Corby exited the room. Laura Bennett was in the parlor tinkling the piano keys. "You play?" he asked.

"A little."

She stood and came forward. His body began to respond.

"Star wanted me to ask if you were taking Sabrina to church tomorrow."

"I don't know. I might be on duty."

"She said you'd say that. We'll take her for you, then."

"I'd appreciate that."

To Corby's dismay, she turned her back and returned to the piano, busying herself with the sheet music stacked neatly on top. He let himself out, wondering why the snub bothered him so.

It bothered him all during the ride back to town and while he made his nightly rounds of the area. Since it was a quiet night, he left his senior deputy in charge of the jail and retired to the boardinghouse, but quickly regretted the decision.

"I'm not in the mood, Mariah. I'm sorry," he said when she let herself into his room.

"You're just all tense and worried about this and that," she cooed, unbuttoning the front of her blue wrapper. "I know how to make you feel better."

Corby got out of bed, the erection outlined by his drawers having nothing to do with her. "Please leave," he said, pulling on his trousers.

Mariah stepped closer, her long hair glistening in the dim light of the bedside lamp. "I need a man, Corby. I need *you*."

Corby said nothing, backing up against the bed when she pressed close. He felt himself soften. "Mariah—"

"You need me, too," she said sharply, tying her wrap closed. "You need a wife. You need someone to make a home for your child. Why won't you marry me?"

"I can't answer you. I'm sorry."

"You should be sorry." She began to pace the small room like a caged lioness. "You should be sorry. After all I've done for you through the years. How long has it been, Corby? How long?"

"I don't know. I moved in here two years before I married Daisy, then came back after . . . I don't know how long. Seven years total?"

Mariah pounced. "Try ten. And don't forget the extra times you stopped by to *visit*."

Daisy's dead face came back to haunt Corby, and he grabbed his discarded clothing from the chair near the bed and left, dressing in the hall, needing to get away.

Wearing her jeans and T-shirt, Laura crept down the stairs and outside. She went to stand beneath the second-floor balcony at the side of the house and tried to trace the way she'd rolled when she fell as she tried to reach the dresser-drawer knob. She went down the little hill, her Reeboks sliding on the dirt and small stones.

This must be where she'd landed—the bits of brush were still broken. She sat and meditated the way Jake had taught her, easing herself deeper and deeper into stages of relaxation until she felt she was almost floating above herself. She was going home.

Her trip was cut short when the large hand shook her.

"Just what do you think you're doing?"

Laura gave Corby Hillhouse the evil eye and stood up. "Who, pray tell, appointed you to be my keeper?"

Corby scowled. "It sure looks like you need a keeper from where I'm standing. Anybody could have come up behind you and done Lord knows what, and you wouldn't even have noticed them. Where was your mind, woman?"

"About a hundred years away," she mumbled, going back toward Star and Jason's house. Corby followed, and she faced him again when they crested the rise.

"What are you doing out here at this hour, anyway?" She put her hand to her forehead. "Don't tell me, let me guess. You came to play 'daddy dearest' because you know full well Sabrina is asleep."

"You are way out of line, Miss Bennett."

Laura thrust out her chin. "And you are one crappy father figure, judging from the little I've seen and heard."

Corby strode away and mounted the horse he had left tethered to the porch railing.

Chapter 18

LAURA WOKE WITH a raging headache that kept her in bed for an extra hour. It faded to a dull pain that gradually retreated with each tick of the small clock on her bureau. Once she was able to think straight, she wondered if the meditation attempt had anything to do with it.

Maybe she couldn't go back. Maybe whatever brought her here wouldn't let her leave until it was good and ready for her to go.

She wasn't thrilled at the prospect of this rustic living, but all in all, it didn't seem so bad. There was basic indoor plumbing. *Very* basic indoor plumbing, but at least she didn't have to visit an outhouse in the dead of night. True, having to manually fill the water-heater tank and empty the bath and sink tubs was a chore. Still, it could be worse.

She could live with it for a bit longer, especially if it meant no more brainsplitters in the morning.

When the knock sounded on her door at eight, Laura flinched, but the headache did not return. "Come in."

It was Sabrina.

"Aunt Star wants to know are you coming to church? We're leavin' soon."

Not being much of a churchgoer, she'd planned to beg

off, but she changed her mind now. "I'll be down in just a minute."

Sabrina beamed.

Laura answered with a smile of her own.

She stared at the closed door for a moment. She didn't want to get close to Corby's daughter. It wasn't good for either of them, her situation being so ambiguous, but how could she not let herself get wrapped around those little fingers?

Sabrina was a beautiful little girl with an infectious laugh and a million-dollar smile. She had a wicked sense of humor too, judging from the impression she'd done yesterday afternoon of the woman who owned the boardinghouse where Corby stayed.

"She looks like this," Sabrina had said, crossing her arms in front of her, tilting her head forward, looking up through her dark lashes with eyes colder than stone.

You'd have thought the kid had grown up watching *Dynasty*'s Joan Collins at her bitchiest. Mariah Nitakechi certainly didn't sound like a very sociable person.

While Laura sponged off with the water from her bureau pitcher, she reflected that living around such an attitude might account for part of Corby's coldness where Sabrina was concerned.

Perhaps this Mariah would be at church, and she would be able to check her out in person.

As was customary, the large Hillhouse family gathered in front of the church, and Laura was introduced to the clan. There were Jason's parents, Elan and Martha; and the second son, Jacob; his wife, Talulah; and their four sons. Peter and Libby were there with their daughter, Jacy, and the youngest Hillhouse son, Lucas, soon arrived with his fiancée and her parents. Star's father and stepmother came next, and the family began to enter the church en masse.

As usual, there was no sign of Corby, which prompted Talulah to remark (also as usual, according to Star), "I swear, that man hasn't set foot in this church since we buried my sister."

She and the other members of the family were openly surprised when he appeared near the end of the service and stayed for the monthly lunch social.

"Look out!" Elan Hillhouse said, pointing to the tall church steeple. "I think it's going to fall over. It's not used to having Corby in its presence."

"Aw, Uncle Elan, it hasn't been that long."

"Yes, it has," Talulah Hillhouse said, breaking the light mood.

Laura watched Corby's boyish grin evaporate, and he walked away toward the tables where the food was being set up. She followed.

"I take it you and your late wife's sister don't get along."

"It's not anything I care to talk about," he said, never looking at her.

"If you ever change your mind, I've been told that I'm a good listener."

Laura waited for a response. There was none. Corby simply watched the young women of the congregation go about their work of lining up the filled picnic baskets each family had brought. They watched him back. And smiled. Often.

"If you change your mind, I'll be around."

Corby turned and watched her go. Heaven help him, he wanted to tell her. All of it, about Lorena and her father, about Daisy and his affair with Mariah. But of course, he wouldn't. Not today. Not ever. It was none of her business. It was nobody's business, and he preferred to keep it that way.

Laura went back to the family. She sat on a blanket next to Star while Dr. McNamara and Jason took the older children to get their food.

"What were you and Corby talking about?"

"Nothing. He blew me off."

Star shook her head. "You say the strangest things, but they seem appropriate somehow." She sliced a thin piece of apple and gave it to baby Matthew. "How *that* woman can show her face in a house of God I will never understand."

Laura looked over her shoulder, trying to follow Star's cold gaze. Some chesty woman in a yellow dress was slithering over to Corby. She had "bitch" written all over her. "Who's that?"

"Mariah Nitakechi."

Laura looked away, wanting to laugh.

"What's so funny?" Star asked, handing the baby another piece of apple.

"Sabrina did this impersonation of her yesterday. You had to be there."

A strange little noise drew Laura's attention to Matthew. "He's choking."

"Daddy!" Star shrieked, trying to reach into Matthew's mouth.

Chapter 19

"No! YOU'LL MAKE it worse!" Laura snatched him, turned him over her knee, and performed the infant Heimlich maneuver that she'd learned at the YMCA.

The apple piece popped free. Laura handed the crying baby to his equally shaken mother and moved off the blanket so Jason could take her place.

"You saved his life," Star said in a voice very unlike her own.

Jason wiped away his son's tears. "We're much obliged."

"It was nothing," Laura said quietly, praying that she hadn't upset some weird cosmic balance. Of course, if she hadn't intervened, Matthew might not have lived to adulthood. On the other hand, if she'd never arrived, Star might not have been gossiping . . .

Feeling a twinge in her temple, Laura eased out of the way, walking in the direction of the horses, which were corralled in a roped-off area.

Not a bright idea, she told herself when the smell of horseflesh and other horse accoutrements hit her nose. She turned and ran smack-dab into Corby's solid chest. His smell was an entirely different matter indeed.

"Whoa now."

The hand Corby put out to steady Laura seared her through the thin material of her ruffled shirtwaist, the heat spiraling down way too deeply for her comfort. She took a step back.

"Forgive my clumsiness." She tried to step around him. He shifted to block her way.

"Thank you for what you did back there. They almost lost Matthew when he was born, the cord was around his neck . . ." Corby cleared his throat and took a breath. "It would kill Jace and Star both to see anything happen to any of their kids. You saved my family a lot of grief."

"I did what needed to be done."

He nodded. "Still. We appreciate it."

"Excuse me," a male voice said from behind him.

Corby looked over his shoulder, not pleased to see Star's newspaper editor/reporter, Abel Potts, behind him.

"Excuse me, Sheriff. I'd like to speak to Miss Bennett." He looked around Corby's broad back. "It is 'Bennett,' isn't it? With one or two *t*'s?"

"Two," Laura said, stepping to the side. It surprised her when Corby stepped to the side as well, further blocking Potts's view. She reached past Corby and tugged on the smaller man's coat sleeve, coaxing him forward. "You aren't going to make a big deal about this, are you?" she asked, leading the reporter away and leaving Corby staring after them.

Corby rubbed his tense jaw. That woman was a real pistol. She had more nerve than three Stars combined. She sure was something else, a woman the likes of which he'd never met. There couldn't possibly be another one like her in all of the Indian Territory. She was nervy—and mouthy—but, Lord, she was attractive.

And apparently he wasn't the only man to have noticed that fact. Corby's back stiffened as he watched the single men of the congregation (and a few of the married ones) fuss over Laura Bennett. He walked toward the throng, becoming more annoyed with each step. Damn harebrained men. Didn't they have anything better to do than fawn over some stranger who could be on the run from the law, for all any of them knew?

Looking at those fools, you'd think Miss Laura Bennett was the first woman ever to set foot in Warburton.

She certainly wasn't the first, but she sure was the most interesting.

Corby was barely aware that Mariah had come up beside him until she slid her arm inside his jacket.

"Who is she? One of Star's hoity-toity Boston relatives?"

"No. She's new to town. Fell and got hurt behind Jace's house. I guess they're letting her stay on a while. Pretty lucky they did, all things considered."

"It looked to me like she was tryin' to kill that baby, snatching it up the way she did."

The words had barely sunk in when Corby caught sight of Jason with one of his twin daughters. An invisible knife stabbed Corby's heart. When Laura came into view, holding Sabrina by the hand, he felt the knife again, along with a stab of jealousy.

Mariah followed his line of vision. Her mouth drew into a taut line. "Would you hitch up my buggy for me, Corby?"

He made no reply.

She asked again, this time jabbing him in the side for emphasis.

"You came with Potts, didn't you? Get him to do it," Corby said tersely, walking way, his eyes fixed on Laura and Sabrina, who were laughing at something that fool Potts was saying as he ladled out cups of lemonade for them.

Corby strode to the refreshment table and took the lemonade cups from the startled reporter. "Mariah needs you. Said it's important."

Potts looked at Laura. "Well, if it's important. I daresay you'll be in good hands with the sheriff," he said, letting out a little laugh. "Good day, ladies."

"Good-bye, Abel. I'll let you know about Tuesday."

Corby bit back a growl as Potts's simpering smile grew wide.

"I'll look forward to it, Miss Bennett."

Corby handed Laura and Sabrina their cups. "What was that about?"

Laura blinked. Twice. "What?"

Corby frowned, partly because Laura was playing coy,

partly because his daughter was trying to hide behind Laura's skirts as if he were some monster. "That Tuesday business."

Laura shrugged. "He asked me to go for a walk." She turned and walked away, Sabrina close behind.

With a few strides of his long legs, Corby caught up and stepped into Laura's path. He took his daughter's lemonade cup, handed it to Laura, and picked up the startled little girl. "Mr. Swanson fetched the pony from the livery. Let's get you to the front of the line for a ride."

With an encouraging nod from Laura, Sabrina's weak smile grew steady. "Okay, Pa."

Following Corby through the crowd, Laura snuck a quick look at the church. *Thank you.*

Following the pony rides, the men gathered for a game of *ishtaboli.* Galen and Jake had explained it to Laura, saying it was a combination of lacrosse and insanity.

Laura wasn't ready to agree on the insanity part, but it certainly was rough-and-tumble, with the men doing anything and everything to keep their opponents from getting the leather ball to goal for a score. There were cuts, scrapes, and bruises galore fifteen minutes into the match, and Laura no longer wondered why Dr. McNamara began setting up a first-aid station as soon as the game was mentioned. By game's end he was tending to swollen ankles and elbows, and what appeared to be a broken wrist.

Sabrina came barreling into Laura's arms, shrieking, "Pa and Uncle Jace's team won!"

"They certainly did, sweetie," Laura said, watching the bare-chested Corby get in line at a large wooden tub to soak his head for a moment.

Laura's eyes were glued to him as he came through the crowd, running his fingers through his dripping hair, laughing at something someone said to him—stopping to speak to some petite, doe-eyed woman who offered her shawl as a towel.

It took three tugs on her sleeve before Laura realized Sabrina was trying to get her attention. "What is it, hon?"

"Can I go wif' Nita May to get a lemon ice?"

"Okay. I'll be here when you get back."

"I'm back," Corby said in a low, oh-so-sexy tone.

Laura turned her head, her gaze following the progress of a water droplet that fell across his broad shoulder to his taut, bronzed chest, over his erect nipple . . .

"Our side won, but nothing new there," he said lightly, reaching for the shirt he'd left in Laura's care.

"I figured that out," she answered, barely aware that she'd handed it to him, that his long, rough fingers were brushing over hers, lingering for an awfully long time. She watched him don the shirt and fasten the buttons, moving like a big cat, full of grace and power. She sighed.

"You all right?"

She gave her head a quick shake to clear it. "Yeah. Can I get a cold drink for you?"

"That would be mighty fine."

He smiled.

She smiled back.

Laura sighed inwardly when Corby gulped the cup of lemonade she brought him. Who'd have thought the sight of a bobbing Adam's apple could be a turn-on?

"You shouldn't step out with Abel Potts."

Laura gaped. "Step out? You mean go out? Why not?"

"You just shouldn't, that's all," Corby said, swallowing the final drops of lemonade.

"You have to have a reason."

"I just don't think it's a good idea."

Laura rolled her eyes. "You have to have a reason. Did he do something? Did some woman file a complaint against him? Will he make me pick up the tab? What?"

Corby folded his own arms, entranced by the fiery glints in her eyes. "Never really cared for Potts, that's all. He's too"—he paused, searching for the word—"he's too prissy."

"Maybe I like prissy men. Did you ever think of that?"

Corby felt a rush of heat and told himself it was just the sun setting behind him. "You do what you want, then. I don't care."

Laura watched him go, a small part of her wishing he did.

Chapter 20

RESTLESS THE FOLLOWING morning, Laura offered to take Star's grocery list to the general store. "It's Cassidy's, right? The store we passed going to church?"

"Yes, but it's rather far."

"That's okay. I know how to ride. Could I borrow one of your horses?"

"You can use the brown mare. And I have tomorrow's editorial in my office, if you wouldn't mind taking it to Potts."

"No problem."

Laura considered putting on her jeans as she tried, with little success, to mount the horse, her long skirt getting in the way. She knew, however, that she should try to fit in as long as she was here. There was no point in being an obvious misfit.

Corby was coming down the boardinghouse steps when Laura entered town. Mariah Nitakechi was standing in the doorway, gazing longingly at him, smoothing her hair into place, adjusting her bodice.

Corby must have had lunch. Or something.

He waved. Laura waved back and went about her business.

From the end of the street she saw Corby go into the jail.

Maybe she'd stop by after she ran her errands. Just to let him know that Star was keeping Sabrina for the rest of the week while Libby and Peter got the last-minute details in order for their move.

Corby was sitting outside the jail when Laura emerged from the *Choctaw Sentinel* office. Mariah Nitakechi was on her own porch as well, wiping the front windows, which, Laura was certain, hadn't had so much as a single streak when she rode in earlier.

"Hello, Corby."

"Hello, Miss Bennett," he said casually, barely taking his eyes off the scrap of wood he was shaving with a knife.

"Laura," she said, leaning against the square post that supported the roof. "My friends call me Laurie."

He looked up again, only this time his eyes were smoldering coals boring into hers. "Hello, *Laurie*."

He said her name in a tone that created a swarm of buzzing bees in her stomach. "How's the sheriff business today?"

"Same as usual. What are you up to, visiting Potts?"

"I had to take him some papers and stop at the general store for Star. In fact, Mr. Cassidy offered me a job as a clerk. He said he'd even fix the empty space upstairs into a room for me if I couldn't get a room at the boardinghouse."

"You can't stay at Mariah's," Corby informed her.

Laura straightened. "Doesn't she have a spare room?"

"She has two unless I'm mistaken, but that's no place for you."

Laura's attraction to those sexy eyes began to fade. Was he afraid she'd catch him and the merry widow in the act? "Where do you get off telling me what I can and cannot do every time you see me? This is the *third* time you've done it."

Corby turned back to his whittling.

Laura simmered. "Sabrina is going to be staying with Star and Jason for the rest of the week—not that you care."

His head shot up. "I care about my daughter very much."

"I'm sure."

He looked back to the wood.

Shaking her head, Laura returned to the general store, where her horse was tethered.

Corby felt her leave. He watched her with quick glances. It would be fine to have her working at the mercantile, but he sure as hell wouldn't see her live at the boardinghouse. Not with a dozen men who'd be after her like a hound after an errant chick.

When the doorbell rang as the Hillhouses were sitting down to dinner, Laura offered to get it.

Corby took off his hat before stepping into the entrance hall, and Laura noticed that he'd changed his shirt. She also noticed how good he smelled, with a mixture of some spicy cologne and the tang of tobacco.

"Come in," she said. "Sabrina is just about to have her supper."

Jason peered out of the dining room. "Come on in, Corb. There's plenty of food."

"I don't want to be a bother."

"Get in here."

Corby gestured to Laura. "After you."

Laura found it all but impossible to eat the roast she'd helped Star prepare. Her stomach was ajitter with both pleasure and pain. Pleasure at having Corby so close, his elbow brushing hers on occasion, pain at seeing the way little Sabrina could barely look her father in the eye. Somehow, she had to bridge the chasm for that poor little thing.

"Sabrina really liked the pony rides at the church picnic. Do you think you might get her a pony of her own?"

The girl perked up. "Can you, Pa? Please? Uncle Jace said Mr. Swanson is gonna sell his. Can I have it? Can I?"

Corby stared down at his mashed potatoes. "I don't think so. There's no place for you to keep it."

Star added her few cents' worth. "Libby told me that she and Peter offered you their house. They have a barn, you know."

Corby turned to Laura. "Are you going to be taking the job at Cassidy's?"

"I don't think so," she said flatly, looking at Sabrina, who was toying with some boiled corn.

"She's considering another position," Star chimed in. "Outside of town."

"Oh," Corby said, his tone duller than Laura's had been.

The remainder of the meal passed with Star and Jason making small talk.

Laura offered to clear the table afterward.

Star refused. "Nonsense. You're a guest. But I would appreciate it if you and Corby would take the children out to play while Jason and I tend to things in here."

Laura gave her hostess a stern look. "I'm an unwanted guest who can't repay your hospitality. You guys go relax." She turned to Sabrina. "You want to help me, sweetie?"

The girl brightened. "Yeah."

Corby lowered his head, pretending to concentrate on the last of his apple pie.

After the dishes were done and put away and Sabrina had gone to join her cousins for a final game of tag before bed, Laura remained in the kitchen, absentmindedly folding the tea towels and straightening the cups and saucers in the corner hutch.

"Do you need a hand?"

Laura jumped at the sound of Corby's deep voice. "No. I'm done. Is there something you need? A glass of water? Another piece of pie?"

He grinned. "I suppose three pieces of pie were enough."

Laura answered with a halfhearted grin of her own. He was so darned irresistible, why did he have to be such a jerk where his only child was concerned? She set aside the tea towel she'd just folded twice. "I think I'll head upstairs. It was nice seeing you again."

"Laurie?"

She turned, shivering deep inside from the way he said her name. "Yes?"

He slid his hands into his trouser pockets and looked down at his boots, then looked up again. "I was wondering if you'll be at the farewell party Wednesday, the one Jace and Star are giving for Peter and Libby."

She nodded her acceptance. "It's not like my social calendar is full."

His back stiffened. "But you're stepping out with Potts tomorrow, aren't you?"

"You already know that, Sheriff." She brushed past him, hating herself for the quickness of her pulse.

Laura was more angry with herself when Sabrina knocked timidly on her door after ten that night.

"What's the matter? Are you sick?" Laura asked, kneeling, feeling Sabrina's forehead.

Sabrina stared at the floor. "I had a bad dream." She looked up, her big brown eyes misting. She threw her arms around Laura's neck, stifled sobs shaking her. "I'm scared. Don't let the mean man hurt me."

Laura's expression hardened and she lifted Sabrina, cradling her as she had her foster child, feeling the same attachment. "He won't hurt you, sweetie. I promise."

Chapter 21

LAURA HAD TO rely on her old false smile during her date with the reporter, Abel Potts. He was a nice enough guy, but he tried way too hard to please.

"You don't like the cake?" he asked over dessert. "I'll send it back to the kitchen. What would you like? We can ride over to the ice cream parlor in—"

Laura raised her hand. "The food is fine. I just have a few things on my mind. I'm sorry." She felt a pang of guilt at the way he seemed to deflate before her eyes like a brown-checked balloon. "Would you mind taking me home?"

Corby Hillhouse was sitting on the front porch, talking to Jason, when the buggy appeared through the stand of pines. Corby looked at his pocket watch. "It's about time."

Jason suppressed a grin. "Is that so?"

"It never takes Potts three hours to eat supper at the boardinghouse."

"That might be," Jason observed, getting up from the wicker chair and stretching his back, "but I expect his dinner companions at Mariah's aren't so pretty."

Corby shot his cousin a hard look. He was married. How dare he notice how pretty Laurie was? His face became even more unyielding when Laura thanked Potts for the dinner with a quick kiss on the cheek after he helped her out of the buggy.

Jason coughed. "I think I'll turn in. 'Night, Corb."

Laura returned Jason's wave, then stood and watched Potts drive off. Corby's stance grew more rigid by the minute. What was wrong with this woman? She was acting like an out-and-out floozy. Mooning over Jace, *kissing* Potts in public.

It caught Corby unawares when Laura turned to face him. "Did you come to visit Sabrina?"

"Maybe. Maybe I was making my rounds and decided to sit a spell."

She gave her cute little chin a defiant tilt. "*Maybe* you should stop acting like *my* father and spend more time acting like Sabrina's." She was not surprised to see him stalk away.

Laura woke with the same tangle of emotion she'd fallen asleep trying to untangle. The flesh-and-blood Corby Hillhouse was even more puzzling than the photographic one had been.

On the surface not only was he the best-looking man this side of heaven, but he seemed to have an easy, adaptable personality—except where his daughter was concerned. In that regard he was an enigma. The way he'd taken Sabrina for the pony ride at the church lunch and afterward watched with loving eyes as she played with other kids showed that he wasn't "anti-child," but when he turned his coldness on the girl as he'd done at dinner last night it was infuriating. No wonder the poor thing had a nightmare about a mean man.

Staring up at a shaft of moonlight on the ceiling lamp, Laura wondered if she'd been transported here to help Sabrina and Corby bond. Judging from what she could make of the extended Hillhouse family, they'd all grown up with the kind of parental love and support that was often taken for granted.

In contrast, she'd come from the quintessential dysfunctional family. Her parents had married because they'd *had* to, and their unhappiness showed itself often, with her father drowning his sorrows for hours after work and her mother taking "nerve" pills. Neither of them was happy as a person, and they found it hard to be pleased with her.

They never knew that she'd excelled in school to make them proud, to bring them together on a common ground. Even when she'd applied for and won a scholarship to UCLA on her own, they were unimpressed, just relieved that they wouldn't have to foot the bill for their daughter's education.

Grandpa Alex was the one who had really taught her about unconditional love. He'd made his mistakes by not supporting her mother when she needed it, and he'd lost her love as a result. Being there for her daughter was his penance and salvation.

Sabrina Hillhouse needed a loving father, and Corby Hillhouse had the potential to be that father before it was too late.

Laura turned onto her side and pulled the light blanket over her shoulder. She would do her damnedest to make that happen, although she was having some reservations about whether Star's "plan" was the way to go.

"This seems like an abrupt change of heart," Star remarked, layering apple slices in a cobbler. "If you don't want to look after Sabrina, tell me now."

Laura sprinkled on the brown sugar topping. "I'd love to watch over Sabrina, she's a great kid. It's just . . . Don't you think it will go better if Corby is told from the start? I doubt that he'll want to be hit with a surprise house and housekeeper."

Star took the baking dish to the iron range. "What Corby wants and what Sabrina needs are two different things." She brushed a few strands of brown hair off her forehead. "Giving Corby a choice in the matter will simply make him think of new excuses. It's high time for that man to get over his selfishness, or fear, or whatever it is that has kept him from assuming his fatherly duties." She took a mound of sweet roll dough from its proofing bowl atop the stove. "It's sink or swim time for Corby."

That evening it was needling time for Corby. Jason let out a whistle when Corby entered the house.

"I do believe my cousin is trying to make an impression," he said, gesturing at Corby's new suit.

Heads turned in Laura's direction until Corby responded. "Then again, it might be that I split my other pair of pants, and since your brother is paying such a princely sum for my furniture-moving services . . ."

Corby didn't mind taking her out of the spotlight; he couldn't have avoided it if he'd tried. He also couldn't avoid the pull of his own paternal feelings when the dinner buffet was set out. Sabrina had retreated to a corner of the room as her cousins both small and tall were fussed over by their mothers with instructions to fill their plates. He saw her look around—for Laura, he supposed—but she was in the kitchen refilling one of the serving plates.

"'Brina," he said, approaching her, his heart breaking when she shrank back, as she so often did. He held out his hand. "Let's get you something to eat before Jake's boys gobble it all up."

She gave him a shaky smile, then led the way, becoming more animated when they reached the table and Laura approached from the other side with a platter of fried chicken in her hand. "Me an' Laurie made that together, Pa."

"I'll bet it's real tasty, probably better than Aunt Martha's." He grinned at Laura. Lord, but that woman was something when she blushed.

He handed her an empty plate. "You need to join the party."

She shook her head. "There are things to do in the kitchen."

"I'll let you in on a secret," he said, his gaze fixed upon her green eyes. "We all know where to find the kitchen if we need something. Besides, I bet 'Brina would like you to join us."

Warmth flowed through him when she cast a loving smile at his daughter, who answered with one of her own.

They took their plates out to the porch and found a space beneath the second-floor balcony. Corby looked toward the sloping ground where he'd gone in search of a lost baseball, only to find a pale blond angel.

He looked back at Laura, and caught her staring at the hill as well. Was she remembering the day, their brief, potent kiss? Corby's inner warmth grew hotter, making his new suit even more uncomfortable.

"We forgot to bring out something cold to drink," he said, quickly setting his plate on the small painted pine table between Laura's and Sabrina's chairs.

He got two glasses of cider for Laura and his daughter, then took his dinner plate over to where his uncle Elan and Quinn McNamara were standing.

Corby's "all-overishness" grew stronger instead of fading once the meal was over and the children were sent off to bed to give the adults time alone. Star and Libby sang a quiet church hymn in their native Choctaw, and Cousin Luke's fiancée contributed a soothing ballad. Uncle Elan tried to get away with a risqué tune he'd heard from a fellow horse breeder, but Aunt Martha stopped that with a poke to the ribs.

Laura surprised them all by doing a song as well. The music was strange, like nothing they'd ever heard, but the story the song told of unrequited love touched them all.

The suspicious part of Corby's nature came to the fore as he speculated on Laura Bennett's mysterious past and how he might unravel it, but when Cousin Jason took up his cedarwood flute, those speculations ceased.

The ancient courting song drew the assembled couples close and brought home to Corby just how lonely he was, how lonely he'd been his entire life. He stole a glance at Laura, seated alone across the room.

She was in a world all her own, gently swaying in her seat, her eyes closed, a dreamy smile raising the corners of her pink mouth.

She was thinking of someone. Some man. He was sure of

it. Had she been on her way to meet him? Was she running from him?

Corby loosened his constricting necktie, convinced that his discomfort came from the new suit of clothes. He wished now he'd taken a seat nearer the parlor door so he might make an unnoticed exit, but he doubted he would, even if given the chance. He couldn't stop looking at Laura Bennett. He thought of her sad song, the way she and Sabrina took to one another, how she blended into the family gathering and helped without being asked, giving Jason and Star the freedom to enjoy their own party. He remembered how she had saved little Matthew, then brushed it aside as nothing.

He was glad he'd come tonight and not allowed Mariah to cajole him out of it. He'd thought of bringing her but couldn't. She didn't really fit in. He hated to see this night end, but ending it was.

"Thought we were going to have to pry your bottom out of that chair."

Corby stood and followed his uncle, mumbling that he was simply relaxed and drowsy from the soft music. As he waited to retrieve his hat from the stand in the hall, he noticed the way Laura, Star, and Libby kept casting looks at him from just outside the front doors.

He stepped outside, giving them each a questioning look, flattered to be the object of attention.

"Now why do I suddenly feel like a juicy young rabbit who just came upon a den of vixens?"

Chapter 22

CORBY GOT HIS answer nearly two weeks later, the day he returned from transporting the largest of Peter and Libby's possessions to their new home.

After dropping off the hired wagons at the livery, he went to the boardinghouse, intending to get into a hot bath and a soft bed, perhaps with a little company in that bed.

"'Morning, Mariah," he drawled, sauntering in the back door and planning on giving her a long-overdue kiss.

She turned from the sink, her black eyes furious. "Where do you think you're going?"

"To my room."

Corby ducked the dish she threw at his head and barely dodged the bowl that followed.

"Hey!" he shouted as the next piece flew past. He cursed when a saucer grazed his temple.

"Mariah!" he yelled, taking cover behind the pie safe in the far corner. "What in blazes is wrong with you?" He ducked as a maple rolling pin came his way, denting the corner of the small cupboard.

Mariah pointed a finger at him, her eyes filled with more hate than he would have thought possible. "You have lived under my roof for the better part of ten years and you have the nerve to ask what's wrong?"

Corby gulped, trying to remember when they'd last lain together, "You're not in the family way, are you?" He ducked but was hit by a piece of the mug that shattered on the edge of the pie safe.

"No, I am not in the family way, you sneaky bastard!" she shrieked before hurling the rest of the crockery that was within her reach. "You could have had the decency to tell me or come to get your belongings yourself instead of sending Jacob's boys to tell me you were moving out!" Cursing, she searched for new weapons.

"The only moving I did was with Peter's furniture. Where's my gear?"

Mariah didn't answer, but when she turned she had a cast-iron skillet in one hand and a meat cleaver in the other. "I am going to feast on your two-timing hide!"

Corby dove through the open window to the right of the pie safe.

"What do you mean, Taima isn't here?" Corby demanded. He glowered at Ike Swanson, the livery's owner.

"Jake's boys come and got him a couple days back."

"Where'd they take my horse? What are they up to?"

"Don't rightly know, Sheriff," Swanson said, barely containing his amusement. "I tend to rely on you to tell me 'bout the goings-on around town."

A distasteful grumble vibrated in the back of Corby's throat.

"Why, Corby, whenever did you get back?" Star called airily from the livery entrance.

Corby stalked toward her, the pieces of the puzzle settling into place. He should have known. Wiping a trickle of blood from his forehead, he reminded himself that she was family. "Star—"

"I guess Potts was right. That was you running out of the boardinghouse one step ahead of a frying pan. Something have Mariah in a dither?"

Corby scowled, shoving his handkerchief into the rear

pocket of his dusty trousers. "Enough. What did you do with my gear and my horse?"

Star looked shocked. "Why would I want your things?"

"Star," he hissed, the muscles of his neck cording with tension.

"They're home where they belong."

"At your place?"

"No, at *yours*."

"I sold my place when Daisy died," he reminded her, the words falling like a lead sinker in a pond. "Stop playing games, woman, because I'm not in the mood. I'm hungry. I'm hot. I'm tired, and I want my gear." He paused, not surprised that Star did not yield. "For the last time—"

"At Peter's," she said. "He and Libby told you to live there, remember? I hired a housekeeper to look after you and Sabrina."

"Damn you, woman! Can't you ever keep your nose in your own business?" He swore under his breath and fished some coins out of his pocket, tossing them to Swanson. "I'm saddling up the bay."

Chapter 23

LAURA'S PULSE SKITTERED as she dabbed on a little of the perfume Star had sent out from Cassidy's along with the message that Corby was just entering Warburton.

She'd been living a fantasy these past few days, imagining the look on his face when he walked through that door and found her and his daughter waiting to welcome him home. The fantasy ended now as it always did, with Corby welcoming her into his life with a kiss even better than the one they'd shared before.

Laura exhaled a quiet sigh just as Sabrina wandered into the bedroom sniffing the air.

"I snells flowers."

Laura laughed, amused by the mispronunciation. She knelt, dabbing a touch of perfume on Sabrina's wrist. "Now you smell like a flower, too."

Sabrina's crooked smile spoke volumes, and she threw her little arms around Laura's neck. "I love you, Laurie."

"I love you, too, sweetie," she said, returning the hug.

Caring for this child had brought her so much in such a short time that she hated to think it might end as abruptly as it had begun. Still, watching Sabrina come out of her shell made any possible loss worthwhile and made her confident that all Corby needed was a bit of coaxing as well.

Laura stood up, hoisting Sabrina to her hip. "Let's see if those cookies we made are cool. Your daddy should like them."

"You sure he likes me? Is he gonna be a real pa now?"

"I know he loves you. And I'm sure he'll spend lots of time with you now."

"Can you be my ma?"

"I don't know," Laura said. "But I promise to stay as long as I can."

"Okay," Sabrina said, resting her head against Laura's shoulder.

Laura walked to the kitchen asking whatever cosmic forces had brought her here to let her stay forever.

She smiled as Sabrina entered into her job as cookie tester with gusto, one oatmeal cookie in each hand. Laura took one of the chewy cookies for herself, then went to the icebox for the pitcher of milk. She poured a cup of coffee from the blue enameled pot on the stove, then spooned some cream in and gave it a quick stir.

She poured Sabrina a glass of milk and thought how strange it had been to have to get this milk from the natural source instead of a plastic jug, but it had been fun, even with Sabrina giggling at her inexperience.

"Do you think your daddy might like one of those chicken-and-vegetable pies for supper, like the one Aunt Star made for the party? You can help me."

"Yeah!" Sabrina said. The smile on her face waned. "Do we have to cut the chicken's head off like yesterday?"

Laura shuddered. She didn't even want to think about that. It looked so easy, so impersonal when she watched Jason do it, but holding that squawking thing and delivering the coup de grace was not something she wanted to do again. "I think we have enough left in the icebox. All we have to do is make the gravy and crust and cut the vegetables."

She shared Sabrina's sigh of relief and hoped Corby wouldn't balk at her dealing with the butcher in town from now on. There was no way she was going to go to the natural source for a steak or pork chop. Getting milk and eggs was all the adventure she could handle.

Sabrina reached for a third cookie. Laura removed the plate to the top of the tall icebox. "Sorry, sweetie. We have to save some for your daddy. He should be here soon."

Chapter 24

A MUSCLE TWITCHED along Corby's rocklike jaw. How dare Star take it upon herself to run his life, to go behind his back and hire a goddamned housekeeper? He reined the bay to the left, taking the turnoff to Peter's place. Housekeeper. It was probably one of those biddies from church, the ones who *oohed* and *aahed* every time they saw Sabrina, thinking she was the key to igniting his interest in them.

Like buzzards hungry for a fresh carcass, they'd started circling him before Daisy was in her grave a month, bringing by food and baby things and, of course, offers to "help look after the precious little darling."

They'd look after her, all right. They'd be just like the woman his own widowed father had married. They would treat the child like gold in the presence of the natural parent and like pond scum the rest of the time.

You'll get what's coming to you, whoever you are, Corby thought when Peter's spacious log house came into view. *I'm going to toss you out on your fat behind and take Sabrina to live with Daisy's other kin in Krebs.*

Hell, he might even leave town himself. There wasn't much reason to stay in Warburton. There hadn't been for a very long time.

Chapter 25

THE FRONT DOOR banging against the coatrack startled both Laura and Sabrina. Before Laura could do more than stand up and put Sabrina behind her, Corby burst in through the swinging door. He so resembled a fire-breathing dragon that she could almost see flames licking between his lips.

It's not supposed to be like this, Laura thought.

Sabrina inched out from behind her, her innocent face hopeful. "We made cookies, Pa. You want one?"

"Go to your room, 'Brina," he ordered, his eyes skewering Laura. Despite the feelings she roused in him, he had no idea of who or what she was, and the fact that Star would trust his child to the care of a stranger only served to intensify his anger.

"Pa?"

"Go to your room, girl!"

Laura felt the pain visible on Sabrina's face. When the child fled the room in tears, she tried to follow, but Corby's vicelike grip stopped her.

She pulled away. "I have to go to her."

He blocked her path. "She's *my* daughter."

"The day you treat her like a daughter and not an incon-

venience is the day I'll believe that," Laura snapped back, as
Sabrina's distant sobs cut her clean through.

Corby strode after her, grabbing the back of her skirt.
"You're not wanted here. Go away."

Laura let out a caustic laugh. "Go, so you can bully her
some more? If you want me out, then you move me."

Corby was sorely tempted, but he'd never laid a hand on
a woman in his life and didn't plan to start now. When she
went toward the bedrooms he followed, the tense lines
around his mouth easing when he saw Sabrina respond to
Laura as she sat down beside her on the narrow bed.

He felt like a monster when he saw how Laura comforted
his shaking daughter, stroking her hair, wiping her tears,
soothing her with soft, earnest words.

"You're safe, sweetie. Sssh now. You're safe."

"I'm sorry for hollering at you, 'Brina."

She looked up for just a moment, her teary eyes wide, her
little hands scrunching the fabric of Laura's dress as she
clung with all her might, terrified to let go.

She was terrified of him.

The sound of her new cries echoed in Corby's ears, hurting him more than any bullet or knife wound ever had.
Crushed, he left the house, needing to think, to put this impossible situation into perspective.

Corby rode the hired bay at top speed with no particular
destination in mind, then circled back toward town, stopping
at the remains of the small house he'd grown up in. He let
the horse graze while he sat on the withered stump of a
sweetgum tree.

Little was left of the tidy frame house: a few feet of foun-
dation, half the brick chimney, a few warped floorboards.
He was pleased to see that the gnarled maple standing to the
left of the front door was dead. That tree had supplied the
branches his stepmother used to whip him when his father
was away on his overland mail route.

Corby hadn't seen his father's white wife since they
buried the old man fourteen years ago, but still he remembered her clearly, remembered the way she made him do
everything but lick her boots in his father's absence. The

phantom pain of her frequent beatings bombarded him. He'd learned quickly to keep the pain in, to paste on a carefree smile and let no one be the wiser, lest his next whipping be even worse.

Nothing like that was going to happen to his Sabrina. No strange woman was going to waltz into her life and do her wrong.

She's already been done wrong, Corby's conscience told him. *She's been done wrong by you.*

Corby didn't want to listen. He was doing what had to be done. He couldn't take proper care of Sabrina on his own. If she'd been a boy it might have been different, but he couldn't raise a girl. There were things he wouldn't feel comfortable explaining when the time came. She needed a woman for that. A woman who wasn't a stranger.

You're searching for an excuse again and you know it. Corby refused to listen. He headed back toward the house with the intention of telling Laura Bennett she had to go.

A mouthwatering aroma greeted Corby even before he opened the back door, diverting him from his thoughts. He glanced at the sky. It would be dark before too long and it wouldn't be right to put a woman out alone at night.

Woman, Corby repeated to himself. That woman had a name. She was Laurie Bennett. His pretty little one.

His stomach growled as soon as he stepped into the kitchen and was enveloped by the smells of fresh pastry, chicken, and vegetables in the oven and yeasty bread in the center of the pine table. He rubbed his stomach in anticipation.

Hearing laughter from the main room, Corby crept to the connecting door and peeked in. Suddenly he wondered if he could ever make Laura Bennett leave. He stared in rapt silence, not quite believing his eyes. Except for their coloring, Laura and Sabrina could have been mother and daughter, judging by the obvious attachment they shared as Sabrina sat on Laura's lap looking at a homemade storybook. He made no sound, but continued to observe, both pleased and troubled by the sight.

"Do the toady part again," Sabrina pleaded.

"Again? I read it four times," Laura protested weakly. She gave in completely when Sabrina pouted.

Making the face of what Corby assumed was the "toady," Laura said, "Ribbet, ribbet, Nancy Newt. That's my fat cricket." She stuck out her tongue and caught the imaginary insect, then licked her lower lip and patted her stomach. "Ribbet. That was tasty." She paused, then put on another expression, which Corby assumed to be that of the perturbed newt. "Toddy Toad, you are so mean. I am going to have my friend Chef François make a frog leg dinner out of you!"

The burst of male laughter made both Laura and Sabrina jump. Laura's breath caught at the sight of Corby leaning against the doorjamb, his arms folded across his chest, the door propped open with his booted foot. The smile on his face faded when Sabrina whimpered and buried her head against Laura's shoulder.

Laura tilted the girl's face up. "Look at your daddy. He isn't angry anymore." She turned to Corby. "Are you?"

Shaking his head, Corby came into the room. "I'm awful sorry, 'Brina. I didn't mean to holler at you. I was just—tired."

"That's what Laurie said," she mumbled.

Relief showed on his face and he gave her a nod of thanks. "Laurie is a very smart lady and a darn good story-teller."

Laura returned Corby's smile, gently nudging Sabrina out of her lap. "Are you hungry? We were about ready to have dinner."

"Hungry doesn't begin to describe it," he said quietly, his attention lingering on Laura as she took his daughter's hand and came across the room to meet him. "Do I have time to get a bath first?"

Laura nodded. "Your things are in Libby and Peter's room. Star's parents sent over an extra bed they had."

"You didn't take that spare room, did you? It's awfully small."

"It's good enough for me," Laura assured him.

"If you say so," he said, going past her, inhaling her sweet scent.

She and Sabrina were setting the kitchen table when he

came through on his way to the bathroom, which had been added on to the house behind the kitchen to make use of the hot water tank mounted to the wall between the steel range and the kitchen sink.

Corby gestured to the tank. "It's nice not to have to lug water upstairs like at the boardinghouse."

Laura nodded, unable to utter a coherent reply, too overcome by the sight of him undoing the top buttons of his gray shirt.

"I won't be long."

Laura nodded again, her mind swarming with images of him at the church picnic, half-naked, sweaty, flexing his muscled arms as he swung the curved hickory stick in the *ishtaboli* game. Taking a deep breath, Laura forced herself to concentrate on slicing the bread before her. She also tried to recall, in minute detail, Grandpa Alex's cooking lessons in a futile attempt to stop thinking of Corby, so close, so—naked.

Her heart beat faster than the wings of a hummingbird when Corby returned to the kitchen, buttoning his collarless white shirt. Laura's fingers tingled, longing to do it for him, to whisk across that bronze skin, those hard muscles . . .

She didn't realize he had spoken until Sabrina tugged at her skirt. "I'm sorry. I didn't hear you."

"I asked where you wanted me to sit."

"At the head of the table, of course."

He pulled out Sabrina's chair, then came around the table to seat her. Laura could feel his presence radiate through the back of the chair. She was stunned to hear a faint intake of breath as he inhaled her scent.

"You smell almost as good as the food."

"Almost?"

Corby's chuckle rushed through her veins like a flooding stream.

"I might think diffcrent, but I haven't eaten since five this morning," he explained with a boyish grin, taking his own seat.

Laura's stomach flipflopped at the sight of that grin. Maybe he wasn't such a jerk after all.

"Can we eat now?" Sabrina asked.

"Of course, sweetie. Corby, would you like to say grace?"

"I suppose," he said, a look of unease passing over his face. "I haven't had much practice, but here goes." He paused to clear his throat. "Thank you, Lord, for both this fine meal and the pleasurable company."

He and Laura looked up at the same time, their eyes locking for a striking moment, and Corby knew that he could not force her to leave anytime soon. Not without real cause. He tried to pay deep attention as Sabrina detailed her and Laura's adventures during the time he'd been away, but his mind kept drifting, wondering what Laura was thinking when she was stealing glances.

After a while she openly stared, and he watched with amusement as Sabrina tried to get her attention. What was Laura thinking? He hoped they were good thoughts. He couldn't bear to think she might be plotting trouble. He was pleasantly surprised when Sabrina tugged on his sleeve, a pleading pout on her lips. He smiled, letting her know he was pleased to help her get through to Laura.

Leaning forward, he curved his long fingers under Laura's chin and tilted her head until their eyes met. She was soft and warm, and the realization of what he was doing dawned on her slowly, deepening the flush of her cheeks. She colored and smiled sheepishly, and he wondered if that blush extended down into her shirtwaist, tinging the tips of her ivory breasts. He was disappointed when she pulled her head away.

"I think 'Brina wants to ask you something."

"Can I have cookies, Laurie? I ate all my food."

With invisible flames licking her skin where Corby had touched it, Laura went to get the cookie plate. She put two on a smaller dish, then got Sabrina another glass of milk. "We'll take this into the other room for you. I want to talk to your daddy. When I'm done I'll help you get your bath and read another story."

Returning to the kitchen, Laura busied herself with clearing the dishes, then stored the leftover bread in a linen sack and the butter in the icebox.

She told herself it was foolish to feel so nervous because Corby was watching.

"Did you have enough to eat?" she asked at last. "I can make you something else—"

She stopped short, for Corby had wrapped his long fingers around her wrist. Though his grip was featherlight, his inherent strength coursed through her. He grinned the grin that was both boyish and sexy and that turned her knees to jelly.

Letting go of her wrist, he stood up. "What did you want to say to me?"

"I'm sorry for going along with Star and springing this on you." The light of the oil lamp on the table made the deep, rich hues of his skin and eyes glow. She'd never felt like this. Never. "I imagine this caused problems for you with Mrs. Nitakechi."

"A few, but Mariah'll get over it."

Laura stepped away toward the sink. "I'll leave if you want to hire someone on your own, but I would like to stay if that's all right."

She turned her back at that, and Corby was torn between the experience with his father's wife and the warmth he'd seen between Sabrina and Laura. Then she faced him again, awaiting his answer. "I'd like you to stay for a while. Sabrina has taken a real shine to you." It pleased him to see her eyes light up at the mention of his daughter.

"I've taken a shine to her, too. She's precocious and funny." She paused, her eyes growing serious. "Why do you keep yanking her around? One minute you're kind, the next cold. It's not good for her emotional development."

"I have my reasons," he said, shoving the chairs back beneath the table.

"What are they?"

"None of your business."

Sabrina came into the kitchen after her father rushed out, and Laura continued to stare at the swinging door.

"Are you gonna cry, Laurie?"

Laura smiled her practiced smile, then sat and lifted Sabrina to her lap. "I'm as happy as Toddy Toad. Ribbet."

Sabrina's merry laugh almost cheered her.

Chapter 26

OWEN WEBSTER BANGED a heavy fist on his desk with enough force to slosh the contents of his whiskey glass. "No-good, incompetent fools! I should have known better than to let Frank handle it!"

Clint Barker, Webster's sometime foreman and trigger man, waited until his employer's stream of curses had slowed to a trickle, then spoke. "Do you know what train Hillhouse was headed out of Fort Smith on? I'll do the job right. You know that."

Webster downed his whiskey, oblivious to the envy on Barker's face. "How the hell should I know? He took his red ass back to Indian country, I guess. I don't know what the hell kind he is. Something starting with a *C*, I think. Cherokee, Cheyenne, I don't know."

Barker shifted. "You want me to start looking?"

Webster poured himself another drink. "Not yet. We got a lot of work to do here. Hanson is giving me trouble about the water rights again. Take care of it."

Barker checked the ammunition in his revolver. "I been plannin' on paying a visit to *Mrs*. Hanson. I'm sure I can persuade her to get her husband to see the light."

Webster dismissed him with a wave, then turned back to the day's mail.

Chapter 27

CORBY KNOCKED ONCE on the door to Abel Potts's room, then entered.

Potts was standing before the bureau mirror tying his striped bow tie. "Good morning, Sheriff. Is there something I can do for you?"

Debating with himself, Corby went through with the plan he'd thought of during the long, sleepless night. "You used to work at a paper in New York, didn't you?"

"The *Sun,* but that was a long time ago."

"Do you still have friends back east, other newsmen?" Corby asked, his heart telling him to end this now.

Abel combed his sandy hair. "I never had many friends to begin with, which is what brought me out west." He paused, Corby's reflection glowering at him. "Are you thinking of advertising for deputies?"

"This is personal," Corby said, looking down at the toes of his boots. He looked up. "I want to know if Laura Bennett has any criminal charges against her."

Potts's jaw dropped. "Miss Bennett? I can't believe she'd ever do anything against the law. I don't know her well, of course, but you get a feeling about people sometimes."

That woman gives me too damn many feelings, Corby thought.

"If some strange woman was minding your child, wouldn't you want to know about her?"

"I understand perfectly," Potts replied before donning his blue-striped jacket. "It may take some time, of course. Days, perhaps weeks."

"Today, Potts," Corby said, walking toward the door. "I want an answer before the day ends."

Chapter 28

As she had been doing for the past hour, Laura watched miserably while the hands of the wooden mantel clock advanced. Ten o'clock. The day was almost over, and she hadn't seen Corby since dinner last night. He hadn't come back to sleep in his bed, and she decided that he'd patched things up with the widow Nitakechi. He'd probably stayed with her last night and undoubtedly would again tonight.

Of course, it was her own fault if he never came back. She'd told him his hot-and-cold treatment of Sabrina was no good. Maybe he agreed and had decided to leave the relationship at "cold." But why? It was plain to see that he loved his daughter. So what was his problem?

She doubted that he blamed Sabrina for her mother's death. The man would have to be a total bonehead to do that. There was always the chance that he was afraid. Even men of her time had trouble playing "Mr. Mom," and it was probably harder for a man like Corby, whose world had a definite line drawn between the sexes. If only he would say something, she'd do her best to help him work it out. After all, she'd come all this way to help him . . .

You could be here to help yourself, you know, Laura's

loneliness prompted. She sat up straighter on the velvet sofa. That was just plain crazy. She didn't belong here. She wouldn't stay. It was simply a matter of time before the universe got its act together and put things in their proper places. Hopefully, she'd be able to help Corby get his act together as well, but that was it. That was her mission.

Laura looked away from the clock as the minute hand ticked off more time. She should stop waiting. Corby wasn't coming home. He was probably in Mariah's bed right this minute. Not that it mattered to her. He wasn't frozen in those old pictures of Galen's. He had a life, and according to Star, he and Mariah had been something of an item before his marriage, so it was only natural that he would pick things back up. Even if she did have the eyes of a heartless witch.

Yawning, Laura put Corby and his lady friend out of her mind. She was tired. She needed to get some sleep. She yawned again, then massaged her neck and shoulders, still aching from hand-washing laundry.

Why was it that none of her favorite fictional heroines struggled with stiff muscles or rough hands from bending over a washboard and tub of hot water, or strained their backs hauling firewood for the stove, or ruined their knees scrubbing hard wood floors? She didn't even want to remember today's "adventure" of cleaning the horse stalls in the barn. No self-respecting novel heroine would ever have to put her hands in that.

Whoever termed these the "good old days" was a nut—all this manual labor was exhausting. Right now she would love nothing better than to spend a couple hours in front of the boob tube with a box of microwave popcorn and some take-out pizza.

Oh, well. There was no sense pining for what she couldn't have. Laura stood up and took a step toward her bedroom. She stopped. The water in the kitchen tank was still hot. She'd might as well take her bath now instead of waiting till morning and having to heat it all over again. That took forever.

*   *   *

Corby rubbed down his gelding, then gave him fresh feed and water. "Sleep well, Taima. Tomorrow is sure to be a busy day. The miners get paid and the illegal liquor will flow."

The horse whinnied as if to commiserate.

Normally Corby would have been touched by the humor, but tonight he was just too tired. It had been a long day, with lots of little fights breaking out over the foolest things—the livery's prices, the food at the hotel, the low water in the public horse trough. It was like the whole town was as much on edge as he'd been while he was waiting for Potts to get word from his newspaper friends.

That had been a big wait for nothing. No Laura Bennett was known to have committed a crime or had been charged for any indecency in New York City. Of course, that news only made him all the more confused. Was she a liar on the run from somewhere else, using a false name, or was she really an innocent traveler come upon some misfortune she couldn't remember to explain?

The endless questions made Corby's head ache, and he rubbed his temples, then stretched his back trying to get the kinks out. He sure could go for one of Mariah's back rubs right about now—

His thoughts skidded to a halt as he realized he could have simply gone to sleep at the boardinghouse instead of coming all the way out here. Why hadn't he thought of it? Sabrina was the reason, he decided, starting toward the house. He needed to be near his daughter to make sure no harm came to her. Fatherly instinct was what had made him ride half an hour out of his way.

Corby thought nothing of the faint lamplight coming from behind the partially open bathroom door, assuming that Laura had forgotten to extinguish it after bathing Sabrina or that she'd left it on as a guide light. He dropped into the nearest chair, pulled off his boots and socks, then stood and shed his sweaty jacket, vest, and shirt before dragging his weary body to the bathroom. A nice soak in Cousin Peter's roomy copper tub sounded mighty fine.

The unexpected surprise waiting in the tub was like a

physical blow, unsteadying his legs, making his insides burn much as they had the day he'd discovered her. He blinked, then rubbed his eyes, still unable to believe that the sight before him was real—Laura, naked as the day she was born, dozing in the copper tub, her arms resting on the top edges, her head leaning back.

Her skin was a warm ivory in the low light, her lips deep pink and looking sweet enough to taste forever. The heavy fringe of her burnished lashes skimmed her cheeks. Corby expected to see disgust in those lovely green eyes, but she remained asleep, impervious to this violation of her privacy.

Unable to fight his male instincts, Corby continued to gaze down upon her, watching how the suds atop the water pooled around her firm little breasts and clung to her nipples. He let his eyes travel and was at once thrilled and agitated to be able to see the downy curls between her legs. It took nearly all of his self-control to keep from reaching in and touching her, gliding his fingers inside to see if perhaps those blushes heated her in there . . .

From the moment he'd seen her lying helpless in the brush behind Jason's house, he'd wanted to possess Laura in every way imaginable. That want reasserted itself now with a pounding urgency that compelled him to kneel beside the tub to get as close as possible. Without thinking, he reached out to caress her smooth cheek, her neck, her shoulder, her breast . . .

Laura's faint murmur brought Corby to his senses and he stood up quickly. What was wrong with him, taking advantage of a woman this way? He hurried back to the kitchen, picked up a tin plate from the sideboard and dropped it. He heard the bathwater slosh as Laura was startled awake.

"S-Sabrina?"

"It's me. Corby."

"Oh." There was a long pause. "I'll be right there."

The water sloshed again and Corby pictured her stepping out of the tub, the soapsuds sliding down her small, supple body. He stifled a groan as his body reacted and then stifled another when she came into the kitchen, a vision of pure, pale beauty, so inviting. He wanted to take her where she stood, to see that luscious pale flesh joined with his own.

"Corby. Corby?"

"Yes, little one?"

Laura faltered at the unexpected term of endearment and at the sight of that bare chest. She struggled to remember what she'd wanted to say. "Could you help me empty the tub? I put too much water in it."

Corby forced his mind away from his impure thoughts. "Just leave it. I was planning to clean up before I go to sleep."

"It's cold. I kind of dozed off." *And had a dream you would not believe.* His dark eyes captured hers, and she was certain he could read her mind. She blushed and averted her eyes.

"You should be careful. Falling asleep in the bathtub is a dangerous thing. You never know what might happen."

"I'll try to remember that," Laura said, edging past him, unable to shake the feeling that something *had* happened— or was about to.

Chapter 29

"NO ONE'S BEEN here for ages, luv."

"Yeah, but—geez, Galen. I feel she's close. What if she went back to the booze or pills and is hurt somewhere?"

"She didn't, Jake. Laurie feels good about herself now."

"Then where is she? Why did she go off and not leave a note or call us? And that broken railing is not a good sign. It's like she disappeared into thin air."

"People don't disappear into thin air, little bro'. And don't start that nonsense about her being in her room again . . ."

Chapter 30

LAURA HEARD THE voices in her sleep and sat up. "Jake? Galen?" Were they here? Was she home?

Rubbing her eyes, Laura focused on the dim light of the moon coming through the gingham curtains. This wasn't Galen's house. This was her room at Corby and Sabrina's. She tilted her arm to get the dial of her vintage watch into the light. It was three in the morning.

She could have sworn Galen and Jake were close, in this room or right outside. It was like the dream she'd had at Star and Jason's.

Lying back, Laura closed her eyes, the weird dream replaying itself in her mind. Then again, on a sliding scale, this dream was way under the weirdness level of the one she'd had in the bathtub. That had been off the scale. Imagine, Corby all but begging to make love to her. That thought did have a certain cheap-thrill quality to it, but it wasn't going to happen.

After an hour of tossing and turning, Laura realized that returning to sleep was also not going to happen. She dressed in her T-shirt and the jeans she'd cut into shorts and went out back to do her t'ai chi. She hoped it would focus her energy and keep her alert, because once Sabrina woke there would be no slowing down until midafternoon when she could be coaxed into a rest period before they fixed dinner.

Corby dragged himself out of bed, still tired and achy but anxious to get out of the house before Laura woke up. After the wicked visions that had haunted him all night he didn't quite trust himself to see her in her nightgown, even if it would be good to chow down on her fine cooking, look at that pretty face, and hear her tell Sabrina that silly toad story.

Sabrina. What was he going to do about her? He hadn't a clue, but his gut told him that Laura would look after her until he could think of something. Surely if the woman was up to no good she would have acted on that by now. She'd had Sabrina all the time he was helping Cousin Peter move, and the girl seemed fine, happier than he'd seen her in a long time. A couple more days couldn't hurt.

Impulsively, Corby chose to stay long enough to make himself a cup of coffee. He stoked the fire in the stove, set the pot on to boil, then rolled a cigarette, planning to smoke it outside in the hope that the chilly morning air would cool the burning desire he was feeling for his blond housekeeper.

He didn't realize that Laura was outside, about ten yards from the back porch, until he heard her begin to hum a tune reminiscent of one of the flute tunes his cousin liked to play. An unaccustomed pang of jealousy hit Corby then, as he remembered the way Abel Potts's face lit up at the mention of Laura. The jealousy flared when he thought of Potts courting Laura at all.

Corby's stance relaxed once Laura began a strange little dance the likes of which he'd never seen. The grace of her slow movements held him spellbound as much as the sight of her in the unusual, clingy clothing did. She'd hacked the legs off her denims so that now the pants barely covered her cute little behind, and he tried not to speculate on whom she was trying to attract. It took even more effort not to acknowledge the effect the sight was having on his body.

He finished his cigarette, then sat on the top step to smoke a second, still watching Laura's performance until a light coughing spell made her aware of his presence.

She spun around, her long hair blowing in the breeze. "Oh, Corby. I didn't know you were there," she said quickly, folding her arms in front of her.

Corby dropped the stub of his cigarette, crushing it beneath the heel of his boot. He coughed again.

"You should quit smoking. It's bad for your lungs."

Touched by her unwarranted concern, Corby flashed her an indulgent smile. "Those little things aren't gonna kill me. Besides, it's all the time I spent riding drag that brings on the coughing fits."

Laura stepped closer to the porch, excited by the way Corby's eyes were raking over her, lingering on her bare legs. "Riding drag. What's that?"

"A cattle-driving term. It means the men who ride at the back of the herd to keep the slower animals from straggling too far behind. It's the worst position to ride, and lucky me, since I was just a no-account redskin, I got the honor of doing it more than anyone else in the outfit.

"There'd be times when the trail dirt was half an inch thick and whenever I'd move, I'd stir up my own personal dust storm. That grime was terrible, and it got everywhere: in your nose, your mouth, your eyes and ears. It even got into all sorts of places a man can't mention in mixed company."

Laura laughed with him and moved closer until she was at the foot of the porch steps. What a gorgeous smile he had. And what a strong spirit to be able to find humor in a situation she sensed was worse than he'd ever let on. She wanted to know more about him. Everything. She wanted to know about his past, his dreams, his hopes for Sabrina and the future.

"When were you a cowboy?" she asked lightly. To her dismay, Corby's gentle smile fell and he tensed.

"It was a long time ago," he told her, avoiding her gaze. He stood. "You want coffee? I put some on."

Laura sighed when he strode inside. *Open mouth, insert foot,* she said to herself before trudging up the steps.

Chapter 31

LAURA'S EXPRESSION BRIGHTENED when she entered the kitchen and Corby handed her a mug of coffee. "Thank you kindly, Sheriff." She sipped the steaming liquid. "This is good. Maybe you should give me a lesson. I usually make it too strong or weak."

Corby chuckled, remembering the grumbling at Star's last party. "I believe I heard that from Star, and Peter, and Uncle Elan, and . . ." His temperature rose when she blushed. "What were you doing outside? That dance thing?" he asked as she took a seat at the table, one shapely leg crossed over the other.

"It's called t'ai chi. It's a Chinese exercise. I learned it from my *sensei,* my teacher. My friend."

The way her eyes looked at the mention of this *sensei* awakened Corby's earlier jealousy. "Was this a man? A close friend?"

"Yes, to both."

Corby set his cup on the stove and shoved his hands into his trouser pockets. "What happened between you?" he asked bluntly, needing to know.

"He found someone else."

The touch of regret in her voice tore at him, and he

wished he hadn't brought it up. "Did you never find someone else?"

"Unfortunately, I did." She got up and went to the iron
wall rack where the pots and pans were hanging. "Is there
anything special you'd like for breakfast?"

Corby ignored the growl of his empty stomach. "You
don't have to bother."

When she turned with the pan in her hand, her face was
no longer sullen. "It's no bother. That's what I'm here for. Is
an omelet okay?"

"That sounds fine." Corby thought his heart skipped a
beat when she smiled. There was no mistaking the skip
when she brushed against him while putting the frying pan
on the stove.

"I'll go fight the chickens and the cow and be right back."

Corby smiled to himself as he watched her through the
kitchen window, his eyes locked onto the natural wiggle of
her backside. For a little bitty woman she sure had a lot of
wiggle.

"Laurie!"

Corby gave a start at the sound of his daughter's voice.
His first reaction was to go to her, but he hesitated, afraid to
strengthen their attachment any more than he'd already
done.

"Laurie! I had a bad dream!"

Listening to his heart, Corby went to his daughter.

It pained him to have her shrink back, to look past him as
if hoping Laura was there. "Laurie went outside to get milk
and eggs." He opened the curtains to light the room, then
held out his hand. "I'll take you to the kitchen." The fatherly
pride he felt when Sabrina ran to him pushed aside his mis-
givings.

When Laura came back into the house Corby was entertaining Sabrina with the old shell game, in this case a walnut beneath three mismatched coffee cups. Sabrina squealed
with delight when Corby pretended to take the nut from behind her ear, and Laura shared in the laughter, happy to see
them interacting at long last. She began to make breakfast.

The meal was a leisurely one, with all three enjoying each

other's company. Corby enjoyed it most of all, realizing that this was the closest thing to a home life he'd had since the first months of marriage to Sabrina's mother. Perhaps this arrangements of Star's would work out in the end. Perhaps in a way Laura Bennett had been sent to him. He looked at her. She seemed lost in her own thoughts, and he wondered what they were.

His thoughts drifted to what Mariah Nitakechi had said the other night.

That woman didn't just fall out of the sky. Why, she could be a murderer for all you know.

She might be, Corby thought. *But, technically, so am I.*

He said Laura's name, but she didn't seem to hear so he reached over and tilted her face up toward his. "I'd like to take you and Sabrina into town today to have lunch at the Grand," he said, referring to Warburton's lone hotel, which had never quite lived up to its name.

Laura's brain froze the instant Corby's hand touched her face. "I think I'd like that," she answered finally. "Sabrina, would you like to go?"

"Can you take me to see the horsies at the livery, Pa? Does Mr. Swanson have that pony for sale?"

"You don't still want that old thing, do you?" Corby asked, winking at Laura.

"I want it. An' I have a place to keep it now, an' Laurie can help me clean its stall."

"I don't know," Laura said. "Old ponies are pretty smelly, from what I understand."

"You can do like this," Sabrina said, pinching her nose between her thumb and forefinger.

Laughing, Corby chucked his daughter under the chin. "The pony is yours, 'Brina."

Squealing, Sabrina jumped out of her seat and ran to her father, hugging his neck so tightly he had to loosen her arms to breathe.

"Thank you, Pa! Thank you!"

Laura exhaled a contented sigh. If every day could start like this she'd never be homesick.

*   *   *

Star Hillhouse came out of the *Choctaw Sentinel* office when Corby and Laura approached, Sabrina between them, holding their hands. "And how are all of you on this fine sunny day?"

"My pa bought me a pony!"

Star knelt down to Sabrina. "How nice. Now you can ride with your cousins—"

"Help! Corby, help me! I've been robbed!" came a woman's scream from the other end of the street.

Corby gave Laura an apologetic look. "I'm sorry about lunch."

She nodded and watched him run straight to the boardinghouse and Mariah Nitakechi. After speaking briefly with Mariah, Corby mounted his horse, his muscles rippling beneath his clothing. He rode toward his office, stopping just long enough to grab his rifle, then sped off in search of the culprits.

Laura said a swift prayer for his safekeeping, noticing that Mariah was standing on the boardinghouse steps staring at her. Laura did not trust that woman and wouldn't be at all surprised if she was lying just to get Corby in her clutches.

"Don't you worry about Corby," said Star. "He can hold his own." She lifted Sabrina to her hip and started toward the Grand Hotel. "I don't know why Mariah refuses to deal with the bank."

Chapter 32

DARKNESS WAS DESCENDING when Corby came home. Although he was covered with a film of road dust and had a gaping hole in the left leg of his trousers, he was still the most handsome man Laura had ever seen.

"Is 'Brina asleep already?" he asked, removing his gun belt and sinking onto the nearest chair to rub his neck.

"She nearly fell asleep in the middle of supper. She was tired from riding all afternoon with Star's girls."

Laura set aside the pinafore she was mending and stared as Corby peeled off his dusty jacket and vest. He undid the first few buttons of his shirt, revealing the broad bronzed chest that she desperately wanted to touch. She shifted uncomfortably, trying to dispel this craving for him. She was only a housekeeper. "Can I get you something to eat? I picked up a nice big steak for you at the butcher's." *You are only a housekeeper,* she told herself once more when Corby smiled.

"That steak sounds fine, but I'd like to get a bath first. Would you mind getting me a clean shirt and pants?"

Laura almost stumbled over the leg of her chair. "I don't mind at all. That's what housekeepers are for, right?"

"I suppose," he answered, in a tone that left much to the imagination.

Laura picked out a fresh set of clothing for Corby, taking a long time to breathe in and savor the lingering trace of tobacco and Corby's own masculine scent. She cast a wistful look at the big brass bed before returning to the kitchen.

Corby had already gone into the bathroom, and Laura considered keeping his things out here, wondering if he would come out in only a towel to retrieve them. She was afraid to test the theory, certain that her willpower wouldn't support her morals in the face of such temptation.

She knocked on the bathroom door. "I have your clothes. Where do you want them?"

The sound of splashing stopped. "You can leave them on the chair inside the door. Don't worry about offending your sensibilities. I put up the folding screen."

Just my luck, Laura grumbled to herself before opening the door. She set the clothing where he'd asked, then snuck a peek at the wooden screen. Damn. The panels were hinged too closely for her to see anything.

The splashing stopped again. "You aren't trying to ogle me, are you, Laurie?"

"N-no. I-I'll take your dirty things with me. 'Bye."

The quick slam of the door made Corby laugh, and he imagined that she was blushing up a storm right now. That mental image and an even stronger one of her naked in this very tub renewed the pulsing erection that was almost constant these days.

Corby remained in the water until it cooled enough to further quench the fire that Laura Bennett was kindling inside him.

He should get his clothes on and leave. He didn't belong here. It was too risky. Every minute he spent near her made him want her more, despite the mystery surrounding her. She had an inner passion that ignited his own like no woman before her, and if they spent any more time together it was sure to take its toll. If he fell in love with her it would be a disaster for both of them.

For the second time that day Laura felt like a heroine in a

novel, only this time the novel was a suspense story. She set a place for Corby, glancing repeatedly at the dusty envelope she'd found stuffed into the rear pocket of his dirty trousers.

To Sheriff C. H. Hillhouse
Confidential

The fact that it was typewritten made it all the more puzzling. She knew that Star had two typewriters, one at her home and one at the *Sentinel,* but she didn't know if any of the other small businesses used them. Not that it really mattered. The letter couldn't have anything to do with her. She was just being paranoid.

Of course, Potts had seemed pretty ticked off the other night when she didn't accept a second date. But then, it wasn't as though he was some tabloid reporter who could dig up a ton of dirt on her wild years in L.A. There wasn't a thing to worry about. This was probably nothing more than town business.

Still, when she heard Corby whistling as he opened the bathroom door, she shoved the envelope back into his pocket and tossed the dirty clothes into the corner near the back door.

Corby took a deep breath. "My, but that does smell good," he said, giving Laura the sexiest smile she'd ever seen. "Where did you learn to cook?"

"From my grandfather. He loved to cook. We used to have the most fun in the kitchen." She began spooning mashed potatoes onto his plate, then put the thick steak on it. "I miss him."

Corby's back stiffened. "Then why did you leave?"

Laura paused in placing the gravy and biscuits in their respective containers. She shouldn't have opened her big mouth, but it was kind of late to clam up now. "He died unexpectedly. Just before Christmas. He was all the family I had."

Corby relaxed, his heart aching at the pain she tried to conceal with a sad smile.

"Did you catch your robbers?"

Corby let her change the subject. "No. The ground was too hard to pick up much of the trail. I searched every place

I could think of for them to hole up, but there was nothing. Either they found a new place or got clean away. I guess Mariah will be giving free room and board this week."

"With other assorted goodies, I'm sure."

Arching his eyebrows, Corby let that odd remark pass as well. He dug into his delicious dinner, aware that Laura's eyes were on him the entire time. He looked up, she looked away, a twinge of pink on her cheeks. He shifted on his chair, biting down hard on the piece of steak in his mouth. He would just finish this, then go outside for a smoke and straight to bed. That was exactly what he would do.

"Would you like a few cookies for dessert? Some coffee?" Laura asked in a soothing tone that smashed his earlier resolve like a sledgehammer.

"Coffee would be good—even if it's yours," he teased. She laughed, and he regretted his joke instantly, hating yet loving the way that girlish twitter jiggled his insides.

His insides jiggled more when she brushed his arm while pouring the coffee. His innards downright jumped as he watched her clearing away the dirty dishes, her slim hips swaying ever so lightly as she moved, humming a melody like the one she'd hummed while doing those exercises of hers. She was humming a courting song.

Using all his strength to gather his resolve and look at her as a simple housekeeper, Corby leaned back in his chair and lit a cigarette. "Maybe I should play for you sometime. I know more songs than Jace does."

He was surprised to see Laura freeze. She turned slowly, her pretty eyes opened wide. "You play the Indian flute?"

Corby nodded, brushing back the lock of hair that tumbled into his face. "My pa taught me, and I taught Jace when we were kids. I used to charm all the girls at the church socials with my playing."

"You're still charming them, if that last picnic was any indication," she said, turning back to the sink.

"Is that so?" Corby asked, getting up. He extinguished his cigarette in his empty cup, then dumped the mess in the slop bucket before stepping behind Laura to place the cup in the sink.

She turned her head, her face mere inches from his. Her lips were so inviting, her eyes the same. He backed away.

"I'm going out back for a bit of air, unless you need help."

"I'm almost done, but thanks."

Corby took several deep breaths, afraid that his racing heart would explode. That had been close, too damn close. He sat and stared up at the stars, remembering his foolish New Year's wish. He looked over his shoulder. It wasn't possible. It wasn't possible at all.

He made his mind tend to town business and reminded himself to make sure the alert had been sent to the neighboring communities about Mariah's thieves.

"Corby?"

She was in the doorway.

Don't come closer, he begged silently, inhaling sharply when she stepped forward, the porch creaking ever so slightly. He stood up and left the porch. She followed.

"Is something the matter?"

More than you'll ever know. "No. Is there something you need?"

She opened her mouth, then closed it quickly as if she had just bitten back a comment she knew she would have regretted. "I just wanted to let you know how happy Sabrina is with her pony. It means a lot to her."

"It wasn't much," he said, trying desperately not to notice how beautiful she was in the moonlight, how the rays picked out the gold in her hair, the fire in her eyes. *Oh, hell.*

Laura gasped when Corby pulled her to him, but the shock wore off the moment his lips touched hers. He seemed to hesitate, then deepened the kiss, his tongue teasing hers, exploring every inch of her that he could. A river of lava ran through Laura's body and spilled itself into a blazing lake deep in her stomach.

This was it. This was the magic she'd been craving all her adult life. She'd sampled it with Jake, but it didn't compare to this. It was Corby and Corby alone who'd awakened the passion she was feeling now, the passion she'd searched for in all the wrong places with all the worst men.

Overwhelmed by the fierce need, Corby ended the kiss,

regretting it when he pulled back and saw the sexual hunger in Laura's eyes. He slackened his hold, but she kept her arms tight around his waist, pressing so close that one little wiggle of her hips would have sent him clear over the edge. He removed her hands. "I think I hear Sabrina. She might be having a bad dream." He walked back toward the house.

Laura followed, more confused than ever. "Corby?"

He stood near the table with his back to her. "Check on Sabrina. Please."

"Of course," she mumbled. She quickly went to Sabrina's room, only to find the little girl sound asleep.

Corby had wanted to get rid of her, but why? Had she come on too strong? All her novel heroines responded to their kisses without censure. *But their partners are fictional as well, springing from the minds of twentieth-century writers living in the aftermath of the sexual revolution. Here unmarried equals inexperienced virgin.*

Should she let this pass, forget the kiss ever happened? She couldn't, not in a million years. She'd have to find some way to explain her evident experience. A divorce, perhaps. That wasn't too moral in this day and age, but it was an explanation Corby could relate to. She hated lying, but it was worth it. The chance to experience those feelings again was worth any price.

Laura returned to the kitchen, hopeful that tonight might be the start of something grand.

Her hope died seconds after she entered the kitchen and saw the wrinkled envelope on the kitchen table and the mysterious letter in Corby's hands.

Chapter 33

"EXPLAIN THIS, LAURA."

A sickening chill crept along Laura's spine when Corby skewered her with those brown eyes. Gone was the gentle man who'd kissed her until her head swam. Here, confronting her, was the hardened lawman, looking at her the way he must look at those he arrested, those who undoubtedly protested that they were innocent.

"Explain it," he repeated in a voice as tempered and cold as the steel barrel of the Colt revolver he carried while on duty.

Her fingers shaking, Laura took the letter he thrust at her. Like the envelope, it was typewritten.

Sheriff Hillhouse,

As a longtime resident of Warburton and supporter of yours, I feel it my duty to warn you that your housekeeper might not be all she seems.

While I am unable to provide any details at this time, I urge you to be cautious.

A Concerned Citizen

"How do you explain this?"

"How can I explain something I don't understand?" Laura asked. "I don't know who this 'concerned citizen' is, but I do know they're grasping at straws and hinting at things that don't exist."

"Really?" Corby asked skeptically, stepping closer. Towering over her, he snatched the letter from her hand. " 'I feel it my duty to warn you that your housekeeper might not be all she seems.' " He looked up, his dark eyes as emotionless as glass. "What are you? Who are you? Where did you come from?"

Laura's unhappiness formed a huge knot in the center of her stomach. She took a step forward, her heart shattering when Corby backed away like she was some diseased thing. "I'm a woman like any other," she said earnestly. "My name is Laura Ashton Bennett and I was born in California. I lived in New York with my grandfather for the past four years until he died. I'm an interior designer by trade. My friend Galen showed me photographs of Star and Jason's house . . ." She let her words die away, knowing that he didn't believe a single one.

He dropped the letter on the table and shoved his hands in his trouser pockets. "Tell me, in New York do all the women walk around in those funny shoes and tight, clingy shirts and cut their denims so short a man can damn near see their backsides?"

What could she say? He certainly wouldn't believe the truth, that she'd come from the New York of the 1990s. "Those things were made by a friend of mine, they're one of a kind. I told that to Star. Check my story if you don't believe me. And as far as the shorts go, I'm not used to doing all sorts of housework in a long dress. I was getting tangled up all the time . . ."

Corby ran his hand through his hair. "I'm too tired to sort this all out. I'm going to get some sleep. If Sabrina wakes during the night, you just leave her be. I'll tend to her."

"Really?" Laura's hurt pride countered. "You'll tend to her the way you've been doing since she was born, I suppose. She'd get better care left alone on a doorstep."

His back went stiff, his chest expanded, his expression became deadly. "If you weren't a woman, I'd make you regret those words."

"I already do," she whispered as he stalked away.

With hot tears blurring her vision, Laura retrieved the vague, damning letter and tore it into progressively smaller pieces while mentally calling the writer every obscene name she knew.

She threw the scraps in the firebox of the steel range, then went to her room, where she stared up at the ceiling until exhaustion pulled her into a dreamless sleep.

Chapter 34

NINE O'CLOCK! LAURA'S brain screamed when she woke and glanced at her watch. She jumped out of bed, dashed to Sabrina's room, and found the bed empty and unmade. She ran through the house calling the girl's name, getting no response. She ran to Corby's room. He also was gone, but his bed was made. He'd gone to work and certainly wouldn't have taken Sabrina.

Where was she?

Her heart pounding, Laura ran out to the barn, hoping Sabrina had gone to feed her pony. The pony had fresh feed, but Sabrina was nowhere in sight. Corby's gelding was gone as well.

Laura dashed out of the barn, then made herself stop and try to think, her eyes frantically searching the dense woods bordering the property. Sabrina could be anywhere, lost, frightened, injured, or worse.

Stop letting your imagination run wild and think. Where would she go?

To Laura's horror, her mind remained blank. She looked this way and that, wondering if Sabrina had ventured to Star's or into town to find her father. Either way was rife with danger, danger that she was responsible for. How could she have overslept? Why hadn't Sabrina called out or come to wake her as she'd done before?

Suddenly a familiar figure appeared in the distance, and Laura grabbed the hem of her skirt and sprinted forward, barely feeling the rocks poking into her bare feet.

"Jason, I need your help! Sabrina is lost. I overslept. She must have wandered off. Help me find her, please!"

Jason dismounted and held Laura when her emotions broke free.

"It's all my fault. If she's hurt—"

He pulled back. "Listen to me. Listen."

Laura looked up, her teary eyes wide with fright, her lower lip trembling. "You know something."

"Sabrina is fine. That's why I rode over. Corby brought her early this morning."

"Sabrina is safe?"

He nodded, smiling a smile so like Corby's that it tore her already battered heart into smaller bits. Fresh tears trickled down her cheeks.

Jason handed her a handkerchief. "You stop crying. Sabrina is fine. In fact, she was digging into a stack of flapjacks when I left."

Forcing a smile, Laura felt the invisible weight lifted from her chest. It fell again, harder, when Jason took a note from his back pocket.

"Corby asked me to give this to you." He stepped away and looked into his saddlebag, giving her privacy.

Laura's hand shook more than it had with the other note. What did this one say?

Under the circumstances, you might want to look into that job at Cassidy's mercantile. I'd appreciate you relocating within forty-eight hours.

Sheriff C. H. Hillhouse

Laura crumpled the note and shut her eyes tight, determined to keep the tears to a minimum. She must have died in the fall from the balcony because this sure felt like hell.

Wiping her face with her hands, she scrambled to regain some semblance of composure.

"Thank you, Jason. If you see Corby, tell him I understand the message perfectly." She sniffled, and her shoulders sagged. "Will you give Sabrina a hug for me?"

He offered her a sympathetic look. "It'll be my pleasure." He paused. "She's been asking for something you gave her. Toddy the Toad."

Laura managed a weak grin. "It's a storybook we made, I'll get it."

She took the book from Sabrina's room and gave it to Jason. "Don't forget to give her that hug."

"I won't."

Crumpling Corby's note tighter, Laura watched Jason's mount gallop off.

Oh, yeah. This had all the earmarks of a living hell.

At the sound of the kitchen door opening, Corby looked up from his cup of cold coffee, his dull and bloodshot eyes attesting to his sleepless night.

Sabrina sat beside him, her breakfast barely touched. She looked at him, tears filled her eyes, and she ran out, the paper book clutched in her hands.

"Did she say anything?" Corby asked after a time.

Jason poured himself a cup of coffee and leaned against the sink. "She asked me to give Sabrina a hug." He sipped his coffee. "Hell, Corb. If I didn't know better, I'd think she'd borne Sabrina herself. She was so sick with worry, crying, blaming herself for sleeping too long."

Corby was touched, but . . .

"Did you give her my note?"

"Yeah. She wanted you to know she understood the message." Jason paused again, came to sit opposite his cousin. "What happened?"

"Nothing," Corby muttered, staring down at his cup. He rubbed his mouth with the back of his hand, as if the action could erase the memory of her kiss. He looked up when Jason spoke.

"Unlike my lovely wife, I tend to keep my nose in my own yard, but are you sure you're doing the right thing?"

Corby remained silent. Jason continued.

"Granted, her popping up out of nowhere was strange, and normally I'd agree with you, but she seems like a decent sort." He tightened the rawhide lace holding back his long hair. "Giving her the benefit of the doubt for now is easy for me, considering she saved Matthew's life."

Corby pushed his chair back and stood. "I have to head into town. I'd appreciate you keeping 'Brina until I can make other arrangements."

Chapter 35

LAURA RATTLED AROUND the house, busying herself with every chore she could think of. Dusting the hand-hewn pine mantel for the third time, she looked at the clock, leaning close to see if it was still ticking. Noon. This day was dragging on worse than the day of Grandpa Alex's funeral. At least then she'd had her friends to make small talk and take away a bit of the loneliness, but now, without even a TV or radio to fill the silent void, she felt the walls closing in.

She went out to the front porch and sat on the top step, lowering her head to her lap. She wanted to go home, get away from this insane nightmare.

"I can't do it," she whispered, her eyes heavenward. "Whatever you want, I can't do it. I don't want to. It hurts too much."

She clamped her eyes shut. In her heart, Sabrina Hillhouse had become her daughter, but now that was gone. There would be no high-priced lawyers securing her temporary custody, as she'd had with Candace. There was only the loss.

The tears ran their course quickly, and when they were gone Laura picked herself up and went inside to pack the clothing Star had given her. She fed and watered Sabrina's pony, the chickens, and the cow, then saddled the brown mare and rode into town. She would try to make the best of things until she could find a way home or solve the mystery of the accusatory letter.

Corby felt her presence as absolutely as he felt his own skin. He stopped pounding the nail holding the hand-lettered sign he'd made, then looked over his shoulder. Laura was on the wooden sidewalk across the street, small carpetbag in hand.

He wanted to go to her, to say he was sorry, but the lawman in him wouldn't allow it. "Concerned Citizen" had written for a reason, and until he found out what that reason was, things would remain the way they were. He gave the nail a final whack and went back inside the jail, slamming the door behind him. He stood off to the side and peered through the door window. Laura walked away in the direction of Cassidy's store.

Conscious of the four sets of male eyes focused on her back, Laura gave gray-haired Ned Cassidy a grateful smile when he suggested that they talk in his office. She blushed when the men gathered in the "social corner" made various comments, most of them rude.

"Pay no mind to those heathens, Miss Laura."

"It's all right," she said, wondering if she really wanted this job. Then again, what choice did she have? "I won't take much of your time," she said, not accepting the chair that Ned indicated. "I wanted to know if you'd still like to give me a job. I have customer service experience and I'm good at handling money, but I don't really know how long I'll be staying in Warburton. I'll understand if you want someone who can make a long-term commitment, but I'll settle for something temporary, as I'm a bit short on cash at the moment."

"Are you done?" Ned asked when she paused to take a breath.

"I tend to babble when I get excited. I'm sorry."

He chuckled. "That's quite all right. This old town can use some excitable blood. Maybe it'll get all those lazybones away from my checkerboard and back to their crops." He settled back in his padded desk chair. "Let's get down to business."

Corby had moved his own desk chair outside and was whittling a piece of wood when Laura emerged from the mercantile, carpetbag in hand. She walked around the side of the building to the stairs leading up to the unfurnished room above the store.

Laura was followed by Ned's delivery boy and one of the old-timers who whiled away the hours yapping and playing checkers. They were carrying pieces of a bed frame. Two other men emerged with a rolled mattress. The men took the items upstairs, then rushed back down the stairs to gather linens, a chair, a small table, and a new wash pitcher and basin, which they also took up.

Corby stuck the tip of his knife into the wood when Laura at last stepped out onto the small landing visible above the roof of the undertaker's. She gave each man a big, bright smile and a quick peck on the cheek, waving as they went back to their daily business. Then she disappeared inside her room, closing the door behind her.

She certainly hadn't wasted much time getting herself re-situated. The anonymous letter writer must have been right. Laura Bennett was not all she seemed. So much for her concerns about Sabrina and Jason's benefit of the doubt.

Mariah Nitakechi's mouth curved into a self-satisfied smile as she peered through the lace curtains on her parlor window and saw Corby returning from his afternoon rounds. Her little plan was moving right along. The brat was out of the way again and that little blond whore was gone as well. She *was* still in town, but at least she wasn't within sleeping distance of Corby.

Potts had certainly done his job well. Perhaps if she gave him a bit more incentive, he'd finish it, get the bitch run out of town completely. The only real problem was what to do about the advertisement Corby had put up. So far, three women had applied for the housekeeper position. Why he wanted to remain in his cousin's house she didn't know, but she aimed to find out. And she knew just how to coax the information out of him.

Humming a bright tune, she went to the kitchen and removed the plate she'd kept warming. The dish (one of her best, never used for mere boarders) was piled high with Corby's favorites—fried chicken, mashed potatoes, fluffy biscuits, cream gravy, and *to falla,* the traditional Choctaw dish of boiled, cracked corn. Mariah set the plate on a tray, along with a big wedge of peach pie for good measure.

Her self-satisfied smile turned to a petulant pout when Corby did nothing but pick at the dinner she brought him, finally pushing it across his scarred oak desk after taking no more than a bite of each item.

"What's the matter?" she drawled. Reaching out, she ran her hand through his thick hair, letting her fingers glide down across his cheek. To her dismay, he seized her wrist.

"I appreciate you taking the time to bring me supper, but I'm not in the mood," he said dully, the double meaning quite clear.

Mariah sat herself on the edge of his desk. "I could get you in the mood for a lot of things."

"No," he told her, getting up to look out the front window.

Mariah's expression grew hard, then softened. "All right. I can see how busy you are. When you make your rounds later, why don't you stop by for a cup of coffee or something?"

"I don't think so," he said, his eyes fixed upon the right second-floor window of the mercantile.

Chapter 36

STAR CAME INTO the mercantile on Laura's third morning there. After exchanging a few pleasantries with Mr. Cassidy and the unofficial social club, she asked Laura to show her the latest hats, displayed near the front window.

Star picked up a black straw one decorated with silk roses. "Don't you think this has gone on long enough?"

"This hat display?"

Star cocked her head to the side. "You know exactly what I'm talking about."

Laura fiddled with some ostrich plumes on another hat. "Corby gave me forty-eight hours to remove myself and I did."

Star put the hat back and fixed her cinnamon-brown eyes on Laura. "He told us about the letter. I realize it could have been written about anyone in this town with the same results, but if there's any veracity to it, I want to know."

Laura met her stare. "I am not an escapee from an insane asylum. I am not on the run from the law. No, I don't have a reason for being here, and yes, I'm eccentric in my dress and speech, but that's just the way I am."

The little brass bell over the front door jangled. "I have a customer. Please excuse me."

Corby was the recipient of Star's next morning call. She threw the Housekeeper Wanted sign on his desk. "It would appear that I have already taken on the position. When do I get my wages?"

He scowled and walked over to the double jail cell. "Time to go, Sam. You've slept it off long enough."

A bleary-eyed Choctaw dragged himself out the door.

Star was still standing before the desk. "Now that our audience is gone, I expect you to answer my question."

"I'm working on it," Corby said roughly. "I just haven't found the right person to look after 'Brina."

"You could have fooled me."

Corby picked up his hat. "I'll walk you back to the *Sentinel.* I have some business to take care of."

Corby's business of the past three days had consisted of one assignment: finding the "Concerned Citizen." He'd been to every place of business and almost every homestead within thirty miles of Warburton, bringing up the subject of newcomers in every way imaginable, but he had come up empty-handed each time.

Laura was the only newcomer to hit town in two years, and all who had met her at church or at Cassidy's in the past few days had only kind words to say. He'd even stopped at the boardinghouse for dinner last night and had come away with nothing but an angry knot kinking his innards.

There was only one person he hadn't been able to talk to—Star's father, Quinn McNamara—and that was where he headed after seeing Star to the newspaper office. Finding the doctor's waiting room empty, Corby knocked on the inner office door. "You got a minute, Quinn?"

Quinn gestured with his German pipe. "Come right on in. Are you feeling poorly, the rheumatism acting up?"

Corby closed the door behind him, then sat down in one of the maple armchairs in front of the doctor's desk. "I'm fine. I was just wondering if you knew anything about Laura Bennett. Did she say anything when you first checked her over? Anything at all?"

Quinn took the pipe out of his mouth. "The only odd thing

was that she knew she was in Jason and Star's house. Apart
from that and her clothing, the only other unusual thing was
that she kissed you."

Did she ever, Corby thought. "Well, thanks. I appreciate
it."

He started to rise just as another knock sounded on the office door. The caller was none other than Laura herself. She
was carrying a small wooden crate.

Corby's body warmed when her eyes met his, cooling just
as quickly when she looked away. "I'm sorry for interrupt-
ing. Those elixir bottles you ordered are here." She offered
a friendly smile, then handed the box to Quinn.

Corby stood and with two strides reached the door. "I was
just leaving myself. I'll walk you out."

His body warmed again when Laura's lily-of-the-valley
perfume wafted toward him. "How do you like your new
job?" he asked, holding the waiting room door open for her.
She swept past him, the silk of her green skirt rustling ever
so softly.

"It's all right. Standing on my feet is tiring, and I could do
without the leers of those old men who hang out and play
checkers, but the job has its advantages." She stopped on the
wooden sidewalk and held out a piece of her skirt. "Mr. Cassidy let me have this for sixty percent off. It was a return he
couldn't get anyone else to buy."

"The color does do you justice," Corby said, forcing his
eyes straight ahead.

They walked a few feet in silence.

"How is Sabrina?" Laura asked, pausing as two men
came out of the saddler's and stepped in front of them.

"All right, I suppose," Corby said guiltily. "I've been
busy the past couple days. Been sleeping at the jail."

"Oh." Laura continued walking. "Have you been taking
care of the animals?"

Her tone was harsh, as if she'd slap him if he gave the
wrong answer.

"I've had my cousin Jake's oldest tend to them before and
after school."

"The pony gets lonely."

Corby stopped short, taking hold of her hand to stop her. He dropped it quickly. "What?"

Laura blushed, and his temperature soared. Did that pink flush go down past her collar?

"It's silly, I know. She likes being around people, especially Sabrina. She cried when I left her the other day. Actually, she whinnied, but it sounded like a cry."

And 'Brina cried when I made her leave you.

Corby looked away, started walking again. "I'll be sure to see that she gets some company." He crossed the street, leading the way to Cassidy's. "Here we—"

He stopped short again, pulling Laura behind him. The sound of a woman's whimper came through the open transom over the door.

Laura peered around him. A man was in the store holding a gun on a customer.

"You stay here and make sure no one comes in."

Corby gestured to one of the checker codgers through the front window to stay put, then entered the store slowly. The bell barely tinkled.

Laura could hear him through the transom.

"There something I can help you with, Pike?"

"I had enough of it, Corb. I'm gonna kill her."

"Whoa, now," Corby said gently. "We been through this before. Every time you leave to work with the railroad you get these crazy ideas about Paloma."

"They ain't crazy, Corb. A man can tell. I know she's been running with someone else. There's signs."

"Come on now, Pike. Take the gun away from her head. Come on. This is a private matter. You don't want the whole town getting involved."

"I can't stand it no more. I just come home this mornin' and she wouldn't give me the time of day, an' as soon as I go take a little nap she runs out of the house. So I followed her here and you see what she's doing? She's buying fancy soap and silk stockings. She's trying to gussy up for her lover!"

"Pike—Pike, listen, to me. Take the gun away from her head. That's it. Now just listen a minute. If Paloma was running on you, don't you think you'd have been told? You know your ma would have caught wind of it and told you."

"Maybe."

"You know it's true, and as far as not giving you the time of day, I bet she was getting the boys cleaned up and fed and off to school, wasn't she?"

"Well, yeah."

Shooing away the gathering onlookers, Laura peeked in the door window. Corby was edging closer to the gunman.

"A lot of women do their shopping early in the morning, so that ain't so unusual, is it?"

"No, but the soap, the stockings."

"All right, Pike. Take it easy now."

Laura saw Corby gesture with his hands, coaxing the man to lower the revolver once more.

"How long you been off working this time? Three weeks?"

"Four."

"Well, then, don't you think it's possible that she was just wanting to surprise you? To get here and back before the kids and pretty herself up and give you a proper welcome home?"

The man looked at his shaking wife. She nodded vigorously.

"I-I w-was, darlin'."

"Really?" The man said, his eyes glistening.

His wife nodded her head again. He hugged her and Corby pried the gun away and removed the bullets.

"All right. Now why don't you run over to the Grand and order a nice breakfast for you and the missus. I'll join you if you like. We'll do some catching up. It's been a long time since we had a chance to talk."

The man smiled. "That it has, Corb. That it has. You think I could run over to the boardinghouse and clean up a bit? I don't want to go to breakfast sweaty and smelly."

Corby clapped the man on the shoulder. "That's a fine idea. You go on, tell Mariah I sent you. You know where my room is. Ask her to give you one of my shirts to borrow."

Laura gazed at Corby, her anger replaced by admiration.

He sent the man on his way, then told the onlookers to go about their business and went back into the store. Laura followed, busying herself with a display.

"Listen up, Paloma," Corby said in a low, authoritative tone. "What you do is your business, but it's going to get someone hurt if you keep it up. Pike may not be the most pleasant man, but he never hit you or the boys and he doesn't badmouth you or blame you for his troubles. If you want to leave him, then do it, but don't play this game. If it's not you that gets killed, it might be one of your boys."

The woman nodded.

"I'll bring your stuff over to the Grand."

Laura followed Corby out and to his office, where he locked Pike's gun in the jail safe.

"What you did was incredible."

Corby turned, his low spirits bolstered by the admiration in her eyes. "That's what they pay me for. They don't pay much, but . . ."

Laura shared his smile. "Maybe we should compare bad-pay stories sometime."

"Maybe," he replied, needing to get away lest he kiss her again. "I'd best get going."

Later that afternoon, Star paid another visit to Corby. He was seated out front, whittling. "Something I can do for you, Star?"

"I want you to come out to the house for dinner."

He glanced past her toward the mercantile. "I don't feel like it, but thanks anyway."

"It's not a request, Corby."

He looked up, meeting her stern look. If he didn't give in, she'd just keep badgering till he did. Besides, Mariah was getting tiresome with her flirting. "All right. I'll be there around six."

Star greeted Corby at the front door, leading him around the porch to the rear of the house, where the children were playing. Joyous laughter rang through the air from Star and Jason's twin girls and four-year-old son, James, who were playing tag, and even baby Matthew, who sat on the lap of Star's old nursemaid, Rosa.

Sabrina was sitting alone, beneath the oak tree, looking through her paper book, a floppy rag doll across her lap.

"Look at her," Star said, her tone both compassionate and severe. "What's more important—an ambiguous accusation or your child's peace of mind?"

With that, Star went inside and left Corby alone with his conscience.

Laura was getting ready for work the following morning when the knock sounded on the door to her tiny room above Cassidy's.

She opened the door, reeling back when Sabrina launched herself into the room, grabbing her around the waist. Catching her balance, Laura picked the girl up, hugged her back, kissed her cheeks and forehead.

"I missed you, Laurie! I missed you!"

"I missed you, too, sweetie," Laura said, hugging her again. She looked up to see Corby, standing just outside on the landing. "You're welcome to come in."

He stepped inside, leaving the door open. He removed his hat and fingered the brim. "'Brina and I were wondering if you'd like to come back out to the house. To stay."

"Please, Laurie. Please."

Laura smoothed the wisps of Sabrina's black hair that were escaping her long braids. "I don't know if I can," she said, looking to Corby.

"Please, Laurie." Sabrina craned her neck. "Make her, Pa. Make her."

"You can't force people, 'Brina." He held out his hand, "Come on. Let's give Laurie some time to think it over."

Reluctantly, Laura put Sabrina down. "I wouldn't feel right about leaving Mr. Cassidy in a lurch. He's been so kind."

Corby looked at her. Her knees began to melt. "Ned is the easygoing type. I'm sure he'll discuss it. If you want to."

"I do."

Corby cleared his throat. "We'll be at the Grand having breakfast. You can join us if you like."

"Please, Laurie," Sabrina said.

Go, her heart said. *He still doesn't trust you,* her cynical side chimed in. Sabrina's big brown eyes ended the battle.

Folllowing breakfast, Laura finished out the day at the mercantile and was given a warm send-off by the men she termed "the checkers codgers."

" 'Bye, now, Miss Laura."

"Don't be a stranger."

"Ned's goin' outta business without your pretty face to attract the customers."

"The pleasure has been all mine, gentlemen," she said, showing more than a bit of ankle as she mounted the brown mare Star had given her.

Corby was waiting in front of the jail and mounted his gelding when Laura neared.

"Are we picking Sabrina up from Star's?"

Corby shook his head. "Jace said he'll bring her back on his way to Red Oak. He has some business to tend to for the tribal council."

Mariah Nitakechi was on the porch of the boardinghouse talking with reporter Abel Potts. Laura responded to the other woman's wrathful gaze with a friendly wave and a smile.

The smile faded as soon as they passed. "May I ask what changed your mind about having me look after Sabrina?"

Corby glanced her way, then turned his attention back to the dirt road. "A lot of things, I suppose. Mainly it was the way 'Brina missed you. She was happier than a june bug when I brought her in to see you this morning."

"But you still don't trust me, do you?"

He didn't look her way. "Being the suspicious type comes with my job, I guess."

Another awkward silence descended between them. Though both hurt and angry, Laura knew that she really couldn't blame him. This was a far simpler time than the one she was used to. Even at this late point in the nineteenth century, much of the area surrounding Warburton was as provincial as provincial could be. People tended to live for generations in one spot. Strangers were few and far between, and when one came out of nowhere as she'd done, it was only natural for people to be curious, suspicious.

Being hurt or angry wouldn't do much good. All she could do was let it go for now, let Corby and the rest of the town judge her for her actions and think what they wanted to about her "past."

Corby looked over at Laura. She was lost in her thoughts again. Was she worrying that he would soon find out what she was keeping secret? What was that secret?

Does it matter? his heart asked. *She's made Sabrina's life brighter in a few weeks than you have in almost five years. That has to count for something.*

Corby cleared his throat to silence the tiny voice within him. He didn't want to hear how Laura Bennett had changed his own life in her short time here. He told himself it didn't matter that she aroused feelings in him he'd never thought possible, that her kiss was like a gift from above. A gift that might just be powerful enough to erase his deadly past mistakes, to let him love again.

Such things were impossible and he'd be a fool to think otherwise.

He cleared his throat again. "I have some business to tend to back in town. I'll be heading out once Sabrina gets home and you get settled back in."

"Whatever," Laura replied, and said not another word to him.

Chapter 37

"TIME TO WAKE up!"

Laura smiled, hugging Sabrina, who'd jumped on the bed. "Good morning, sweetie. You sleep well?"

"Yep."

To Laura's surprise, Corby stepped into the narrow doorway.

"Get off Laurie before you crush the life out of her."

"I don't mind," Laura assured him. She sat up, kissing Sabrina's forehead. "Time to scoot, so I can fix breakfast."

"Not this morning," Corby answered, his tone smoother than silk. "I started it. Put hot water in the tub, too. The food'll be ready when you are." He held out his hand. "C'mon, 'Brina. You can help me set the table."

"Okay."

Laura tugged at her hair when they left, certain that this was a dream. Wincing, she rubbed her aching scalp, then scrambled out of bed and got her clothing together. She hadn't a clue as to what had brought this on, but she wasn't about to question it. Not yet, anyway.

She felt the potency of Corby's stare as she crossed the kitchen on her way to the bathroom, dress and underthings clutched in her arms. She hoped he couldn't hear how loudly her heart was pounding. She could barely hear the sizzle of bacon in the pan.

Trying to contain a sappy grin, Laura hurried into the bathroom. Like an anxious teenager preparing for her first date, she dropped the soap time and again, washed herself three times, brushed her teeth four, and combed her hair for a full fifteen minutes, all the while silently thanking whoever or whatever was responsible for Corby's change of temperament. She eventually gave up trying to arrange her hair on top of her head and left it unbound.

Corby wondered if Laura had read his mind when he saw her gleaming blond hair hanging loose, the ends curling on her shoulders. The movement of her walking carried the scent of sweet flowers to him, embellishing the lovely picture she made. There was only one thing missing, but he knew how to bring it out.

"If you'd been in there any longer I think I'd have busted down the door to check on you—even if it meant catching you in the altogether."

The flush of Laura's cheeks warmed him all over. "Hold up," he said when she pulled out her chair. "I'm waiting on you this morning."

Laura felt like a queen when Corby seated her, brushing his fingertips ever so lightly across her shoulders. He presented her with a mug of steaming coffee, then brought over a platter of bacon and scrambled eggs and a dish of toast.

She smiled as she took her toast, and Corby had an unconscionable urge to smear her with some of the orange marmalade and lick it off. Realizing that she'd spoken, he snapped back to reality. "Yes?"

"I asked where Sabrina was."

Grinning, Corby spooned eggs onto his plate. "It seems that I forgot the most important part. She stepped out to get it."

He'd no sooner finished the sentence than Sabrina bounded into the kitchen, a bunch of semi-wilted wildflowers clutched in her chubby fist. "Quick, Pa, they needs water!"

"They 'needs' more than that," Corby remarked with a grin as he got up to help.

"There," Sabrina said proudly, presenting Laura with her water-glass vase and bouquet.

Laura hugged and kissed her, feeling like the luckiest woman alive. "Thank you, sweetie."

Corby took Sabrina by the hand. "Let's get this dirt off so you can eat."

What in blue blazes had addled his brain? Corby wondered as he listened to Sabrina and Laura chattering like magpies. He should have stayed away last night, but he hadn't been able to. When his deputy checked in at midnight, he'd felt the pull to come home, to sleep in his own bed, without worrying about Mariah making demands he didn't want to meet.

But the truth of the matter was that he'd barely slept at all. He'd caught sight of Laura through her partially open door and he'd watched her for the longest time, enchanted by her angelic beauty, the air of mystery surrounding her. Finally going to his own room, he'd stared at the ceiling, unable to get the lovely picture of her out of his mind.

But it wasn't just her physical attributes that had him in a fix. He envied the closeness springing up between her and Sabrina. He wanted to share it. He liked the way it felt to take part. That was what prompted him to stay home late, though he told himself it was the day's business that was the true reason.

"I have to testify at a trial in McAlester this afternoon. If you ladies don't have any pressing plans, I'd like to have you join me. I shouldn't be long. You can do some window-shopping, then we can stay for supper."

"Sounds like fun to me," Laura said. "Sabrina?"

She reached out, taking hold of each of their hands. "Yeah."

Chapter 38

THROUGH THE STREAKED window of his hotel room, Owen Webster's dull eyes scanned the passersby below. It was just his luck to be stuck in Indian country overnight after the train carrying him from Oklahoma Territory was forced to delay.

Damned savages couldn't even keep the tracks in repair. The government ought to herd all their red asses onto a desert reservation. Let 'em all dry up, blow away, and leave the country to God-fearing white men like it was meant to be.

Web was turning away from the window when something—someone—caught his eye.

It couldn't be. Oh, but it was. Hellfire. Maybe this was his lucky day after all. "Well, well, well," Web said. There was no mistaking that goddamned swagger or the regal tilt of the head. That redskin below was Corby Hillhouse.

Webster slid open the window as Hillhouse paused in front of an ice cream parlor. Drawing his Remington, he aimed. He'd kill that sonofabitch where he stood, since his man in Arkansas had failed. He pulled the gun back at the last moment when a little black-haired squaw ran out and into Hillhouse's waiting arms.

So he had a whelp now, did he?

A twisted smile settled on Web's face while a plan formed in his head. A plan even better than his previous one.

Ringing for room service, Webster told the maid who answered that he needed to send a telegraph to his ranch in Texas. When she left, message in hand, Web returned to the window.

Hillhouse was gone, but it didn't matter. He would soon pay for his past sins.

He'd pay with his kid's life.

And then with his own.

Chapter 39

ON THE TRAIN ride home, Laura gazed longingly at Corby, who sat with Sabrina on his lap. They were both dozing peacefully, Corby's cheek resting against the top of his daughter's head, her small hand clutching his.

Twisting the little wooden doll that Corby had carved for Sabrina this morning, Laura reflected on their time together today. It had been very nice, though part of Corby had remained aloof, which hurt more than she cared to admit.

She shouldn't be surprised. He was simply being civil to her for Sabrina's sake. She'd have to be clueless even to consider that there was more to his motivation than politeness. The attention he'd showed today was a fluke, the kiss they shared nothing more than a momentary physical gratification that, if it had gone further, would have ended in a meaningless act of sex.

It wouldn't have been meaningless to you.

True, Laura's practical side conceded. But it would have left her feeling empty just the same.

Laura sighed audibly and shifted in her seat to stare out the train's window, the romantic fantasy in her head too painful to bear.

*   *   *

Corby wrestled with his own inner pain in the days that followed.

Why? That was the question he asked himself at intervals
as regular as ticks of the clock on the parlor mantel.

Why had he done such a fool thing as to spend the day
with Laura and Sabrina in McAlester? Why had he continued to spend time with them the next week? Why was he
doing what he swore he'd never do the day he buried Sabrina's mother—let his child love and depend on him?

But most of all, why was he falling in love with Laura
Bennett?

It couldn't continue. None of it. It had to end here and
now.

Laura jumped when Corby came up behind her one
evening while she was giving the barn animals their "bedtime snack."

"You scared me," she said, her body heating from Corby's
closeness. "Did Sabrina wake up?"

He shook his head. "I wanted to talk to you about something."

Her pulse skittered and butterflies sprang to life in her
stomach. "Okay. Let's go outside. I put off cleaning the
stalls today and I'm kind of regretting it."

Chuckling softly, Corby followed her outside. They sat on
the rear porch steps.

"So, what did you want to say?" Laura asked, turning toward him. He was so close. He smelled so good.

Corby stood up and leaned against the porch support. He
looked down at the toes of his dusty boots a long time before speaking. "My deputies have been putting in a lot of
hours. I owe them some time off. I'll be taking the night
shift."

"Okay," Laura said.

Corby looked at her briefly, but it was long enough.

"And," she said.

He left the steps. "I'll probably keep the night shift."

"And?" Laura asked, her tone rougher. She stood up.

He looked her in the eye. "And since 'Brina is up and

about all day, I might as well stay in town to get some sleep."

With that, he went in the house, returning a short time later with a rucksack. "If you need anything, you let me know," he said before going to the barn.

Laura followed, waiting for him to come out with his gelding.

"An explanation would be nice."

Corby looked down at her. "I told you," he said flatly. "My deputies need some time off."

He tipped his hat, then nudged his mount into a gallop.

"Okay," Laura said to the dust cloud settling back to earth in Corby's wake.

The deputies needed some time off. There was nothing unusual about that. Even staying in town to sleep made perfect sense.

Sort of.

"Don't overreact," Laura thought aloud.

The deputies needed a few nights off. That was what this situation was about.

Laura formed a different opinion the afternoon she took Sabrina into town for a new pair of shoes.

The sheriff's office was locked. Laura took Sabrina to the mercantile to get the shoes, intending to check back.

"Have you seen Corby today, Mr. Cassidy?"

"Can't say as I have. Saw Adam a bit ago making his rounds." He whistled to the checkers codgers. "Any of you no-goods see the sheriff?"

Their shaggy heads shook.

"Ain't seen him much at all."

"He's probably still sleepin'. He don't go on duty till almost suppertime."

Laura's skin crawled. The boardinghouse.

"Thank you." She took Sabrina by the hand and led the way to the door. "Gentlemen," she said to the older men.

"You know where to find Corb?"

"I'm sure I do," Laura said.

*   *   *

"I don'ts like her," Sabrina whispered as they waited for the boardinghouse door to be answered.

"We can't like everyone and everyone can't like us, but we still have to be polite. Do you understand?"

Sabrina nodded.

Laura found it hard to follow her own direction when Mariah Nitakechi answered the door, slightly out of breath, her hair falling out of its bun, her dress bodice buttoned crooked.

"May I help you?"

"We'd like to see Corby."

Mariah cast an uneasy glance inside. "He's indisposed."

Laura took a deep breath, the widow's meaning coming across like a bomb. "Tell him we were here."

With a slight nod, Mariah closed the door.

Chapter 40

LAURA ROCKED SLOWLY in the maple rocker on the front porch of Jason and Star's house, gazing lovingly at Sabrina, who was tumbling in the grass with Matthew.

"Thank you," Star said as she took the seat beside Laura.

"Matthew was no trouble at all," she replied, wondering what Jake and Galen would say if they knew she'd been baby-sitting their grandfather.

"What I meant was thank you for giving Sabrina back her childhood. She's been so happy since you've come into her life. I swear, your affection has her growing like a weed."

Smiling, Laura looked at the children again. "If I've done anything to make her happy, she's given the same to me a hundred times over."

"What about Corby?" Star asked bluntly. "Has he given you anything?"

Laura's smile faltered. "He gave me a kiss I'll never forget, and he bought me these jeans when we went to McAlester."

"Just one kiss?"

"Just one."

Laura exhaled a quiet sigh.

"Don't you care that he's not been home, in what, a week?"

"Thirteen days," Laura mumbled. She looked at Star. "It doesn't matter if I care or not. I'm just a housekeeper."

"And his child's mother," Star continued before Laura could protest. "You are the closest thing to a mother she's ever known. If Corby had half a brain in that thick skull of his, he would make it legal and permanent."

Laura said nothing, a strange mixture of excitement and fear running through her. How exciting it would be to have those kisses and more every night for the rest of her life. How frightening even the thought of another relationship was, considering her past failures with men in general.

"Well?" Star asked after a time. "You love him, don't you?"

"I hardly know him."

Star laughed quietly. "You know how he likes his morning eggs. You've obviously found the key to his being a father to Sabrina, however infrequently. And we certainly can't forget how taken you were with the way he handled that trouble between Paloma Colbert and her husband."

Laura sighed again. "There is no denying my feelings for Corby, but the decision is all his and I doubt that he'll ever be interested in me. Mariah seems much more his type lately."

"He and Mariah do go way back," Star consoled.

"Yeah, well," Laura sighed. "I better get home and start dinner."

Corby came in the front door to find the house ominously silent. If he hadn't been distracted by the aroma of yeasty dough coming from the kitchen, he might have taken notice of the vague sense of foreboding his mind tried to create. As it was, he shrugged off the uneasy feeling and went to the kitchen, stepping out to the rear porch when he saw Laura through the window. She and Sabrina were both on Laura's mare, with Sabrina's pony tied behind.

"Where've you been?"

Laura placed her finger to her lips and he came down

from the porch. Sabrina was sound asleep, her head resting on Laura's bosom. What he wouldn't give to trade places with his daughter right now.

Laura whispered, "Can you carry her inside? She's been playing all day."

Corby accidentally brushed Laura's breast when he took Sabrina from her. At the touch, his head spun, and his innards came alive in ways they hadn't since he'd last seen Laura.

He shouldn't be here. This was trouble for both of them. But, heaven help him, he didn't want to be anywhere else. Carrying Sabrina to her room, he laid her gently on the bed. He stopped on his way out of the room, turned, then bent to kiss her forehead. He'd missed her, too. A lot.

Laura was at the sink washing her hands. Although dressed in a combination of boy's long denims and a lady's ruffled shirtwaist, she was breathtaking. She flashed him a smile that made his head spin anew.

"What brings you home?"

He leaned against the icebox. "You expecting a gentleman caller or something?"

She busied herself with drying her hands. "I was just curious," she said quickly. "It's none of my business what you do. I know I'm just the hired help."

She made a beeline for the bowl of dough on the kitchen table and tested it with the tip of her finger.

"I was only teasing, little one," he said, moving up behind her and resting his hands lightly on her waist. She went stiff and he backed away, feigning a cough.

Way to go, Ace, Laura grumbled internally. She looked at Corby, who'd taken one of the cookies from the tin atop the icebox. God, he was sexy when he chewed. If only she could feel those lips again . . .

"Actually, I was expecting someone," she said, kneading the dough. "I thought Toddy Toad might call and bring his girlfriend, Mariah the lice-infested rat."

Corby's hearty laugh reached deep inside her. She seriously considered throwing herself at him, but managed to contain the urge, partly because of her past disastrous affairs but mostly because the date on the little wall calendar assaulted her twentieth-century morals. This was still the Victorian era, and proper women did not ravish men. Even men who turned them on like a barbecue grill.

"So," she said, rinsing her hands again. "You never did tell me what brought you out this way."

"I was making my usual rounds and such," he answered, taking another cookie. It did nothing to satisfy the painful craving building within him.

She sat at the table. "Sabrina needed a new pair of shoes. I put them on your bill at Cassidy's."

"That's fine. You need anything else, feel free. If you need something for yourself, you can buy that too. A new hat, some stockings, what-have-you."

What-have-yous of the unmentionable variety paraded themselves in Corby's mind's eye. How fine she would look in nothing but a camisole and petticoat. Hell, she'd look even finer out of them . . .

"One of those old codgers asked me to go to church with him on Sunday."

Corby's attention snapped back to reality. "When was this?"

"This morning. I ran into him on the way to Star's. He must have been planning it because he had his hair all slicked back and a real shirt on, not that wrinkly old thing I've always seen him in."

"Are you going?"

Startled by his jarring tone, Laura asked, "Do you care?"

Corby started to speak but then said nothing. Any man was a better match for her than he was. He tossed the unfinished portion of his third cookie into the slop bucket near the sink. "I'd best be on my way."

Laura stared at the space he'd vacated for a moment, then rushed after him. He was untying his gelding from the porch rail.

"Are you coming back when you finish your rounds?"

"I wasn't planning to."

"You have to," Laura said, coming down the three steps. "I promised Sabrina that we'd make you a surprise. It's my

Grandpa Alex's specialty. It's called pizza. It's sort of a flat, crusty bread covered with tomato sauce, melted cheese, and whatever else looks good to you."

"You—" Corby adjusted his saddle. "You don't have to worry about me. You and Sabrina do what you planned. She enjoys the way you do things with her."

"She enjoys your company more. You're her father. You can't just play with her like a little doll and put her away when you're bored. Do you have any idea how much she's missed you?"

His expression hard, Corby swung up into his saddle. "I have a job to do."

Laura grabbed Taima's reins. "Your main job is being a father. That's the most important job you'll ever do. Do you have any idea how lucky you are to have a daughter? Do you know how many people never get that chance?"

He said nothing. She continued, her tone less severe.

"It's all right if you can't make it back. We'll bring the pizza to you later. Don't take this away from Sabrina."

"No," Corby said firmly. "I won't have you riding out by yourself at night. I'll eat at the Grand or ask Mariah to send over whatever she's serving at the boardinghouse."

He jerked the reins from her hands, then rode off hurriedly.

Laura's hands clenched into fists at her sides.

"'I won't have you riding out by yourself,'" she mimicked. "Stupid chauvinist man. I have a black belt. I can take care of myself and Sabrina too. You just don't want us to cramp your style with dear old Mariah."

Sabrina's voice echoed from inside the house. "Laurie!"

The tense lines on Laura's face eased. "I'll be right there, sweetie."

Chapter 41

CORBY LOOKED UP from the paperwork he'd been trying to complete since returning to town three hours ago. It wasn't the least bit complicated, but instead of words and figures all he could see was a meaningless sheet of nonsense—and Laura Bennett's delicate face.

"Here's the supper plate you ordered," Mariah called sweetly as she entered the jail. She set her tray on Corby's desk and took a quick look at the two unoccupied cells. Sashaying back to the door, she locked it and pulled the window shade.

"What in blue blazes did you do that for?" Corby asked, moving aside the checked napkin covering the plate. He inspected the sandwich. Damn, but he missed Laura's cooking. Even her too weak/too strong coffee.

Re-covering the plate, he looked up and his eyes grew wide at the sight of Mariah. She was stark-naked from the waist up, her shirtwaist and camisole on the floor at her feet.

"What are you doing?"

She smiled and unfastened her skirt. It fell to the floor with her petticoat. She was not wearing underdrawers. "I need you, Corby. I need you bad," she pleaded, sinking down to his lap.

Corby's response to her kiss was reflexive, his response to the heat of her womanly charms nonexistent. He pushed Mariah off his lap, her bottom landing on the plank floor with a thump.

Far from being annoyed, she leaned back, her hand drifting down across her round hip. "You know I like it rough."

"No," Corby said, getting up, stepping over her. He gathered her clothing and dropped it on her. "I'll wait out front while you get dressed."

Corby stepped out onto the small porch and his jaw dropped. Laura was walking in his direction. Sabrina was with her, a covered plate in her hands.

"I told you not to come here. It'll be dark soon."

Laura crinkled her face. "Don't be silly. You have to eat. Besides, Sabrina knocked herself out making this pizza. You have to try it."

She breezed up the two steps past him.

"Laurie, wait," he said roughly, reaching for the back of her skirt and missing by a mile.

"Oh, my God," Laura said when she saw Mariah getting dressed, a satisfied smile on her swarthy face. A *very* satisfied smile.

Slamming the door, Laura gave Corby a look that made him rear back as if hit.

"You don't understand—"

"But I do," Laura replied, taking the plate of pizza from Sabrina's hands. She dumped it on Corby's head as Mariah came out of the office.

"Laurie," Sabrina whined.

She scooped the girl up and gave her a hug. "Your daddy is busy, sweetie."

Flinging the mess to the ground, Corby charged after her. "Listen to me, woman."

Laura lifted Sabrina onto the mare, then turned and leaned close to Corby, whispering something that he alone could hear.

He stood speechless as she and Sabrina rode away into the lengthening shadows. Never in a million years would he have expected to hear such words come from a lady's mouth.

Corby was still picking tiny bits of tomato out of his hair when Jason came in.

"Quit your preening, cousin, and open up one of those cells."

Corby did as asked, frowning at the drunken citizen Jason was holding up by the lapels of his stained jacket.

"Sam, Sam, Sam. Won't you ever learn? Didn't I just haul you in a couple days back?"

Sam slurred something in Choctaw.

"Then why do you do it?" Corby asked.

"Tastes good."

The cousins shook their heads as they helped the man into the cell. Corby set a wooden bucket on the floor between Sam's feet. "If you feel the need to vomit, aim for the bucket this time."

Jason locked Sam's pistol away in the safe, then took a seat on the edge of Corby's desk.

"What?" Corby asked, irritated by Jason's knowing grin.

"Nothing," Jason said, brushing a chunk of soggy mushroom off Corby's desk. He followed when Corby went out to the horse trough and rinsed his hair. "Star and I ran into a friend of yours a bit ago."

"Did you?" Corby asked, shaking the excess water out of his hair. He combed it with his fingers, more annoyed than ever at Jason's grin.

"Then again, I should probably say 'former' friend."

Corby scowled and untucked his shirt to dab away the drops of water near his eyes. "Just say what you came to say."

Jason removed his hat and brushed off imaginary lint. "I don't mean to tell you how to run your life, but you can't have two women at once, you know."

Corby approached the jail porch. "I don't have any woman. Don't want one, either."

Laughing, Jason scratched his head. "I'm going to believe those words coming from a man who had a naked woman in his office while the one he keeps at home is out front, throwing food on his head in a fit of jealousy?"

Corby's expression went blank for a moment. "I didn't lay a finger on Mariah, and if you think Laura Bennett is jealous over me, you're plumb crazy."

"I'm crazy?" Jason asked. He got up and tapped Corby on the head. "You have a brain in there? The woman kisses you the first time she sets eyes on you, she lives in your house, she washes your clothes, she cooks your meals, and she loves your child to pieces. Of course Laura is jealous of you being anywhere near another woman."

Corby ran his hand through his hair again. "It doesn't matter anyway."

"It won't ever matter unless you try to patch things up."

"I have a prisoner."

Jason laughed again. "Whatever she dumped on your head really soaked into your brain, didn't it? Running into old Sam was pure coincidence. Star sent me here to relieve you so you could go home. And I have been told that if I cannot persuade you to go, *I* will be sleeping alone for a long time."

Twice during the ride home Corby almost turned back, afraid Jason was mistaken, more afraid that he wasn't. He wanted Laura to want him. He wanted to hold her, to kiss her, to love and care for her forever, but how could he when there were so many unsettled things in the way?

Corby stopped his gelding a third time, still unsure what to do. After a moment, his horse decided for him, heading toward home at a canter. Corby prodded him into a gallop.

Laura was alone in the parlor when he arrived. She was sitting on the sofa, her feet tucked up beside her, her head resting on the wood-trimmed sofa back. She was asleep.

He cleared his throat. When she did not stir, Corby's broad shoulders slumped. It was a fool idea, anyway. He went to get a clean shirt, then went to the kitchen intending to grab something to eat before heading back to town.

Chapter 42

CORBY WAS SITTING at the kitchen table when Laura's sharp intake of breath drew his attention. "How long have you been here?"

He gestured at the food scraps on the plate before him. "Long enough to eat some of your—pizza?" She nodded and he watched the play of lamplight on her golden hair. "It tasted pretty good, considering. Didn't do much for my white shirt, though."

She blushed and came toward the table. "I'm really sorry. I had no business dumping that on you. What you and Mariah do is your business."

"Mariah and I haven't done anything in a long time. I hightailed it out of that office as soon as she pulled her things off."

Laura looked down. "Still. I overreacted."

"Did you?"

She looked at Corby. "Didn't I?"

"That depends."

Before Laura could respond, Corby pulled her onto his lap, taking possession of her mouth in a way that made her ache for so much more.

She wound her arms around his neck, tangled her fingers

in his thick, damp hair, and gave herself over to the waves of pleasure, her passion for him swelling every cell of her body.

Don't let this be a dream, Laura prayed when Corby's hands undid the buttons of her bodice. She knew it was very real when he stripped off her camisole and cupped her breasts in his large palms. "Heavenly" was the only word that could describe the feel of his lips on her skin. She shuddered and squirmed when he teased her tingly nipples, first one, then the other.

His arousal pressed her from beneath, and she reached down to touch him, reveling in her own feminine power as she felt him grow harder.

A moan resonated deep in Corby's throat. Unmarried women weren't supposed to do this, but damn, he didn't want her to stop. He kissed her mouth, pulling her back just enough to look into her heavy-lidded eyes. "Laurie . . ."

"Yes, Corby. Yes," she whispered, kissing him so deeply he almost went over the edge.

He stood, lifting her as though she were weightless. Kissing her long and hard, he headed toward his room. He set her down and studied her beautiful face in the shaft of moonlight falling between the curtains.

He wanted her. He needed her more than he'd ever needed a woman, but when she held out her hand to him, her eyes so trusting, he froze.

He could not do this. Not to her, not to himself. He looked away, dying a little inside. "I can't. I'm sorry."

"Corby . . ." she said in a weak voice.

He looked back before slipping out the door, the single tear trickling down her cheek burning him like caustic acid. He'd brought death to two women. He wouldn't be responsible for a third.

The slam of the front door woke Sabrina, but Laura was thankful. At least she had a reason not to break down and cry.

Corby wanted to break down too, but instead he rode, like a demon, trying to put as much distance between himself and his turmoil as possible.

He succeeded for a time, until his gelding grew tired. Not wanting to return to town to face his cousin's smart-alecky attitude, Corby decided to head home. It was a fool thing to do, but he had no choice. Being near Laura would hurt like the devil, but at least in her presence he felt alive.

Soft crying sounds woke Laura in the middle of the night. She got out of bed, rubbing the sleep from her eyes, and lit a candle. This would be the fourth time Sabrina had had the nightmare about the wild-eyed man, and Laura wondered what could be causing it. In the absence of cable TV and Stephen King novels, the only option was that the girl had heard either her father or Jason discussing some criminal they'd come up against.

"It's all right, sweetie."

Sabrina was sound asleep, cradling the little wooden doll her father had carved for her during their train ride to McAlester. Laura leaned in close to see if there were tears on Sabrina's cheeks. There weren't.

Thinking that perhaps she'd been the one dreaming, Laura left the room. The sound came again. From Corby's room. She knocked lightly on the door. "Corby. Are you there? Are you all right?" Receiving no answer, she entered, setting her brass candleholder on the bureau.

Corby was huddled on the side of the brass bed, his muffled crying dying away. She softly called his name.

Like a sleepwalker he turned toward her, his face dotted with beads of cold sweat, his tousled hair damp with perspiration, his chocolate-brown eyes wide and staring blankly. He reached a quaking hand out to her.

"I'm sorry. I should have known. I should have stopped it." A single tear slid down his cheek. "I never wanted to see you hurt."

Confused, Laura sat on the edge of the bed wanting to comfort him until his vivid dream passed, never guessing that he would grab hold of her.

Before Laura realized what was happening, Corby pulled her close, crushing her body against his. Her breasts flattened against the corded muscles of his bare chest. His skin was hot, scorching her through the thin fabric of her nightgown. She gasped when his large hands roamed down to cup her buttocks and press her against his arousal, covered only by the light blanket.

"Tell me he didn't touch you," Corby pleaded before devouring her lips with his own. He invaded her mouth with his tongue, then gently explored every moist inch. His kisses moved to her throat while his hands snaked between their bodies to fondle her.

"I'll show you what it is to be a woman," he whispered against her neck, his fingers kneading her sensitive flesh.

Physical pleasure spiraled down to Laura's feminine center.

"Let me love you," Corby whispered in her ear, his breath hot, his voice husky.

"Yes, Corby. Yes," Laura sighed, her body turned to a mass of wanting by the skill of his hands and mouth. She whimpered when he pushed the blanket away from his lower half and rolled her over, his shaft hard against her thigh.

He captured her lips with his once more, teasing her with his hips until she parted her legs. He chuckled deep in his throat, continuing to kiss and suck on the soft skin of her neck, his hands moving down to raise the hem of her nightgown further, his fingers soon finding what they sought.

Moaning, Laura shifted, drawing his fingers deeper inside. "I want you to touch me. I've wanted it for so long . . ."

Corby continued his intimate massage as he kissed her mouth again, gently, sweetly, the consummate lover. He nibbled on her jaw, her ear, the base of her throat, until she could hardly stand it.

"It will be good for you. I'll go slow I promise. I love you, Lorena."

Lorena.

The unfamiliar name ricocheted through Laura's brain, shattering her delicious living fantasy. "No," she mumbled, pushing against Corby's shoulders. "No," she said again. "Let me up."

Corby stopped his love play but did not move off her. He

knelt, took her face in his hands. "Don't be afraid. I won't hurt you, 'Rena."

Bitter tears scalded Laura's eyes while her frustrated body tried to override her mind. She pulled back her hand and delivered a vicious slap to Corby's cheek. It knocked him off balance and brought him back to his senses.

Laura scrambled off the bed, adjusting her nightgown. She took the candle from the bureau and used it to light the oil lamp next to it. By the time she turned around, Corby was standing with his back to her, fastening the buttons on his pants. When he turned around, she was relieved to see he was truly awake.

Corby's thoughts were still blanketed in fog, and he tried hopelessly to figure out why he'd been naked with Laura here in her nightdress. He ran his fingers through his hair, pushing it back from his forehead before he sank down to the edge of the bed. He looked up to see Laura studying him with a strange expression that combined pain and pleasure in equal measures.

Lord, she's beautiful, he thought, watching the way her honey-gold hair gleamed in the lamplight. She gave the illusion of being both an innocent and a seductress with her full, rosy lips and her round little breasts pressing forward beneath the fabric of her gown. Her slim hands were clasped directly in front of her, her fair cheeks tinted with a deep blush.

How he loved her! He needed her to take away the chill that covered his heart. "Laurie, I—"

"You were dreaming," she interrupted, taking a step forward. "You were calling to someone named Lorena." She stopped when his gorgeous eyes filled with pain. "Do you want to talk about it? Sometimes it helps."

She waited for a reply, only now realizing that he'd said *her* name just now, using the same raspy inflection as he'd used earlier when they were so close to making love. "Corby—"

He stood up, his body a mass of tension. "Go away. Please."

"No." Laura came forward, gripped his hand in both of

hers. "Tell me. I have to know what's going on. Why did you stop before . . . Who is Lorena? Do you love her? Where does she live?"

"She's dead. She's dead and it's my fault."

He sank to the bed again, sat staring at the floor.

"Was she a prisoner? Did you fall in love with her in your custody?"

Corby looked up, shook his head. "You don't want to know. It's an ugly, ugly story."

Laura sat beside him. "I *need* to know. I need to know about the woman who drove you away from me tonight. You thought I was her just now."

Corby said nothing, but he took her hand in both of his, rubbed his thumb back and forth across her palm, drawing invisible comfort from the act.

"She was a cute little thing, but not pretty like you. She didn't have half your spunk, either. She was a frightened girl and she looked to me for protection, but I couldn't give it when she needed it most." He paused, then let go of Laura's hand. "This is not your burden."

"It's a burden I want to share."

Studying the compassion in Laura's eyes, Corby followed his aching heart.

"I left here when my father died, traveled around, did odd jobs, finally hooked up with a cattle outfit in Texas. The boss's name was Owen Webster. About six months after I signed on, I caught the foreman fiddling with the books. I got the crap kicked out of me, but I took it to Web anyway. He didn't care much for the color of my skin, but I could read and write and was good with figures, so I got the foreman's job.

"With the paperwork I got to spend time at the big house, and that's where I met Web's daughter."

"Lorena?"

Corby nodded. "She was a frightened kitten, always on guard. I thought it was because she was just fifteen and not used to a man's attention, so I played along, stealing kisses now and then, just sitting with her late at night watching the stars. It was pure chance that I found her one night, trying to hang herself . . ."

Laura used her free hand to brush back the locks of hair that tumbled into Corby's haunted eyes. She let her fingers caress his cheek, exerting just enough pressure to make him face her. "Tell me the rest."

" 'Rena wanted to die because her sixteenth birthday was around the bend and when it came, Web planned to take her to his bed."

Corby swallowed hard, not wanting to dredge it up, but knowing it was too late to turn back now. "She said he'd been leading up to it for years. He told her no man was good enough for her. No one would love her as he did. I wanted to kill him or try to turn him over to the law, but Lorena made me see that no one would take the word of a 'feeble-minded' girl and an Indian over Web's.

"We ran off to Mexico. I married her because I thought he couldn't hurt her if she was my wife. I never tried to consummate the marriage, though. I wanted to wait until she was ready. I planned to bring her here, to make a home for us. We found out Web had put a price on my head for kidnapping his daughter."

Laura squeezed his hand. He brought her hand to his lips and kissed it before continuing.

" 'Rena wired him one day while I was out working. He sent her a message back saying that if she talked to him and told him herself that she loved me, he'd leave us alone. I rode three horses to death trying to catch up to her, but I was too late. By the time I got to the ranch the damage had been done. He did unspeakable things to her, then shoved her down the steps.

"I couldn't break her fall. I wanted to pick her up and get her out, but she had too many broken bones. She apologized for getting me involved and then you know what? She did the damnedest thing."

"What did she do?"

Corby took a deep breath. "She looked up those stairs, blood dripping down her face, and she said, 'I forgive you, Papa.' " Corby paused again. "She died right there in my arms. Web shot at me and I ran. I didn't even have the guts to bury my wife."

"I'm so sorry," Laura said, her eyes filling with tears.

"It's Lorena who deserves the pity," Corby said flatly. "I should have stopped it. I should have shot him the minute I saw him, but I couldn't move. I saw him violating my wife and all I could do was throw up." Corby got up, turned his back.

"It's not your fault," Laura insisted. "You can't blame yourself for that."

Corby spun to face her, his expression a mask of disgust. "Did you hear me? I caught him hurting her and I did nothing. I had a gun and a knife. But I didn't use them. I'm as guilty as he is!"

Laura leapt to her feet. "You are not! You were still a kid yourself. The only thing you're guilty of is being in shock. Being confronted with something that horrible is what stopped you from reacting. Trust me—I know that firsthand."

From the fear in Laura's eyes Corby knew she was plagued by her own demons. He wanted to drive them away, to listen as she had for him, but his guilt wouldn't let him. He grabbed his shirt and boots. "I have to go."

For the second time that day Laura watched Corby turn his back on her. She closed her eyes, aching at the memory of the brief ecstasy she'd felt in Corby's strong arms. She berated herself for ending it, for wanting to be called by her own name, for wanting Corby to acknowledge that he was making love to her and her alone. She wished now that she hadn't awakened him or the emotional monster that tormented him.

Laura returned to her own room, but she could not sleep. Instead she began to relive her own nightmare, the one that had set her on the road to ruin. She, too, could have done something, should have done something, but she hadn't and to this day she didn't know why.

"But I do know this, Corby," she said to the darkness surrounding her. "I know that if you keep blaming yourself you'll be as self-destructive as I once was, and I won't let that happen."

Chapter 43

L AURA NEITHER SAW nor heard from Corby for the
next three days.

And although Star assured her that he was sleeping at the
hotel, Laura's jealous, lonely heart suspected he'd spent
ample time in Mariah Nitakechi's arms.

Laura wanted to cry, but she didn't. If Corby chose
Mariah over her, she really couldn't fight it. But she could
do something to end the torment he felt about not keeping
his first wife from harm.

On the fourth morning after hearing Corby's story, Laura
dropped Sabrina off at Star and Jason's, then collected an as-
sortment of boards and bricks. She would get through to Corby
Hillhouse in the most dramatic way she knew—or die trying.

Corby was out investigating a robbery at the church when
Laura arrived in town. She asked Adam Ofahoma, Corby's
senior deputy, to help her carry the things she'd brought.

"You plannin' on building something, ma'am?"

"No. I'm going to use this to slay a dragon I set free."

"If you say so, ma'am."

As Laura waited for Corby to return, she used the time to
meditate and focus her energy for her performance, the way

Jake had taught her. He'd abhorred doing such "parlor tricks," but he had nevertheless instructed her in them, having found through the years that displays of raw power tended to get one's point across when mere words failed.

"Is something the matter with Sabrina?"

Laura's pulse pounded at the sight of Corby. He filled the doorway, his hair tumbling into his eyes when he removed his hat. She put her thoughts back on track. "Sabrina misses you. I've been telling her that you're very busy and will see her as soon as you can, but I really don't know how long she'll believe it."

Corby stepped further into the office, gesturing toward the bricks and boards that she'd arranged waist-high in various places around the room. "What's this for? To knock some sense into me about neglecting 'Brina?"

"No," Laura answered, ignoring his attempt at humor, knowing that with it, as with the carefree smile they'd both perfected, he was trying to cover up the pain that still gnawed at him like a cancerous beast. "I want to talk to you about Lorena."

Corby stiffened and edged back toward the door. Laura stepped into his path, her grip on his wrist much stronger than he expected. "No, Laurie. I said all there was to say."

"Well, I haven't." She let go of his arm, then closed the door and pulled the window shade to shield them from the prying eyes of those congregating outside. "You cannot keep blaming yourself for what happened to Lorena. I know, because I was in a similar situation. I could have protected myself from being brutalized, but I didn't and I almost died because of it."

Corby's stomach twisted at the thought of violence being directed toward her and he wanted to make the one who'd done it pay. No wonder she was so secretive. And yet . . .

"It's not the same thing. You're just a little bitty woman. How could you protect yourself? I'm a man. I had weapons. Owen Webster is a fat, drunken, piss-poor shot. I should have stopped him—"

"And I have been trained to protect myself against a

dozen assailants." Laura's eyes blazed. "I have a black belt only one level below what's considered a master."

"What are you talking about?"

"Karate," she said. "It's a Japanese form of self-defense. I am capable of killing a man, any man, with my bare hands."

"Don't talk crazy, Laurie."

"I'll show you how crazy I am," she said in a tone that defied argument.

Corby's jaw went slack when Laura's dainty hands smashed the boards and bricks with lightning blows, left, right, left, right. She paused upon reaching the last obstacle: two solid floor planks resting one atop the other. Together they were a good six inches thick. She would shatter her bones. Never be able to use her hands. "Laurie—"

She looked at him, her expression going blank. Without warning and with only a strange little cry, she slammed her forehead into the wood, splintering the planks like two pieces of kindling.

Time stopped and Corby could not move. She was on her feet, but for how long? She'd killed herself before his eyes and he'd done nothing. She would crumple to the ground any second, her beautiful face crushed . . .

Laura shook her head to clear it, then turned to look at Corby. There wasn't a mark on her.

Corby had to grip the edge of his desk to steady his trembling knees as wave after wave of relief ran through him.

Laura pointed to the debris she'd created. "I can do that, but I couldn't bring myself to hurt the man who raped and beat me, so you see, I know the hell you've been through. I lived there for a long time and tried to drink the pain away until I couldn't even remember my own name."

She continued before Corby could speak. "I probably would have drunk myself into an early grave if my grandfather hadn't been there. He helped me see that no matter how badly I screwed up I could not go back. I could only accept my mistakes and keep living."

She came across the room. "You have to do the same. You tried to help Lorena. It was her father who did the damage.

The only thing you did was to react the way any normal human being would: by being too shocked to think straight."

Corby took a deep breath while avoiding her unwavering gaze. She was right. He'd known it all along, had been trying to tell himself the same thing for years, and yet the guilt remained. He had one more demon weighing down his spirit.

Laura was disappointed by Corby's withdrawal, but she was far too exhausted to argue now. "At least think about what I've said. I don't know what any of this has to do with Sabrina, but I know it ties in. You can't do this. You can't distance yourself over something she had no part in. She misses you so much. She thinks you hate her."

She waited for a reply that never came, her spirit sinking lower than ever. She wanted to fight him on this. She wanted to rant and rave and, yes, knock some sense into that thick skull, but she couldn't. She'd used up what fight she had. "I'll get out of your way for now, but I'll be back. I will *not* let you keep hurting Sabrina."

"She doesn't deserve me," Corby muttered under his breath.

Laura stopped with her hand on the door. "What did you say?"

Corby glanced at her, his eyes damp with misery. "Sabrina deserves better than me for a father. I'm the reason her mother died."

Confused, Laura came back toward him. "Star told me it was a difficult birth, that Daisy hemorrhaged while you were on duty."

Corby cringed, the lie he'd perpetuated cutting like a knife. He needed to tell the whole truth, knowing full well that she would hate him for it.

"I wasn't on duty when Daisy died. I cut my rounds short and went to see Mariah while my wife was lying in our bed bleeding. If Star and her father hadn't stopped by on their way from church, Sabrina would have died too. I got home just as Quinn was delivering her . . ."

Laura recoiled, but when Corby broke down, her initial disgust waned. She needed to ease his pain. Stroking his bowed head, she spoke softly. "You made a mistake. Even if you had been home sooner, Daisy might have died."

Corby's head shot up. "*Might,* Laurie. But she might have survived if I'd been where I belonged and had gotten Quinn to her sooner." He rose to his feet, wiping his face on the sleeve of his blue shirt. He started to take hold of Laura's hand but stopped himself.

"I'd told her the night before that I would come straight home and take her to church, but I didn't, because I was too damned horny," he confessed. "Daisy lost our first child, miscarried early on, and when she got pregnant with Sabrina, she wouldn't let me touch her, or hold her, or even kiss her. I understood, but nine months is a long time . . ."

"And I'm sure Mariah reminded you of it every day," Laura blurted, regretting it instantly when Corby shrank back. She took his hand. "I'm sorry for that." Trailing her fingertips along the side of his face, she wiped the last trace of wetness from his cheek. "Did you cheat on Daisy the entire time?"

"Not the entire time. And I never laid with Mariah except that once. I didn't plan it. She asked me in for a cup of coffee and it just . . . happened."

Laura bit back another caustic comment about Mariah. "It happened and Daisy died."

Ashamed, Corby looked down, but she cupped his face in her hand and made him face the truth. "You'll never know if you could have made a difference. Daisy died and nothing can bring her back. Hating yourself can't give Sabrina her mother."

She held Corby while he let out the last of the pain he'd carried for so long. When he broke away she let him, watching as he sat on the edge of his desk to regain his composure.

"Shame is what's kept you from Sabrina. You don't resent her at all, you hate yourself."

Corby nodded. "I hate myself for betraying Daisy and I'm afraid that if 'Brina needs me I'll be useless like I was for her mother and for Lorena."

Laura placed her hands on Corby's shoulders. "Worrying about something that might never happen isn't the answer. Sabrina needs you now. She loves you so much, and she's been blaming herself. She thinks you don't like her because her mother died having her."

"I love that little girl with all my heart."

Laura managed a tiny smile. "Then let her know it. It will do you both a world of good." She moved her hand, but Corby took hold of it.

"What about you, Laurie? Knowing all you know, knowing how I strayed, can you ever feel anything for me?"

Blinking back her own tears, tears of happiness, Laura went into his arms. Corby Hillhouse was no flawless fictional hero, but he was hers if she wanted him. She wanted him very much.

"I love you and I love your daughter, and I'd like to start over from right now. Can we do that and put everything else out of the way, where it belongs?"

Corby flashed that famed Hillhouse grin. "Maybe. If you ask real nice . . ."

Laura gave him a playful punch and laughed with him. This had to be the best day of her life, and she wanted it to last forever. "I expect to have you home for dinner. What would you like to have?"

"Anything, just as long as I get you for a bedtime snack."

Laura shivered at the thought. "You'll have to ask real—" The press of Corby's lips silenced her.

Corby came home early, bathed, then helped Laura and Sabrina prepare their dinner. He passed the evening indulging in the luxury of his daughter's company, playing games with her, combing her hair after she bathed, and rocking her to sleep while Laura read that silly Toddy Toad story.

His eyes lingered on Sabrina's angelic face as he and Laura left her room. He closed the door, exhaled softly. "I missed so much. Her first steps, her first words. What a dumb ass I was."

Laura banished his regret with a kiss.

"Don't worry about what you missed, think of what's waiting. She may be a girl, but you can still teach her to fish and play ball, and you could even teach her to play the flute the way your father taught you."

Corby astounded her by sweeping her off her feet and kissing her with reckless abandon.

"What's this all about?" she asked in a faltering voice, when he began carrying her toward the parlor.

He took Laura out to the front porch and set her gently on the porch swing. "You just reminded me of something I left in my saddlebag."

He disappeared inside, then returned carrying a cedar-wood flute. Laura shivered despite the warm temperature. "You have no idea what that music does to me."

He grinned that grin of his and leaned back against the hand-hewn porch railing, one foot resting on the support post. When he began to play, passion swirled Laura's blood into a tempest and raised her temperature to a dangerous level.

Oh my, oh my, oh my, her soul cried as it soared on the night air with the lilting melody of the traditional love song. Corby's playing was beyond anything she had ever imagined. It put the professional musicians on Galen's CDs to shame.

The music intensified Laura's desire for him until it filled every corner of her being. She squirmed on the swing, not sure if she could take much more.

Corby, too, became aroused as he watched Laura's face flush and saw the sexual hunger come to life in her eyes. He'd been wanting her since the moment he first saw her, and tonight his dreams would come true. The fire in his blood blazed white-hot when she licked her lips and said his name in a ragged whisper.

"Corby, please make love to me."

He wanted to take her here and now, but the gentleman in him wouldn't allow it. "You're sure?"

Her reply was a sweet smile. He put the flute down, then pulled her into a crushing embrace, telling himself that the pounding growing louder was the pounding of his heart and not the hoofbeats of an approaching rider.

"Corby!" Jason called, reining his gray to a quick stop. "All hell is breaking loose at the boardinghouse. Somebody got hold of whiskey, and every man except Potts is running wild."

Corby grumbled, then looked at Laura, who clearly wanted him to stay.

"You have to come, Corby," Jason said point-blank.

"Clay and Adam got beat pretty bad. Quinn is patching them up. I have only one of my men heading there."

Corby gave Laura a swift, hard kiss. "I'll get this settled soon. Wait up for me."

"If I doze off you wake me."

"I promise, little one."

It mattered little to Mariah that all but one of her boarders had been hauled off to jail or that most of her possessions had been broken or damaged in the brawl. What mattered was that her plan had worked and Corby Hillhouse was here, coming across the street toward her instead of staying at home with that blond whore who fancied him.

Still wearing the shirtwaist that had been torn at the beginning of the fracas, Mariah let the front placket gape open, exposing a good part of her bosom. She was not pleased when Corby's gaze remained focused on her face.

"I need you to make a list of what was broken and how much it will cost to replace. I'll send for the judge tomorrow and see that they make restitution. I deputized a couple of men to watch over the jail tonight. Unless you need anything else, I'll be heading back home."

Mariah placed her hand on Corby's arm. "Don't go yet. It's late. It's dark. Why don't you stay here till morning? Your old room was locked. It's in fine shape."

"No, Mariah," Corby said, removing her hand. "It's over. I want Laura. I'm going to marry her."

Mariah's black eyes grew fierce. "You've known me for twenty years. You bedded me for ten, but you never thought to marry me, did you?"

"I'm sorry, Mariah. I truly am."

She spat on him. "You'll be sorry. You'll be very sorry when I tell your precious Laura that you were in my bed while your wife was dying having your baby."

Corby winced but stood tall. "She knows about Daisy. I told her everything and she still wants me," he said proudly.

Mariah shook with anger that her one hold on him was gone. "She's trouble, Corby Hillhouse. You mark my words, you'll regret the day you welcomed her into your life." She pointed her finger at him as he turned away. "You will regret it."

"I'll never regret loving her, Mariah—never," he declared, ignoring the tiny suspicious part of his nature that reminded him of all the things he still didn't know about Laura Bennett.

Chapter 44

LAURA THOUGHT THE lingering kiss was a part of her dream, but when her body instinctively arched forward and pressed against a warm, hard torso she knew that this Corby Hillhouse was no dream lover. Her eyes opened slowly, and she drank in the rugged physical beauty of this man who had suffered so much heartache. "What time is it?"

He nibbled her ear playfully. "It's about time I had my midnight snack," he teased, lifting her from the sofa and carrying her to the bedroom. He set her on her feet, then closed the door slowly, taking care not to wake Sabrina across the hall.

Laura reached for the top button on her shirtwaist, but he stopped her. "Let me."

She didn't need to be asked twice, surrendering herself to the handsome sheriff, feeling more than a little sinful when he caught sight of her modern bra. Her breathing quickened when he ran his large hands over the lacy cups, kneading her breasts, dipping his head to suckle her through the sheer fabric. It was sweet torture when he scooped her up and carried her to the bed, laying her in the center while he undressed.

Laura turned onto her side, her eyes glued to him as he exercised his catlike grace, revealing each sinewy inch of his bronzed flesh with a slowness calculated to arouse. She committed his body to memory, noting a few scars on his abdomen and a larger rounded one on his right thigh. When he turned around to adjust the lamp, she had to bite her tongue at the sight of the faint crisscrossing scars on his lower back, buttocks, and thighs.

She'd seen similar marks while doing volunteer work at a shelter for abused children. Corby had been beaten savagely and often, and Laura wished she had the power to go back further in time to prevent it. She couldn't, but now she made a silent vow to see that their days together were filled with nothing but love and happiness.

Corby climbed into bed beside Laura, turning onto his side. He traced the outline of her face with feathery brushes of his fingers. "Your mind is wandering, little one. What are you thinking?"

"How handsome you are. How lucky I am to be here, and how badly I want you to kiss me."

He grinned. "My pleasure, ma'am."

His kiss was a seduction that poured liquid passion everywhere his lips touched—her mouth, her throat, the edges of her bra. Laura was a quivering mass by the time he eased her onto her back and ran his hands over her midriff, slipping his rough fingers just inside the bottom band of her bra and the waistband of her skirt, teasing her, tempting her with things yet to come. Pleasures that he doled out with excruciating slowness.

"You're killing me," she said as he took hold of her own searching hands and held them out at her sides while he flicked his tongue across the base of her throat.

"You want me to stop?"

"That will kill me for sure."

Corby's laugh was racy, his touch incredibly tender as he undid the front hooks of her bra. She moaned when at last his hands were on the soft globes of her breasts, his mouth close behind. It was torture, fabulous, unbelievable torture. And she loved it.

It was torture for Corby as well, for his burning body urged him to get down to business, but he held back. He wanted this perfect time to last, he wanted to satisfy every creamy inch of Laura's own hot body.

As they had on his very first time, Corby's fingers trembled when he reached for the top button of Laura's skirt, but once the second button came free, he regained control, peeling off her skirt and petticoat with a few quick tugs. A lusty growl rumbled deep in his chest when he saw her tiny drawers held in place with nothing but black satin ribbons at the sides. He pulled both ribbons loose at once, tugging the lacy triangle free from her bottom.

Laura shuddered when Corby's breath fanned her burning skin. Where on earth had he learned such a thing? He blew again, his fingers skimming the tops of her thighs. "Open for me, little one," he begged, trailing kisses along her hip.

Closing her eyes, she did as he asked, lifting for him when he cupped her bottom. She glimpsed paradise when his mouth touched her there, and she thought she'd die when he swirled his tongue around the sensitive bud where the passion throbbed.

He stopped when the climax shook her and pulled back. He muttered an oath, and in that horrible instant Laura realized what he was seeing and she felt so very ugly.

"What happened to you?" he asked softly. "Who did this?" Feeling freakish, she curled onto her side, looking back when Corby coaxed to look with a gentle prod of his fingers. "Tell me. Please."

Laura let him cradle her and they sat against the headboard. "I was in love with my best friend's brother, but it didn't last long. Then I turned to the first man who paid attention to me. He was older, exciting, a singer. I loved the parties and all, but he had a mean side. I left him, but he found me. He beat me, cut me with a broken bottle. He said no man would ever want to look at me again . . ."

Corby held Laura tighter as she let out her hidden pain. Tenderly stroking her tousled hair, he murmured words of comfort. "I will always look at you, little one. Everything about you is beautiful. No one will ever hurt you again. I won't let them."

He kissed away her tears with infinite care, and before

long the kisses turned passionate and Laura responded with all she had to give, stretching out beneath him, rising to meet his hungry touch as he explored her body once more.

"I think I fell in love with you the minute I set eyes on you." His voice was thick as velvet, the words warming her as they fell from his lips.

"It was the same for me," she said. "I've been searching for you my whole life."

The look in Corby's eyes spoke volumes, and as his mouth descended to hers, Laura arched upward, her body quaking when the swollen crest of his shaft pressed against her entrance.

Corby tensed. "I'm hurting you."

"It feels wonderful."

Laura smiled, staring deeply into those brown eyes just as she had dreamed of so many nights. She wrapped her legs around him, sighing his name, pulling him inside.

"You feel so good around me," he whispered in her ear. He moved slowly, his self-control fading quickly. "I don't think I can hold back," he warned, his body increasing the tempo of his hips.

"Don't even try," Laura said, meeting his movements with natural timing, the pleasure taking her higher and higher.

Corby shuddered when Laura's inner muscles gripped him like a hand. What was she doing? How was she doing it? He groaned into the pillow beneath her head as he exploded within her for what seemed an eternity, and she, too, hit the peak, once, twice.

He heard his heart pounding in his ears, felt hers against his chest. He sought out her mouth, savoring her lips and the experience with which her tongue teased his, experience that showed itself in the way she tickled the cleft between his buttocks, prolonging the ecstasy as her passage throbbed around him, sapping his strength.

With suddenly weak fingers he brushed the damp honey-blond curls away from her forehead, licked away the deliciously salty beads of perspiration, then peered down at her gorgeous, sated face. "You sure know how to please a man."

He regretted the words at once, not meaning what they implied. He'd done it again, hurt the woman he loved. He turned her face back toward his. "I'm sorry. I didn't mean it to sound that way."

He moved off her, surprised when she turned onto her side and rested her head on his shoulder. He wrapped his arm around her.

"Things are different where I come from," she said after a time. "I'd take it back if I could. I wish I could be a virgin for you."

Corby kissed the top of her head, smothering the jealousy that wanted to grow. "My past being what it is, I'm not going to judge yours."

Corby wrapped his arms more securely around her. "It was like the first time for both of us, because I never felt this way before. Not in my body, not in my heart."

Touched by the beautiful words, Laura sighed quietly, let her hand roam down across his taut belly. "I bet the second time will be even better."

"I suppose," Corby drawled, letting his own hands roam as the effect of her touch became evident. He felt a flare of jealousy again when she tempted him with soft, sweet lips, until he ached in places he didn't know he had, but when she straddled him and looked deep into his eyes, he knew that he was the only man to possess her soul and that was all that mattered.

Laura smiled when Corby awakened her as only he could.

"I didn't mean to take you like a rutting bull, but I couldn't help myself," he said after a while.

"You didn't take anything I wasn't happy to give."

When he smiled, Laura knew that she could never deny him anything at all. She leaned forward to give him a deep, promising kiss.

"No," Corby said quietly, moving her hand away. "'Brina will be wanting breakfast soon." He kissed her lightly, then moved off her.

"What do you want for breakfast?" she asked as he got out of bed and pulled on his pants.

"Nothing. It isn't even daybreak yet. You go back to sleep."

Laura sat up. "I'm not tire—" Her yawn gave her away, and she felt herself blush when Corby chuckled. "I'm just a little tired."

"I can take care of Sabrina. It's high time I did."

He kissed Laura lightly, growing weak in the knees when she brushed her hand against his groin. "You rest now. We have tonight and tomorrow."

"A hundred tomorrows."

"A thousand," Corby promised. "A lifetime."

God, I hope so, Laura thought as he pulled the light blanket up over her. She shivered as he left the bedroom, suddenly feeling uncertain and terrified that fate or whatever it was that had brought her here wouldn't let her stay and hold on to the happiness she'd found.

Chapter 45

CORBY LEANED AGAINST the doorjamb to watch Laura sleep. Her golden hair spilled over her face, glowing like a halo in the rays of sunlight that streamed through the window, her skin pink against the whiteness of the rumpled bed linens. A warm breeze fluttered the curtains of the partly open window, carrying her tantalizing smell to him. He inhaled, savoring the flowery fragrance of her perfume as it mixed with the lingering musky scent of their lovemaking. A satisfied smile curved his wide mouth when she stirred, murmuring his name, reaching out to his side of the bed.

Although much of her life was a mystery she was not ready to share, he didn't care. All that mattered right now was that Laura Bennett was in his bed, dreaming of him, loving him, believing that he posed no threat by returning her love. And for the first time in his adult life, Corby felt at peace, secure, and more happy than any man had a right to be.

Laura woke to the haunting sound of the Indian flute and in her half-conscious state she whimpered, afraid that she was still in the twentieth century, that she'd never known the joy of Corby Hillhouse's love except in dreams inspired by an old picture and a few CDs.

She rubbed the sleep from her eyes and scanned the room,

the icy fear melting once her gaze fell on the tall form of her man, looking so handsome in his dark suit. He was gazing at her with a mixture of pride and lust. The quickness of her heartbeat and the feeling of contentment settling over her told her that this was no dream. "Good morning."

"Good afternoon," he corrected.

Afternoon! Laura blanched and looked at her watch. "It's two o'clock! Why didn't you wake me?" She rooted for her clothes on the floor. "We missed church and we were supposed to go to the McNamaras' for lunch and Jason's birthday dinner is today and—"

She was silenced when Corby dove onto the bed and pulled her down on top of him. She made a feeble attempt to escape but was vanquished the moment he kissed her. She was a willing captive when he turned her over, tenderly parted her thighs, and showered the sensitive petals of her sex with soothing kisses. She scrunched the sheet in her fists when he sent wave after wave of delight through her body, pushing her pulse into a frantic rhythm.

She fought to catch her breath, curling up beside him when he took her in his arms. "You're going to give me a heart attack."

He laughed softly, feeling her hot body ripple like water beneath his fingers. Giving without taking had never felt so good. "Hell of a fine way to go, if you ask me." He leaned over to kiss her and narrowly avoided having his nose smashed when she shot up to a sitting position.

"Sabrina."

She tried to scramble away. He stopped her. "Sabrina is at Jason's. They promised not to start the party until we get there."

Laura's eyes glittered, and a wicked smile spread over her flushed face. "In that case," she said coyly, deftly loosening his tie and undoing the buttons of his vest and shirt, "I guess they can wait a bit for us to get there."

Laura helped Star clear away the cake plates and coffee cups from the dining table as Jason led the rest of the family to the parlor.

"I think I'll have to print up a proclamation to honor you," Star teased. "I have never seen Corby in such fine spirits."

"I feel higher than a kite myself," Laura said brightly "It's kind of scary, though, like it's almost too good to be true."

"I know the feeling," Star agreed, setting the china plates in the sink. "It seems sinful that Jason and I can enjoy each other so." She put the silverware in next and filled the sink with hot water from the wall tank. "Speaking of sinful, you should have seen the ladies in church. Corby's smiles had them all in a dither."

"Really?"

"Really. If he hadn't been carrying Sabrina out after the service, I do believe more than a few would have literally thrown themselves at him." Star laughed. "I daresay those very Christian ladies are harboring some unchristian thoughts about you this afternoon."

"Isn't that too bad?" Laura laughed with Star, her smile fading as she dried the dishes and a nagging doubt asserted itself. "Before we join the others, can I ask you something?"

Star dried her hands. "Of course."

Laura hesitated, afraid of what the answers might be. "Was Corby this way with Sabrina's mother?"

"He cared for Daisy, but I don't think it compared to what he seems to feel for you. He's barely taken his eyes off you."

"What about his first wife, Lorena—" She wanted to crawl into a hole and die when Star's jaw dropped. "You didn't know about Lorena?" She stepped closer to Star. "Please don't say anything. It was tragic. Corby can't find out I opened my big mouth. You can't even tell Jason."

"Can't tell me what?" Jason asked, coming in through the swinging door from the hall.

Star gave Laura's hand a reassuring pat. "I've promised not to tell how we compared notes about you and Corby in certain personal areas. I wouldn't want to damage your fragile ego."

"Is that right?" Jason asked his wife, obviously put out.

"Yes. Your cousin always was skilled on the dance floor, so I suppose it's natural he'd excel at—"

"Excuse us, Laura," Jason interrupted.

"Of course." Laura hurried out, blushing when she heard the suggestive whispers of her friends' great-grandparents.

Her amusement diverted her attention from the raised corner of the carpet runner. The toe of her pointed shoe caught the rug and she stumbled, bumping against the side of the solid oak staircase, her head colliding with the edge of a step.

Pain shot through her temple and the hallway darkened and grew fuzzy, pulling back into focus with unnatural slowness.

Something was wrong.

The deep-pink roses scattered over the wallpaper were too bright, the wainscoting below too old.

A telephone rang in that annoying electronic beeping way she hated.

Laura clamped her eyes shut and leaned her throbbing head back against the spindles supporting the banister. *Don't let this be real,* she begged as Galen's recorded voice filled the stillness.

"It's a machine, luv. You know what to do . . ."

Chapter 46

CLINT BARKER TOOK a long swig from his canteen. The whiskey he'd brought from Texas had been so watered down that it hardly had any kick at all. Wiping his mouth with the back of his hand, he pulled a crumpled hand-drawn map out of his vest pocket. He'd been from one end of Choctaw country to the other and was still empty-handed.

Hillhouse had to be in one of the towns he hadn't yet scouted. Barker looked at the smudged map. Weren't too many left. Red Oak, Krebs, Warburton. He was tired of this goose chase, but he sure as hell couldn't go back to the ranch with no proof of the killings Web was paying him to do.

Polishing off the last of the whiskey water, Barker stuffed the map back into his pocket, then headed to the next town.

Chapter 47

"WHERE DID LAURA go?" Star asked, looking around the crowded parlor.

Corby's brow creased with worry. "I thought she was in the kitchen with you."

"She was, but she left when Jason came in to—discuss something."

Just as Corby rose from his chair, Laura darted in from the hall, knocking him back down. She sat on his lap, clinging so tightly to his neck that he could hardly breathe.

"Hold me, Corby," she mumbled into his shoulder, shaking like a frightened child. "Please hold me and don't let go."

Corby peered past her, embarrassed by the curious stares of his relatives. He was grateful when Star stepped in front of the chair, shielding him and the sobbing Laura.

"Jason, why don't we take your gifts out to the porch? It's such a warm afternoon."

Corby waited until his extended family had filed out before prying Laura's arms from his neck. He cupped her tearstained face in his hands, brushing away the wetness on her cheeks. "What's the matter, little one? Where did you run off to?"

"Nowhere. Back home."

She cried again and Corby held her, countless questions running through his mind. She sniffled away her tears and mumbled into his jacket front. "I tripped on the rug in the hall and I was home. I was so afraid I'd never see you again. I don't know how I got back."

A strange, numbing cold seeped into Corby's bones. He gently untangled Laura's arms from his neck and coaxed her to sit in his place. "Stay put. I want Quinn to look at you."

"I don't need a doctor. I'm fine."

"Do it for me?"

She nodded.

Laura sat silently and stared down into the glass of water Corby brought her while he and Dr. McNamara conferred on the other side of the room.

"The bruise on her temple is slight. I suspect she had a momentary blurring of vision, perhaps stumbled into Star's office and imagined she was in a different place until her vision cleared."

Corby nodded.

"Do we have to?" Laura asked the following morning in response to Corby's suggestion that they ride up into the hills for a daylong picnic.

"We don't *have* to, but I thought you might like to."

"Of course I would," she said quickly. "I know Sabrina would love it, but . . ."

Corby waited for her to continue. She didn't. "But what?" he asked, doing his best to suppress the suspicious part of his nature.

Laura looked down at the breakfast she'd barely touched. What could she say? *I'm afraid to move because I might be zapped a hundred years into the future and never see you again?* "I feel kind of—blah today."

Sabrina dashed in from her room. "Can we go now? Can we have our picnic?"

Corby pulled Sabrina onto his lap. "I think we'll have to wait. Laura is feeling poorly today."

"Oh."

Hearing that sad little voice, Laura forced a smile. "Maybe I just need some fresh air and sunshine. We'll go."

Corby studied Laura as she packed the leftover food and plates away in the spare saddlebags he'd brought. Something was still not right with her. It wasn't a bodily sickness but something inside. She was worried, afraid—but why?

The answer, when it came, was so simple that Corby wanted to curse himself for suspecting something more. She was on edge because he'd been such a jackass. She'd been in his bed for two nights now and they'd coupled so many times he'd lost count. She might be carrying his child right now. No wonder she seemed ready to jump out of her skin.

Corby's suspicious side reared its ugly head again. *You sure that's it?*

Of course he was sure, and he knew how to fix it.

When they returned home, Corby put his plan into action. "I'm going to make a quick run into town to check on things. I'll be back to help you put 'Brina to bed."

Fear leapt into her eyes. "You'll come right back?"

"Of course I will, little one." He playfully chucked her under the chin. "I might even bring you a surprise." He was surprised by the force of her hug, the distress in her voice.

"All I want is you. I wish you could hold me forever. I want to stay with you and Sabrina."

"You will, Laurie," he said softly, smoothing back wisps of hair from her face. "This is where you belong. This is where you'll stay."

"Always," Laura said, wrestling against the doubt deep within.

She watched Corby ride off and hugged her arms in front of her. She felt so cold, so afraid that her dream was over. She'd gone to her own time. She had and it might be a sign that she would go back for good. Then again . . .

Laura seized the fleeting hope that her "trip" had been a fluke, the cosmic powers' way of letting her know that Galen and Jake were alive and well. She'd been brought here because she belonged here. She and Corby belonged together.

*   *   *

Corby was home before dark, and he waited until Sabrina was asleep to give Laura his surprise.

"I know it's not much, but it's all Ned had in stock. The diamond is real even if it is kind of small. We'll save up some money and then I'll have him order the best one he can."

Laughing, he began to shake his hand to match the nervous trembling of Laura's. "Hold still, so I can get it on your finger."

Laura held her left hand steady with her right as Corby slid the sparkly little engagement ring on her finger. She threw herself into his arms, covering his face with kisses.

"Whoa, now. I didn't even ask you to marry me yet."

He paused and grew serious. "I should have asked you long before now. I should have taken you to the altar first and the bedroom second. If anyone's been soiling your reputation, I'll set them straight."

Laura caressed his face, loving him more by the second. "I don't care what other people think. The only ones who matter to me are you and Sabrina."

"It matters to me," he said, drawing her near. "I asked Reverend and Mrs. Graves to come over for supper tomorrow so we can make the plans. Is that all right with you?"

"That's fine. It's perfect. You're perfect."

Something crossed over her face then, and Corby felt her small body tense. "What is it, Laurie?" He let her pull away, then followed her outside to the front porch. She looked at him, her green eyes filling with pain. "We can be married tonight if you don't want to wait."

"It's not that." She paused, took a step forward, then back again. She twisted the little diamond on her finger, speaking without looking up. "Would you like more children?"

"Of course I would. And don't you worry if you're pregnant now. We'll be married in plenty of time." Corby took her in his arms, but she remained stiff.

He loosened his hold, his mind spinning a web of doubt. "Is there something I should know? Are you carrying someone's child now?"

"No," she said, her eyes even more sad. "I may never

have children. The doctors weren't too optimistic . . . I'll understand if you want to end it now. You need someone who can give you everything you need." She walked away.

Corby felt a piece of himself go when Laura left the porch, and he rushed after her, pulling her to him. "You are what I need, Laurie. You are all I need."

He carried her inside, and satisfied her until the wee hours of the night, and although Laura was secure that he loved her despite the physical flaw and the past she could not explain, she couldn't rest. Life was perfect for her, more perfect than she could ever have imagined—and that was the problem.

Life simply wasn't perfect. Especially a life acquired through something as bizarre as time travel.

Chapter 48

LAURA WAS TIRED when Corby woke her in the morning, but she pushed aside the drowsiness and the lingering qualms, deciding to make the most of each day that dawned.

She walked him out after breakfast, entranced by the grace of his movements as he rubbed his gelding down and saddled up. How proud she would be to stand up before the church congregation and have him take her as his bride. "Do you think you might come home for lunch?"

Corby smiled as he led the horse forward. "Of course I will. Can you make that thing with the cheese and tomato sauce?"

"Pizza?"

"Yeah." Corby flashed a wicked grin and slipped his arms around her waist, pulling her close, then sliding his hands down to knead the soft mounds of her bottom. "Why don't you try to save some of that sauce, then maybe after the Reverend and his missus go home and Sabrina goes to sleep we can use it."

"For what, Sheriff?"

"I'll think of something."

*   *   *

Clint Barker felt a tingle in his crotch when he raised the field glasses to his eyes and saw Hillhouse kissing and feeling up a white woman. She was doing the same in return, and Clint thought they might actually go at it right out in the open, but they didn't. Hillhouse took off on his horse and the woman watched him go. She wasn't too bad-looking, and from what little he'd seen, Clint supposed she'd be good on her back.

He could go down now, sample her charms for himself, then snatch the kid—but no. He'd gotten a reply from Web when he finally located Hillhouse, and the old man had a change of plan. He wanted the kid alive, wanted to kill her in front of her father.

He hadn't said it in those words, but that was what he meant. All Clint had to do was bide his time until Web could meet up with him—another week, two at the most.

Clint looked through his glasses again. The woman was wearing snug men's britches and doing some crazy-looking bending and stretching. She wasn't bad at all, for an Indian-lovin' bitch. It would be a pleasure to show her what a real man could do for her.

"The Reverend will be here in a little while, sweetie, so why don't you put on that new dress your daddy brought home for you?"

"Okay!" Sabrina said, skipping off to her room.

Laura looked toward the bathroom door, considered surprising Corby, but put her mind back on preparing dinner. She added some spices and stock to the enameled baking pan containing the chicken, then stuck the chicken back in the icebox and set aside a pan to make gravy. All she had to do now was slice the carrots and potatoes and place them in their respective pots.

Her hands began to tremble. She couldn't believe this was happening. In less than an hour she'd be sitting down with a nineteenth-century preacher to discuss her wedding plans. Laura's nervousness took a firmer hold. She was going to have a real wedding, be a real wife and mother. She was almost thirty years old. It was ridiculous to be so jittery, but she couldn't help it.

She knocked one carrot to the floor and bumped three potatoes off the table with her other hand. If this was any indication, she'd better lock herself in a padded room the day before the wedding. She bent to pick up the potatoes and hit her head on the table's edge when she tried to stand up.

Blood rushed through Laura's ears in a deafening roar, and the air around her seemed to erupt in a burst of neon colors just as it had the day she fell off the balcony.

Nooo! her mind screamed as the world went black.

"Help, Pa! Help!"

Corby stumbled getting into his suit pants, half falling out of the bathroom to find black smoke coming from the oven and Sabrina screaming in the parlor doorway.

"Hush, now. It's all right."

He cursed when he burned his hand on the hot oven door, then grabbed a towel from the sink to remove the pan of charred bread. He dropped the pan into the sink, then opened the back door and window to clear the smoke before picking up his frightened daughter.

"Where did Laurie go?"

"I dunno."

Corby walked to the back door and scanned the area between the house and the barn. He stepped out to the porch, calling her name. "Laurie, where the hell are you?" When there was no reply he set Sabrina down. "Look for her in my room while I get my shirt and boots on."

Corby went back to the kitchen after dressing. He picked up the paring knife and potatoes from the floor under the table. It looked like she just dropped everything and ran, but why?

"I can'ts find her, Pa," Sabrina said, tears gathering in the corners of her big brown eyes. "Where's Laurie? I want my Laurie."

Unsure if he should be angry or alarmed, Corby held out his hand. "We'll look for her."

Chapter 49

THE ROAR IN Laura's ears subsided, the layers of un-consciousness falling away by fractions. She became aware of smells surrounding her. The smells of age, of decay, of—marijuana?

"No," she whimpered, forcing herself to open her eyes. "No!" she shrieked, getting to her feet, staring in terror at the kitchen. It had been so clean, so lived in a minute ago—now it was shadowy and filthy, with broken Formica-topped counters, an avocado-green refrigerator missing its doors, a decrepit electric range.

Groaning, Laura rushed into the barren main room. Scraps of paper were scattered among animal droppings. She looked at the stone fireplace with the wooden mantel that Peter Hillhouse had carved when he built the home. Stones were missing, the pine mantel she'd polished that morning was now warped and splintered. "No," she said again, hurrying to the bedrooms.

Nothing.

There was nothing but an old stained mattress in Corby's room along with some broken beer bottles. There was no sign of Corby or Sabrina. It was as if they'd never existed.

Laura fell back against the peeling door frame, her knees

giving out from the despair pressing down upon her. She cried until there were no tears left, but she remained on the dirty floor, unable to get up, unwilling to leave this link to her family. What must Corby think? What must Sabrina think?

"Miss? Miss?"

Laura looked up to see a balding man in uniform. A sheriff's uniform. He wore a badge that reminded her of Corby's, and her pain found fresh tears.

"Don't cry, Miss. Who are you? Are you Laura Bennett?"

Laura said nothing. He helped her to her feet, the badge so like Corby's that it held her transfixed. Maybe if she wished on this tiny star hard enough it would take her back home. "Take me home," she whispered. "Please take me home."

"I will, miss."

"You can't," Laura said weakly, allowing him to lead her to his patrol car.

She stared blankly out the window, growing nauseous from the barrage of trappings from the late twentieth century. Here were satellite dishes, mobile homes, cars—all the things she'd never wanted to see again. She clamped her eyes shut and tried to imagine the old Warburton she'd grown to love, the one with bluer skies, unoccupied land, and the people she loved more than life itself.

Laura opened her eyes when the car turned and slowed, remaining in her own world until a familiar face peered through the window at her. She sprang to life, pounding on the glass with her open hand. "Jake! Jake! Help me. Help!"

Jake yelled for his sister as the sheriff unlocked the rear door of the cruiser.

Laura launched herself into Jake's arms and clung to him for dear life, "Help me, Jake! Please help me get back to Corby. Please."

"I think we should take her for help right now," the sheriff said to Galen, tapping his index finger against his head.

"We'll get her what she needs, Sheriff Mitchell," Galen answered.

The sheriff watched Jake lead the frantic Laura up the

broad porch steps, then turned back to Galen. "It was the damnedest thing. One of my deputies chased a bunch of kids out of there not ten minutes before, and when I swung back around to make sure we got all their booze and pot, there she was, like she came out of nowhere all dressed up for Halloween."

Not Halloween, Galen thought. *She looks like she just stepped out of my great-grandmother's photo album.*

"Thank you again," Galen said, shaking the sheriff's hand. "We can handle things from here."

Laura was sitting next to Jake on the antique sofa, her arms crossed in front of her as though she were freezing. She rocked back and forth, muttering the name "Corby" over and over.

When Galen entered, Jake gave her a puzzled look and a shrug.

Galen knelt on the floor in front of Laura and took hold of her clammy hands. "Are you all right, luv? Do you need a doctor?"

"I need to get home," Laura mumbled. She looked at her friends. "I need to get back to Corby. Please help me."

Galen looked at her brother. "Laura, the sheriff said he found you after he broke up a drinking party. He said they found dope there, too."

Laura snatched her hands away and sprang to her feet, the reproach in her eyes impaling her friends. "You think I've been holed up someplace on a binge."

"Well, Laurie—"

"Don't you 'Well, Laurie' me," she shouted, pointing her finger at Jake's nose. "How can you believe that I've been off boozing it up?"

The twins said nothing, but their expressions said everything.

Laura threw up her hands in disgust. "I do not believe this." She pushed past Galen and paced the flowered carpet, her hands on her hips, her head shaking to and fro. "I have not been on a bender. I have been right here in Warburton the entire time. I have spent hours in this very house. I was here the day before yesterday!"

"You weren't here, Laurie," Jake said quietly. "We searched. The sheriff searched. The highway patrol searched."

"Well, you didn't search in 1899, did you? That's where I've been. In the Warburton of 1899. I've been here with your great-grandparents. I baby-sat your grandfather."

The look the twins gave each other crushed Laura, but she did not cry. "Look at me," she ordered. She lifted the hem of her long brown skirt to reveal her high lace-up shoes and old fashioned long underwear. "Where do you think I got these clothes? Your great-grandmother gave them to me when she hired me to work for Corby Hillhouse. I've been taking care of his daughter, and yesterday he asked me to marry him." She thrust out her left hand with the little diamond ring. "Look."

Galen and Jake looked at the ring, studied her clothes. Galen spoke. "When we were at UCLA we all liked to scour garage sales and thrift shops for vintage clothes. You still do."

Laura's eyes were furious as she started pacing again. "I don't know why this surprises me. Your ancestors think I'm a flake too, because I can't explain where I came from. I didn't dare tell them I was born in 1968, not 1868. They think I'm some runaway hooker or something."

Galen and Jake said nothing. They didn't have to.

Laura threw up her hands again. "I'm going upstairs to think of a way to get back."

"She shouldn't be alone," Galen whispered.

She and Jake followed Laura. The telephone rang.

"You get it," Jake said. "It might be the sheriff with more news."

Galen brushed off the photographer who asked for Laura and was hanging up the phone when her brother shouted, "Laurie, no!"

Galen reached the master bedroom in time to see Jake dodge a vicious karate punch that left a gaping hole in the wall just behind where his head had been. Galen's scream froze in her throat as Laura lunged toward the repaired balcony railing.

Jake seized the hem of her long skirt and jerked her down on top of him, rolling back inside, deflecting her punches until he managed to gain the uppermost position. He grabbed Laura where her neck and shoulder joined, compressing her carotid artery until she lost consciousness.

Kneeling over Laura long enough to catch his breath, Jake then picked her up and carried her to her room, making certain that the window, outside shutters, and door were securely locked. He brushed his long hair behind his shoulders and leaned back against the door.

"If she wasn't out of practice, Sis, you'd be scraping pieces of me up off the floor." He massaged a sore spot on his side. "I taught her too well."

"What was all that about—" Galen stopped herself upon hearing the incessant beeping of the downstairs phone. Jake followed her down and took a seat on the stairs. Galen set the receiver firmly in the cradle, then asked her question again.

"She wanted to jump," Jake said softly, placing his hand over his sister's. "She said she traveled back in time when the rail broke and she fell. She said she rolled down that little hill and she woke up to find our ancestor bending over her." He paused, nervously stroking his chin. "I think she needs professional help, but who?"

"I don't know, bro'. Let me ring Aunt Ida over in Talihina. She works at the tribal hospital. Maybe she knows someone."

"Well?" Jake asked as Galen hung up the phone.

"Ida's going to get in touch with a community health rep and have him call right back."

The twins stared at the telephone, except for stealing occasional looks up the stairs. Galen pounced on the phone when it finally rang.

"Yes, I understand. Don't worry. I'll pay for it personally. Thank you. I appreciate it." She hung up. "Bloody jerk."

"No good?"

Galen sat on the bottom step. "It's okay, just bureaucratic

bull. A shrink will be by first thing tomorrow to evaluate her. How long will she be out?"

Jake shrugged. "I'm not sure. I didn't have time to gauge the amount of pressure I used. It could be minutes or an hour."

"Then one of us should stay with her until the doc comes."

"One—meaning me?"

Galen patted her brother on the knee. " 'Fraid so, little bro'. You can handle her physically."

"I hope."

"Where is she, you bloody moron?" Galen yelled when Jake opened the door of Laura's room the next morning.

"She's right here." The last word faded away when his eyes fell on the empty bed. The bed that hadn't been empty a moment ago.

He and Galen made a mad search of the room, checking the closet, under the bed, behind the door, behind the draperies.

Jake looked at the psychiatrist, who was standing in the doorway carefully observing the scene.

"She was here all night. I was sitting with my back to the door. She couldn't have gotten past me. She was sleeping when I moved the chair to open the door."

"The window and shutters are still locked from the inside," Galen said, meeting the gaze of the doctor, who removed a small notepad from his jacket pocket.

"Why don't you both have a seat and tell me about your— friend?"

Chapter 50

THE POUNDING IN Laura's head was like a war drum, reminding her of how Corby had playfully taunted her their last night together. As always, he'd teased her with his lips and hands until she could hardly stand it, and when she accused him of being a barbarian, doing it on purpose, he just grinned his sexy grin, making her squirm even more.

What do you expect, little one? I have the blood of Choctaw warriors in my veins.

Corby. She missed him so. What she wouldn't give to see him again, to hear his deep voice, to hold his hand, to pick up his dirty socks . . .

When at last the pounding in her head subsided, Laura opened her eyes and stared up at the plaster medallion in the center of the ceiling. Although her vision was blurred by unshed tears, she noticed that Galen and Jake had redone her room and contacted the glassblower she'd lined up to repair the painted hanging lamp.

Wait!

Laura rubbed her eyes and sat up. There was no electrical cord threaded up through the brass lamp chain. She looked around the room. What she saw sent her heart into palpitations. This wasn't her room at Galen's future B&B. This was Star and Jason's guest room.

She jumped out of bed and looked out the window. Horses grazed in the morning sun not far from the rear of the house, among them the spotted foal she'd watched Jason deliver last week.

She dashed out of the room, nearly colliding with Star, who was carrying her youngest.

"Laura?"

"I'll explain later," she called, bounding down the stairs, tearing through the kitchen, startling Star's other children, who were having their breakfast.

She yelled to Jason as he was leaving. "Wait for me, please!"

Jason halted his mount and waited for Laura to catch up. His expression bordered on unforgiving. "Corby is worried sick. I was about to get a posse together to look for you."

"It's a long story that I hardly understand myself," Laura said between deep breaths. "I just want to go home."

Jason hesitated, then dismounted and handed his horse's reins to her. "Hang on to Shubuta while I get you a mount."

Laura's spirit soared as the spacious log home appeared on the horizon. Her pulse pounded at the sight of Corby sitting in the middle of the porch steps, his head bowed, his forearms resting on his knees. A circle of cigarette butts surrounded him as he puffed on yet another.

Hearing the hoofbeats, he looked up, and Laura saw relief in his eyes, but too quickly it passed and was replaced by a cold, dark expression. He stood up, dropping his cigarette, crushing it with the heel of his muddy boot.

Laura nearly fell in her haste to dismount. She ran to Corby and threw herself at him, hugging him until her arms ached.

He held her close, then moved her to arm's length "Are you all right? Where the hell were you?"

"I was kind of at Jason's—"

"What?" Corby glared at his cousin.

Jason held up his hands. "I don't know when or how she

got there, so leave me out of this." He took the reins of the horse he'd lent Laura. "Good-bye."

Laura pulled Corby's head down for a kiss. He did not kiss her back.

"Where in blazes have you been? How could you up and leave like that? The food you left cooking damn near burned the house down. Do you know how upset Sabrina was, how embarrassed I was when Reverend Graves got here?"

Laura stepped forward, his bitterness tearing her to pieces. She reached out. He stepped back. "I didn't run away. I hit my head on the table and . . . and the next thing I knew I was back where I came from." She paused, needing him to hear the truth. "I come from your future, Corby. I was born in 1968. I was helping my friends fix their house—Star and Jason's house—and I fell off the bedroom balcony and back through time . . ."

Corby's growing disgust took her voice away. Soon the disgust turned to anguish. "Tell the truth, Laurie. Don't you want to marry me? Are you still married to the man who cut you?"

Laura reached for his hands, but he shoved them in his trouser pockets. The pain in her heart strained her voice. "What I said is true. Why can't you believe me? I saw your picture in my friends' family album. I wanted to meet you so badly, and—I don't know—it just happened."

He dismissed this with an angry gesture. "People don't flit a hundred years back in time, then back and forth again."

She grabbed his hands, holding so tightly he couldn't pull away. "I did just that, Corby. I don't know how, but I traveled through time, and I'm afraid that if it happens again I won't get back here. I want to be your wife, and I'm not married. I was never married." She let go of Corby's hands. "In my time a lot of people live together without being married."

Corby turned his back. "I'm leaving. Sabrina is with Uncle Elan and Aunt Martha. I'll give you twenty-four hours to clear out."

He stalked toward the barn. Laura followed, trying to get him to listen to her nonsense. He ignored her. If she was getting cold feet, why didn't she just say so? Why did she have to use that cockamamy story? If she only wanted to live together without the ring or the paper, he would, even though it went against everything he had been brought up to believe. Why couldn't she be honest? What other secrets did she have?

Laura ran after him when he rode his gelding out of the barn, jumping in front of him. Only Corby's quick reflexes saved her from being trampled as she tried to grab him.

"Please believe me! I love you! I love you . . ."

Corby tore past her, her words dying on the swoosh of wind in his ears. He rode hard, telling himself his eyes were misting from the cool morning air the higher he went into the hills.

He stopped when he reached a ramshackle house made of mismatched boards with paper windows and a sagging little porch. He pounded on the door with his fist, not caring that it started coming loose from one of its rusted hinges. "Sam Choate, get your drunken ass out here!"

Corby bellowed the man's name again, and soon he came out of his house, pulling his suspenders over his stained undershirt. He ran his stubby fingers through his sparse gray hair. "I ain't done nothin', Sheriff."

"I don't give a rat's ass if you have. I want a bottle of liquor."

"I-I give it up—" The man broke off as Corby's arms shot out and lifted him by his shirt.

"I want a bottle of whiskey and I want it now."

Corby took the illegal liquor to the ruins of his childhood home and drank the bottle dry, reminding himself with every gut-burning swig of what Mariah had said last night when he'd gone into town in search of Laura.

I told you that woman was trouble, Corby. Send her on her way before she does more damage.

Send Laura Bennett on her way. That was what he would do, all right. He told himself this again and again while darkness fell and he threw up the cheap whiskey he'd guzzled to drown his sorrows.

And yet Corby's heart refused to believe what his mind told him, insisting that he remember the joy she'd brought into his life. It reminded him that she had accepted his deadly mistakes as simple human failings and had given him permission to forgive himself.

It pointed out that Laura was the one who gave his daughter the motherly attention she thrived on. It told him to consider that Laura was the one who made him look forward to the dawn of each new day—something he hadn't been able to do since his mother's death when he was a boy.

Lastly, it reminded him of his New Year's Eve wish.

You asked the Lord to send you a woman to love. Maybe He did in His own mysterious way.

Corby hauled himself up off the ground and walked over to what was left of the gnarled tree his father's second wife cut her whipping switches from. As he touched the dead, crackly bark, he thought back to the night he and Laura first made love.

She'd touched her fingertips to the scarred skin as though the wounds were still fresh, her eyes full of concern. "Who did this to you?" she'd asked softly, as if afraid to dredge it up at all.

He'd told her, letting out the gruesome details that he'd spent a lifetime concealing. "It hurt, Laurie. It hurt like hell, and sometimes I can still feel it. I still wonder what I did to make her hate me so much."

You told Lorena. You told Mariah. You told Daisy, but it was Laura who cried for you. It was Laura who kissed those scars and took the pain from the deepest part of you and made it her own.

It was Laura Bennett who made you feel whole and loved for the first time in your life.

The cat in Laura's dream flicked its wet tongue over her left ear, then nipped at her earlobe. She giggled when the cat's tongue magically became human lips, searching, insistent, intoxicating, just like Corby's lips. She whispered his name, too afraid to open her eyes, too afraid that this was only a dream.

"Wake up, Laurie."

Laura looked into those brown eyes and melted inside. "You believe me."

"I believe you cared enough to come back to me."

Disappointment squeezed Laura's hopeful heart, but she

focused her energy away from the pain. Corby was here, cupping her face in his strong hands, bringing his mouth to hers.

For the moment, nothing else mattered.

Laura wanted the kiss to go further, but she knew it wouldn't. Still, when Corby settled back on the sofa, his arm around her shoulders, she rested her head on his chest, not minding at all that he could use a bath.

"You deserve an explanation," she said when the silence began closing in. "I wish I could give you one you could believe. I didn't run out. I wouldn't do that to you or Sabrina."

Corby tilted her face up toward his. She didn't have the eyes of a liar, but he simply couldn't accept her version of the truth, despite the wild pleading of his soul. "We can start over from today. Like you said before, the past is gone and we can't do much else but learn from our mistakes."

Laura nodded, biting down hard on her tongue to hold in her tears.

"Oh, hell," Corby muttered. "I have to help Jace transport those federal prisoners tomorrow. We'll be gone for a week."

"If you don't trust me with Sabrina, I'll understand." She started to rise. "Maybe I should just leave."

Corby took hold of her hand, then stood and looked down into her eyes. "I want to start over, Laurie. I know you love Sabrina. You've cared for her like she was your own. I know you'll watch over her for me."

"I promise."

He gave her a fleeting smile. "I'm going to get cleaned up and get some sleep."

Lying next to Corby was like being in heaven, although Laura wanted so much more. "Star told me about those prisoners the other day when she brought over the dress for Sabrina. Be careful."

Corby turned onto his side and stroked her cheek with the tips of his fingers. "They'll be shackled. We'll be safe." He pulled the cotton blanket up over them. "Maybe if you ask real nice I'll let you cook me a big going-away breakfast."

The return of the playfulness that Laura loved so much eased the numbing cold she'd been unable to shake this long, long day. "Even coffee?"

Corby chuckled softly in the darkness. "I'm brave, but I'm not quite that brave. Good night, little one," he added lightly.

Laura savored the deep kiss, the feel of Corby's hard chest through her nightgown. Hope took root within her. He would believe the truth. Perhaps not today, or tomorrow, or next week, but someday he would believe. It wasn't much to go on, but it was something. And when Corby turned onto his side, she turned toward his back, her arm lightly over his middle. He twined his fingers through hers, gave her hand a gentle squeeze.

Drifting off slowly, Laura slept soundly until she woke with a start. She was certain she'd just heard Galen and Jake call to her from the parlor.

Laurie? Can you hear us? Are you here?

Laura screwed her eyes shut and snuggled closer to Corby, her fingernails digging into his side, leaving bloody half-moons.

"Laurie. Laurie, hey," Corby said, prying her fingers loose. His tone softened when she began to tremble and choked back tears. "What's the matter with you?"

"Hold me, Corby. Hold me tight and don't let me go."

"I won't," he promised, laying his cheek against the top of her head. "Did you have a nightmare?"

"Yes," Laura lied, longing to tell him the truth he would not believe. She raised up on her elbow, allowing her eyes to adjust to the dim light just taking hold outside the window, and saw the cuts her nails had made. "I'm sorry. Let me bandage that."

Corby pulled her back down. "I've had worse. Let's get back to sleep for a while."

Laura kissed him and rested her head on his solid chest. "I love you and Sabrina more than anything."

"I know."

Laura raised her head. "Promise me that you'll remember I love you. No matter what. If anything happens—"

Corby touched his fingers to her lips. "You stop fretting. I've transported mean prisoners before. Jace and I will be fine, back before you know it."

"Okay," Laura said, trying to regulate her quick, nervous

breathing. She settled as best she could, holding tightly to Corby's hand, anchoring herself to him, to this time.

Hot tears slid down her cheek. She kissed his hand.

If you believed, it might keep me here . . .

Chapter 51

A SLEW OF curses spilled from Jason Hillhouse's lips. "If you can't sleep, Corby, then fidget over there!"

Corby moved his bedroll far from his cousin's, then ran his fingers through his tousled hair. "I'm sorry, Jace. I just feel all-overish for some reason. I can't wait to get home."

Jason nodded as he rearranged his blankets before the campfire. "I can't blame you. It gets to me, too, sometimes. When I'm away from Star and the children it feels like I left a piece of myself behind."

"Yeah," Corby said, lying back down.

For a long time he stared up at the silvery stars twinkling in the black sky, unable to shake the feeling that his all-overishness was only partly due to missing his family.

There was something bad in the air, his instincts had been telling him all day, and yet he couldn't pinpoint the source. He only hoped it had nothing to do with Laura.

Clint Barker left the telegraph office in McAlester, muttering obscenities. Another goddamned delay. Shit. He had been having the worst streak of luck in his life with this goddamned job. If he had the guts he'd tell Web to screw hisself six ways from Sunday.

That goddamned Hillhouse had been gone for days, and he could of killed the little squaw, then had a go at the blonde taking care of her, but no. Web wanted to be in on it. Shit. He'd wasted more time in this godforsaken territory than he'd ever wanted to, and it looked like he was in for some more waiting.

When the time came he would do the job with pleasure, if only to make them all pay for his boredom now.

Chapter 52

A GROAN THAT was half pain, half pleasure echoed in the back of Corby's throat when he and Jason crested the last hill and he saw his house in the distance.

"My sentiments exactly, cousin," Jason said, turning his mount left. "Home sweet home, here I come."

Corby kicked his gelding in the flank and raced home, the blood pounding in his veins like Taima's hooves pounding the ground. His blood surged more when he rounded the house and saw Laura out back dressed in her short denims and clingy white shirt. She was punching and kicking the air as if fending off invisible attackers, each move she made accompanied by that strange sharp cry he'd first heard the day she'd broken those things in his office.

She performed a rapid series of movements that both surprised and impressed him, ending with a high, spinning kick, only to lose her balance when she saw him. She landed on her backside, and he laughed, then dismounted to help her to her feet.

The moment his hand touched hers, it was like the first time, and he pulled her roughly against him, smothering her lips with his. The hunger appeased, he let the kiss turn leisurely, dipping his tongue into her honey-sweet mouth, his hands gliding up and down her back. She grew warm, her body rippling like a mountain stream when he cupped her firm bottom.

Corby let his fingers tickle their way along the frayed edges of her short denims. She was bare beneath and moaned deeply into his mouth when he stroked her moist flesh. The feel of her so hot and ready was almost too much to bear.

"Where's Sabrina?" he asked in a raspy whisper.

"Your aunt Martha is keeping her and Star's kids until tomorrow."

Without another word Corby swept Laura into his arms and carried her inside, setting her down near the kitchen table. "I don't mean to be indelicate, but I want you so bad I can't wait." He tugged at the metal closure of her pants, stripped off her shirt, his hands kneading her soft, warm breasts.

"Who wants delicate?" she teased back, popping open the buttons of his fly, pulling off his vest and shirt, kissing and suckling his small, hard nipples. He tilted her face up toward his and she clung to him, thrilled by the way her breasts throbbed at the feel of his skin next to hers, the way his tongue stroked hers as his hands did the same to her back. His muscles were tight and on fire, his skin so hot and musky.

Laura's own temperature rose higher when Corby let out a long moan as she licked his shoulder, her fingers sliding down to stroke him intimately.

He lifted her to the edge of the table, driving his full length into her with one thrust. He leaned her back, his hands supporting her shoulders, and took her hard, loving the way she wrapped her legs around his waist, meeting his moves with unbridled lust.

"Don't stop," she begged when he paused, reaching the peak.

"Never," he promised, driving into her again until her own climax came. He let her catch her breath, then sat on one of the chairs, with her straddling his lap.

"You must have missed me," she cooed, wriggling against him.

"How can you tell?" he teased.

Her laugh was delightfully wicked, her kiss infinitely sweet.

They made love again, right there, as they were, exploding together, the passion more intense than before.

Corby felt Laura's tears drop onto his shoulder, and he pulled back, cradling her flushed face in his hands. "Am I hurting you?" He tried to lift her from his lap, but she wouldn't allow it, wrapping her limbs around him again. Concern lined his face when her tears fell like rain upon his chest.

"I missed you so much."

Corby held her close, caressing her with feathery touches, sensing there was more to this than simply missing him. When Laura's tears subsided and he had dried them with his fingers, he gazed into her eyes, feeling her pain.

"What happened? Was there trouble with Sabrina or Mariah?"

She shook her head and sniffled. "No. I just missed you. I was afraid you wouldn't get back before—"

"Before what?"

Laura hesitated, feeling his muscles grow tense while his shaft grew flaccid within her. "Before I had a nightmare like the one I had last night. It was so real. I dreamed those prisoners hurt you."

Corby gave her a fatherly sort of look and hugged her. "It was only a dream, little one. Only a dream."

"Just a stupid dream," she echoed. It hurt to lie but it hurt more to know that Corby would never believe her fear stemmed from being sucked back to her own time.

It was going to happen. She knew it. She felt it, and sensed that only sheer force of will had kept her here this long. And when it happened, what then? He would assume she had run out on him and he would turn to Mariah Nitakechi.

"A penny for your thoughts."

Forcing a smile, Laura ruffled his hair. "I'm thinking it's been a few days since you had a decent bath."

Corby's laugh jostled her, and she felt a little of the sadness ebb.

"Then let's see if that tub's big enough for two."

Corby swiped a piece of buttered bread across his dinner plate to sop up the last of the rich brown gravy, his eyes on Laura the entire time. She'd been quiet all day and now was lost in her thoughts again, staring at her own plate, the food barely touched. He dropped the bread onto his dish, then reached across the table to turn her face up toward his.

She blushed, and as always he felt the fire seep into his blood, but there was something else, something hidden. "Are you feeling poorly? You hardly ate."

"I'm just tired," she said, taking his hand in hers. She planted a tender kiss in his calloused palm, then pressed his hand to her cheek. "I love you, Corby Hillhouse, and I always will. Always."

Corby stood and pulled her into a light embrace. "It's the same for me, Laurie."

He gave her a lingering kiss, and she let the fears be subdued for now, determined to make the most of what time they had.

Sitting outside later, Corby played the flute, and the smooth, soothing sounds of the native music captured Laura, overpowering and lifting the invisible shadow that had been disheartening her for days. For the first time in a week she felt as free as a bird, her troubled spirit soaring on the night air with the haunting melodies, her body tingling everywhere, her temperature rising steadily higher until she thought she would liquefy.

When Corby's final song ended, he set down the cedarwood flute and stepped forward, his sweltering look making his intentions quite clear.

Corby loved her slowly this time, with immeasurable care as though she were an innocent virgin, using his hands and his mouth to pleasure her over and over until she felt woozy and pleaded for more.

Laura watched the flickering golden light of the bedside lamp as the flame consumed the last of the fuel. Once it sputtered out, her attention was drawn to the steady rhythm of Corby's breathing. She was exhausted, but in a delightful way, feeling like every romantic heroine she'd ever loved reading about.

Of course, those lucky women lived the happily-ever-after in their fictional worlds. Never did one get to this point and have to worry about it ending. If only she could close the paper cover and live this wonderful life for all eternity.

She continued to stare into the darkness, rummaging through every corner of her mind. What could she say, what could she do, what could she possibly leave behind to help Corby understand that she had no real control over whether she stayed with him or left him?

The idea, when it finally came to her, was so simple that Laura wondered why it hadn't occurred to her before. She slid out of bed and went to the kitchen to write a letter she hoped Corby would never have to read.

Corby was shocked awake when his arm fell on a cold tangle of bedsheets instead of the warmth of Laura's body. He called her name, the knot in his stomach loosening when her voice answered in the distance.

"Hold your horses—I'll be right in."

She appeared in the doorway moments later, carrying a tray laden with eggs, bacon, toast, and coffee. The tray wobbled in her hands when she ran her eyes over him.

"Laurie! I'm home!" Sabrina yelled, banging the front door open.

Sighing, Laura gave Corby a long smile. "Wait a minute, sweetie," Laura called, pulling the sheet over Corby.

Corby caught her wrist and pulled her down for a kiss, telling of things to come. He released her when she began to respond.

Her cheeks were flushed, her breathing quick, her smile bright. "Coming, 'Brina."

Later that afternoon, Laura and Sabrina rode into town to

have an early supper with Corby at the Grand. He met them at the livery.

"Why don't you and Sabrina go on ahead?" Laura said. "I want to stop by the *Sentinel* for a minute."

The cheerful expression Corby had been wearing faded. "Is Potts giving you trouble?"

"Heavens, no. I just wanted to tell him an idea I had for an article."

"Why don't you tell Star?"

Laura shrugged. "I haven't had time to talk to her. I'll just be a minute."

"We'll go with you. It's on the way."

"I wanna eat!"

Thankful for Sabrina's interruption, Laura forced a smile. "Go on ahead. I'll just be a minute. If he axes my idea I'll feel like a goof in front of you."

Corby eyed her suspiciously. "Should we order for you?"

"You can, but I won't be long. I promise."

Laura watched Abel fight to get a new ribbon into his typewriter. Was he the one who'd written that stupid letter to Corby?

"Star isn't in today. She's only here Tuesday, Thursday, and Friday till noon."

"I know," Laura said. "I need a favor. From you."

Potts looked up. "A favor?"

Laura took a small envelope from the waistband of her skirt and handed it to him. "I want you to keep this in a safe place and if anything should happen to me, if I leave without warning, give it to Corby at once." She paused. "I can trust you on this, can't I?"

The reporter nodded.

"Thank you."

Laura's mood was lighter as she strolled down the street toward the hotel.

"Hey!" a rough male voice shouted, catching her unaware.

Laura jumped back, barely avoiding a collision with a

horse and its rider as she crossed the street. The man, who reminded her of a New York cabbie, sneered at her.

"Look where you're going."

"Well, excuse me all over the place," she shot back, punctuating her words with a rude hand gesture.

The man snarled, muttered something under his breath, and galloped away.

Laura crossed to the other side of the street, then stopped and looked toward the cloud of dust that the obnoxious man had stirred up. Had he called her an "Injun-lovin' bitch"? That meant he must have been from out of town. Everyone in town knew Corby and respected him. Also, she had a good memory for faces, and this man's was not one she would easily forget, not with the pockmarks on his forehead.

She went on to the Grand Hotel, stopping outside the front window of the dining room, moved by the sight of Corby and Sabrina entertaining themselves by trying to snatch bits of fruit appetizer from each other's plates without being caught.

Laura's smile fell away at the thought of never seeing them again, and she carved this moment into her memory. She would remember this scene always, remember the beautiful sight of Corby and Sabrina hugging one another and laughing together.

Sabrina noticed her and waved. Laura waved back, tingling all over when Corby gave her his sexiest smile. She hurried inside to join her family and savor this time together.

Clint Barker glanced over his shoulder. Hillhouse's woman was one hell of a looker up close. He'd caught sight of the kid, too. She was cute, but one less Indian would make the world a better place. It was too bad she hadn't been at home last night. He could have snatched her right out of her bed without anyone being the wiser. Hell, the way Hillhouse and his woman had been going at it, the whole house could have come down on their heads without them noticing. He couldn't wait to get his turn with the blonde. Too bad she'd have to die when the time came.

Chapter 53

CORBY'S PLEASANT FANTASY ended when his gelding balked for the third time and tried to pull south. He jerked on the reins, correcting the horse's direction but never taking the time to speculate on the cause of the animal's unusual behavior.

"Come on, Taima. Having to work these past three nights was bad enough without you giving me grief."

Once the horse resumed his trot, Corby smiled to himself. He and Laura were so close he was beginning to pick up some of her unusual expressions.

Lordy, he loved that woman, though he hated the empty feeling it gave him when they were apart. The night she'd taken off had been pure hell, and the thought that she might never come back had made him break down and cry. Why had she done it? He hadn't wanted to press her for an explanation, but he was pretty sure it was because she was skittish about committing to marriage. And yet he couldn't help but wonder if there was any truth to her crazy story about switching places in time. It would explain why she was so different from the other women he'd known, why she dressed the way she did, spoke the way she did, loved the way she did . . .

A hot tide of passion pulled Corby's thoughts in another

direction as he pictured her waiting in bed as she'd said she would—wearing nothing but those alluring lacy underthings, a dish of tomato sauce she'd saved from last night's supper on the nightstand beside her. A slow smile spread across his face as he thought of the last time he put the "war paint" on her and licked it off, inch by delicious inch.

His body tightening in anticipation, Corby kicked his gelding in the flank and sped toward home and the sensual pleasures that awaited.

When he arrived, he tossed his hat on the kitchen table, took off his gun belt and placed it atop the icebox, then pulled off his jacket and vest. He started to unbutton his shirt as he walked through the parlor, his blood pumping like mad as he imagined Laura in bed and waiting.

"P-Pa?"

Corby spun at the plaintive sound of his daughter's voice. He knelt and she threw herself into his arms, dissolving into tears. "It's all right, 'Brina. You're safe. Sssh. You don't want to wake Laurie."

Sabrina pulled back. "She-she's gone."

Corby stiffened. He wiped Sabrina's tears with the tail of his shirt. "You mean Laurie didn't hear you call for her."

Sabrina shook her head, her pigtails whipping her face. "S-s-she's gone."

Corby's blood ran cold as he stood up, holding his terrified daughter against his chest, his emotions a tempest swirling out of control between stark fear and scalding fury. Laura hadn't run again. She couldn't have. She wouldn't have dared leave Sabrina unattended. She was sleeping, that was all. Quinn told him yesterday that she'd been restless while he was away last week. She was just exhausted and hadn't heard Sabrina's cries. "The bedroom is still kind of dark, darlin'. You didn't see her. I'll show you."

No! Corby's heart cried when he entered the shadowy bedroom and found no sign of Laura. She wouldn't do this to him, to Sabrina.

He heard the disembodied voice of Mariah Nitakechi in his brain. *I warned you, Corby Hillhouse. I told you she was no good.*

Corby blinked back the stinging wetness in his eyes and hugged Sabrina tighter. He forced himself to look harder at the empty bed as the sky lightened, brightening the room. His side of the bed had been slept in, the faint impression of Laura's head visible on his pillow.

His knees growing weak, Corby walked to the bed and sank onto the mattress. The life seemed to be draining out of him.

"I want Laurie," Sabrina mumbled, her head on his shoulder.

"So do I, 'Brina. So do I." Corby hugged her close, trying to sort out the hows and whys. He couldn't.

Just then, a ray of light glinted off something on the nightstand. The silver-plated gravy boat that Laura had put the extra pizza sauce in after supper. Confused, Corby stared at the container, then touched it. If she was running out on him, then why would she bother to sleep on his side of the bed? Why would she pretend to be going through with their "kinky sex," as she called it?

What the hell was going on?

Corby looked toward the bureau and was both pleased and troubled to see that Laura's shoes were where she always put them. Both pairs were here, the black-heeled ones Star had given her and the strange ones he'd found her in. "Reeboks," she called them.

Sabrina whimpered when Corby took her off his lap.

"Don't fret. I need to look at something." He got up to look in the bureau drawers. It was comforting to see Laura's petticoats, camisoles, and underdrawers where they belonged. He went to the wardrobe cabinet, his hand shaking as he gripped the brass door pull. Finally he yanked it open.

The audible breath he exhaled sounded like the hiss of a punctured balloon. Laura's clothes were here. Her two dresses and three skirts were hanging in their place, with her shirtwaist. Her long denims and the cut-off ones were folded on the bottom shelf next to his own pants. Even her clingy little top, the one she'd called a T-shirt, was in place. All of her clothes were here. All of them.

All except the daring underthings she'd promised to wear when he left to go on duty last night.

She wouldn't have run, not half-naked.

Corby's emotions settled down as his instincts, honed from almost a decade of law enforcement, took control. He fastened the sash lock on the window, then sat on the bed. He took a moment to mask his unease before speaking to Sabrina.

"You and Laurie like to play hide-and-seek, don't you?"

"Y-yeah."

"Well, Laurie was telling me about a hide-and-seek game they play back east, and I bet she's hiding outside now to surprise me." Sabrina gave him a questioning look, and he answered with one of the carefree smiles he'd used to mask his pain for so long. "We're gonna surprise her back, okay?"

"Do we hafta?"

"Yeah, 'Brina, we do," he said, picking her up along with her doll and the picture book Laura had made for her. He carried her to the spacious wardrobe. "You hide here behind Laurie's dresses and I'll find her. You stay right here until I come and let you out. Do you understand?"

Sabrina nodded, struggling to hold back her tears.

Corby kissed her forehead. "I'll be back real soon."

She gave him a hug. "I don'ts like this game. It's not a fun one."

Corby forced his best smile. "I know, and once we find Laurie we'll never play it again."

He shut the wardrobe doors, then retrieved the spare revolver from behind the nightstand on his side of the bed. He checked inside the house, found nothing out of the ordinary, then went outside. Around back, beneath the bedroom windows he found the sign he'd been dreading.

A man's footprints.

A big man, judging from the depth and size of the tracks. He'd come from the woods a hundred yards away. He'd gone to Sabrina's window, to the main bedroom, then back again before returning to the woods.

Corby looked around again, troubled that he saw no tracks that were Laura's. True, she was a little bitty woman and she moved lightly, but surely there would be some sign of her if she'd come out to investigate noises made by an intruder.

Chapter 54

LAURA'S LAUGH WAS low and throaty when Corby's raspy tongue tickled her behind the knee.

Wait—Corby didn't have a raspy tongue.

Her eyes flew open and she shrieked when she saw that the tongue belonged to a mangy striped cat who hissed and darted out of the room.

The decaying room.

The room littered with empty beer cans, broken bottles, and a used condom in the corner.

The room where the air was dank and pungent with the odor of marijuana.

Laura screamed again as it all sank in with sickening finality, stopping only when a terrifying realization hit her like a slap to the face.

Sabrina was alone!

Laura jumped up. If anything happened to that beautiful child she would never forgive herself. She wanted to cry but didn't. She looked at her watch. Before, when she'd slipped back, the time had been the same in both centuries. Corby should be home by now.

He would hate her for leaving, but perhaps once Abel

Potts gave him the letter he'd understand and find it in his heart to forgive her.

She stayed there a while longer, hoping against hope that she'd be taken back. But soon the truth became all too clear. This was the end of her wildest dream, her perfect, happy life.

Jake Hillhouse froze in midstride. He was not seeing Laura Bennett walking from the woods wearing nothing but a bra and panties. He didn't believe she was real until she began running and threw herself into his arms, collapsing against him as sobs shook her thin body.

Watching at the kitchen window, Galen Hillhouse felt the same disbelief. What in bloody hell was going on with Laurie?

This was not normal. Galen's fear for her friend's sanity struggled with the tiny voice inside that reminded her of Shakespeare's line about there being more things in heaven and earth than can be imagined.

The authoritative voice of the local psychiatrist intruded upon Galen's jumbled thoughts with his opinion of Laura's "problems."

Delusional, suicidal, manic. A threat to herself and others . . .

Galen looked from the window to the telephone and back again before she took the psychiatrist's business card down from the bulletin board near the phone.

Chapter 55

JASON AND CORBY dismounted near a shallow stream to water their horses. The day was hotter than usual for this time of year, and the strain of exertion showed on both animals and riders.

Jason splashed some of the cool water onto his face and neck, then waited while his cousin did the same before he spoke.

"Let's head back, Corby. We've been out for six hours and haven't found anything since a mile from your place."

A muscle tensed at Corby's jaw. His swarthy face clouded in anger. "If it was Star missing, would you give up after only six hours?"

"No," Jason admitted. "I'd go to hell and back for her." He paused. "But she never ran out on me."

Corby took a menacing step forward. "Laurie didn't run. All her clothes are at home. She wouldn't just up and leave Sabrina alone. She wouldn't go off in nothing but her underclothes." He paused, his expression growing darker.

Jason pushed a strand of long black hair out of his eyes. "I know how you feel about Laura, but in the light of things, it's possible she knows who was at your house this morning."

Corby's fist shot out. Jason deflected the first punch, but not the one that followed.

"Stop!" Star shouted as she rode into the clearing. She sprang off her horse and rushed toward the stream. Filling her hat with water, she threw it in the men's faces, grabbing hold of her husband's arm to end the fight. "Settle down, both of you."

Cursing under his breath, Corby stalked away.

"Has there been any word?" Jason asked, massaging his jaw.

Star took an envelope from the rear pocket of her denims. "Potts brought this to the house when he heard."

She went to Corby. "Laura left something for you."

He spun to face her. "When? Did you see her? What did she say? Is she all right?"

Star handed him the letter. "I didn't see her. No one has. She gave this to Potts a few days ago and asked him to give it to you if she left without notice."

Corby's shoulders sagged as the ugly reality seeped in. "Did you read it?"

Star shook her head. "She told Potts that it was for your eyes only." She gave his hand a sympathetic squeeze before leaving him alone.

Corby took a long time studying the envelope, tracing his name, picturing her writing it, knowing full well she would go, never thinking to tell him the truth, never even hinting. How could she do this? How could she treat him this way?

How dare she place his daughter in danger by leaving her alone?

Crumpling the letter in his powerful fist, Corby drew back his arm to hurl it into the stream but stopped at the last instant. He had to read it. He had to know why.

Corby—my friend, my love, my life,

    Fate brought me to you and I'm afraid Fate will take me away as quickly.

    The second I saw your picture I knew you were special and when I met you, my heart told me what a part

*of me always knew—that you were the man of my
dreams, the man I'd waited a lifetime to meet.*

*I only wish we could end our days together, but if
you're reading this, then it can never be. We come
from different worlds that only wishes can unite.*

*I love you, Corby Hillhouse, and I wish now that
our worlds had crossed sooner, but they didn't and I'll
have to make do with the memories, the wonderful,
magical memories of our time together.*

*I don't know when I'll leave, but know that I'm not
going willingly. I came to accomplish something and
since I have done that, I can't stay, but I pray that in
time you'll understand and if possible forgive me
enough to remember the love.*

*I will always love you. You and Sabrina are the fam-
ily I longed for and dreamed of, and I don't want to
hurt either of you, especially Sabrina, but it's not my
choice to make.*

Please believe me.

*I would give up my other life in a flash to stay with
you. And if I can find a way back, I hope you'll accept
me. If not, well . . .*

*Forgive me if I hurt you. I didn't want it to end this
way.*

*You and Sabrina will always be in my heart. Al-
ways.*

Laurie

Corby was numb for a long time after reading the letter.
He was tempted again to throw it away, but he didn't.

He folded it haphazardly and shoved it into his shirt. He
trudged back to Star and Jason, feeling older than his thirty
years, wishing miserably that she'd used that time-traveling
nonsense to explain her absence. At least then he would
have something to cling to, some reason that would stop this
growing hatred he felt toward her.

"You all right, Corb?" Jason asked.

Corby swiped his hand across his face. "I think I got a piece of dirt in my eye. You know how it is."

"Yeah, I know." Jason reached for his wife's hand as Corby turned away. He spoke when Corby turned back. "It's your call. Where do we head now?"

Corby shrugged. He felt like standing here forever and letting life pass him by. "Your place, I suppose," he said finally. "I'll collect 'Brina, take her home, try to explain why Laurie up and left her like that."

"The letter didn't?" Star asked.

"Not really."

The trio rode in silence and were halfway back to Jason's when Corby's deputy Adam Ofahoma overtook them.

"Did you find Laurie? Did she come back?"

"No, Sheriff. It's Sabrina. She's gone." He looked at Star. "Your housekeeper sent word."

"Sabrina was with the twins when I left. Did Rosa search the house?"

"I don't know nothin', ma'am. All I know is they can't find her." He turned to Corby. "Clay went to check your place. I told him we'd meet him there."

Corby was gone before Adam finished his sentence.

Chapter 56

GALEN HUNG UP the telephone seconds before Jake brought Laura inside. She hugged her trembling friend. "We've been worried sick, luv. Are you all right?"

"I'll never be all right," Laura mumbled, pulling away from Jake. "I'm going to get some clothes on."

Jake remained by her side.

"You don't need to follow me."

"Laurie—"

She silenced him with a look. "I am getting dressed. I'll be down in a minute. I will leave my bedroom door open."

"I'll wait on the stairs."

"Whatever."

Galen followed her brother out of the kitchen. Laura gave them a reproachful look as she ascended the staircase.

"She seems so—resigned," Galen said quietly.

"Did you call the psychiatrist?"

"I couldn't."

Jake tore his gaze from Laura's door. "Why not? She needs help, Sis."

"But what kind? The psychiatrist thought *we* were bonkers until the sheriff told him that Laurie was real and not a figment of our imaginations."

"But—" Jake broke off when Laura came out of her room.

Dressed in jeans, work boots, beige T-shirt, and blue flannel shirt, Laura trudged down the stairs like a condemned prisoner, her hands shoved in her pockets. "Where should I wait?"

"Wait?" Galen asked.

Laura smirked. "For the men in the white coats. With my track record you can probably get me thirty days' commitment easy."

She walked past her friends and went to the parlor, trying desperately to picture Corby sitting in the wing chair he always took when visiting his cousin. As she sat on the sofa, she ached just being there.

Tears glistened in Laura's eyes when she looked at her friends, who stood watching her as though she were some freak. "Go ahead and call a psych hospital. If I'm lucky they'll dope me up so much that living without Corby and Sabrina won't hurt this bad."

Laura tried but failed to contain her emotions. When Jake sat next to her, she let him hold her while the tears ran their course. She snatched the tissues Galen offered her, her grief turning to anger with the certainty that her tragic love affair would be considered nothing but a drunken illusion.

She pulled away from Jake, stood glaring at him and Galen. "If you want to think I've been drinking myself into another world, you go right ahead. I know the truth. I know where I've been."

"Tell us," Galen said quietly.

Laura let out a sharp laugh. "I did tell you. I fell back a hundred years and fell in love with one of your ancestors." She threw up her hands in disgust. "Why am I even bothering? You don't believe me. You didn't before."

"We might now," Jake said.

"Why?"

"Because you vanished from a room I secured with my own hands."

Laura smirked again. "Maybe I hypnotized you. Maybe I knocked you out."

Galen came forward, stepping into the path of Laura's pacing. "We won't apologize for being skeptical, but we're willing to listen."

"I'm sure." Laura rolled her eyes. "Why are you so open-minded all of a sudden?"

"Because you mentioned Sabrina." Galen glanced at her brother. "The last time we saw you, just before you and Jake got into that brawl upstairs, someone called for you, some photographer from Oklahoma City. She called back yesterday. She said she found some information she thought you'd be interested in. It concerned a Sabrina Hillhouse, Corby's daughter."

Laura blanched as a sick feeling overcame her. "What about Sabrina?"

"I didn't ask. It didn't seem important at the time."

Laura tore at her hair, paced frantically. "I have to call her. I have her number. Where is it?"

Jake took hold of Laura's shoulders to keep her in place. "We'll find the number, but first tell us. Tell us everything that happened to you."

Chapter 57

SABRINA WAS GONE.

She'd disappeared without a trace, just as Laura had.

She'd been out back with little Matthew while the three older children did one of the chores they'd neglected earlier. Matthew had wet himself and Star's housekeeper went to change him. Sabrina asked to stay behind to watch the birds eat the crumbs she'd scattered.

"Oh, Miss Star. I was only gone a minute. I surely would have seen her running off if she was chasing the birds." Rosa wrung her plump hands. "It's like someone reached down and plucked her up."

Jason looked at the others in the kitchen and voiced the thought that was on all of their minds. "We have to assume she was kidnapped."

Star tried to disagree. "Sabrina would have run or screamed if someone had tried to abduct her."

"Maybe not," Jason said. He stole an embarrassed look at Corby. "She wouldn't have been afraid of—"

"Don't say it, Jason," Corby warned, his stomach churning violently, his battered heart steadfastly denying the obvious.

Star gasped. "Oh, Jason, you don't think—"

"Laurie," Corby said, the agony he felt weakening his voice. He bowed his head, staring down at the pine table as the pieces fell into place. Her sudden appearance, her eagerness to care for Sabrina, her secretiveness, her disappearances.

The man at the window. Who was he? Her accomplice? Her lover? Her husband?

"Corby."

"Not now, Jace. I'm gonna be sick."

Corby bolted from the room, making it as far as the rear porch before heaving up the cup of coffee and sandwich he'd had earlier. He flinched when Star stepped up beside him. He sipped the water she handed him, then dumped the remainder down the stairs. "I'll clean up the mess."

"Leave it."

Star rubbed his back, furtively massaging the muscles that were like iron bars beneath his shirt. "Forgive me, Corby. I feel so responsible. I always considered myself a good judge of character, and all the children took to her so easily. Even Nita May. You know how tough she is to please."

"Like her mother."

Star attempted to smile at the feeble jest, but tears filled her eyes. She hugged Corby.

He pulled away. "I'm going to head out again. Maybe I can pick up a trail before dark."

"Perhaps Laura was kidnapped too," Star said hopefully. "Whoever is behind this might have forced her into luring Sabrina away."

Corby closed his eyes a moment, then took out the letter Laura left behind and let Star read it. "She doesn't spell it out, but I don't need your college education to tell me that what she was sent here to accomplish was taking 'Brina."

His eyes grew cold, his features bleak. "Heaven help those responsible for this. I will get my child back, and if I have to, I will kill them all."

Chapter 58

LAURA CHEWED HER thumbnail as she waited for the fax to arrive through Galen's machine. After telling the twins her story, she'd called the photographer in Oklahoma City who had copied Corby's picture for her. Angel Lazlo said that she'd come across some old newspaper articles while working at the Oklahoma Historical Society.

Angel's evasiveness when pressed for details chilled Laura. She prayed that it wasn't linked to her disappearance and tried to concentrate on what Galen was saying to fill the empty minutes.

"I could kick myself for never bothering to look at the historical society for copies of our great-grandmother's newspaper. I assumed they only had information from statehood and after."

Laura got up and began to pace the office to keep her thoughts from turning morbid. "Angel told me they have almost every newspaper published here, even during the Indian Territory days. I think the oldest goes back to 1844. The *Cherokee Advocate* or something."

Galen was about to comment when the fax came. Laura looked at the machine, then turned away, feeling as though the breath was being pulled from her lungs. "I can't read it. It's awful. I know it. Read it for me, Galen."

The atmosphere in the sunny room grew heavy, becoming unbearable after Laura heard the fax paper being torn from the machine. "It's bad, isn't it?"

Galen remained silent and held out the paper to her as Jake positioned himself between Laura and the door. Laura took the paper but didn't look at it, instead transferring her attention to the carved rosewood desk, which stood in the same place Star had it. She remembered Star hinting at some of the things she and Jason had done on that desk.

Clinging to the lightness of that moment, Laura looked at the fax, a copy of one of the microfilmed *Choctaw Sentinel* issues on file in the historical society's newspaper department.

> *The body of Sabrina Hillhouse, four-year-old daughter of Sheriff Corby Hillhouse, was found yesterday in a gully five miles past Gox Creek by a posse headed by Sheriff Hillhouse and his cousin, Light-horse Captain Jason Hillhouse. Sabrina was abducted from the home of Captain and Mrs. Hillhouse Tuesday morning by persons unknown.*
>
> *Citizens are asked to come forward at once with information on an unidentified man approximately six feet, weighing in the area of two hundred pounds, and his possible accomplice, Miss Laura Bennett, who was Sheriff Hillhouse's housekeeper. She is just over five feet with medium-length blond hair . . .*

The paper fell out of Laura's hand. "Nooo!" she cried, looking at her friends desperately. "This can't have happened. Today is Tuesday, isn't it?"

Galen nodded.

Laura ran to her. "I went to sleep Monday night in 1899. This didn't happen yet, not all of it. Sabrina is still alive. I know it. I feel it. I have to get back to save her!"

"How, Laurie? You don't know how it happened, how you traveled."

Laura ran her hands through her hair, a few strands pulling loose. "I have to try! Corby can't think I did that. I love his daughter like she was my own."

Another fax came. Galen took it. "Laurie, you should see this."

Laura held up her hands. "No."

"Laurie."

She pushed it away. "No, Galen."

Galen read it. "Sheriff Corby Hillhouse was found dead by his own hand following the funeral of his daughter, Sabrina, whose body was found Wednesday . . ."

Laura's face went ashen and she raced for the door. She tried to shove Jake aside when he intercepted her. "I have to get back. I have to get back! I have to!" she shouted, her voice rising steadily higher until she was hysterical. Jake slapped her. She slapped him in return. "Hit me, Jake. Do that knockout thing you do. Maybe it will send me back again."

Jake did nothing even after Laura began to pummel his chest with her fists.

"Do it, Jake! Do it. Please!"

Jake grabbed her wrists. "No, Laurie. It's dangerous."

Laura stopped struggling and looked up at him through a wall of tears. "But I have to try. Sabrina is only four. Her fifth birthday is next month. We were going to make her a chocolate cake with buttercream icing and gumdrop flowers. She loves gumdrops, e-even the icky licorice ones . . ."

Jake held Laura, rubbing her back and shoulders in a vain attempt to soothe her. He looked at his sister, asking the silent question, receiving a shrug and a rare puzzled look in return.

Laura pulled back, wiping her cheeks with the sleeve of her flannel shirt. "Please, Jake. She's still a baby. She can't die. Corby can't die thinking I did that."

Laura stared into Jake's dark eyes, so similar to Corby's that the pain ripped her insides to shreds.

He glanced at his twin, then back at her. She felt the gentle brush of his fingers on her neck, and as his lips skimmed her forehead, the world went black.

A barrage of images like disjointed scenes from a biographical movie filled Laura's head, the one constant being Corby's smiling face.

With torturous slowness, physical awareness seeped back into Laura's body.

She was lying on the sofa, its leather surface soft and supple. It was the sofa in Star's office.

Yes! Her mind screamed, confident that she had gone back. She opened her eyes.

"Laurie, are you all right?" Galen asked softly.

Laura heard nothing further. She was still in the twentieth century.

Sabrina was going to be murdered.

Corby would believe that she was responsible and then he would die too.

Help me, God. Help me, Grandpa Alex. Someone. Anyone.

Help me . . .

Chapter 59

SECONDS FELT LIKE hours, with only the ticking of the oak calendar clock on the wall to break the horrible silence.

Laura held her breath, hoping her prayers had been answered, that she'd gone back at last, only to have the hope dashed by the hourly chime of Jake's digital watch beeping its annoying electronic beep.

She bit back a scream of frustration and straightened, her heart beating like a runaway train, the blood pounding in her head until her brain ached.

Maybe I'm having a stroke, she thought bitterly. *If I'm lucky, maybe my brain will be so fried I won't remember anything or anyone.*

No, she realized. She didn't want to forget any of it. Sabrina and Corby were far too precious and she loved them much too deeply to brush them aside to ease her own heartache.

She raked her fingers through her hair and stood up. "I have to get out of here. I have to think."

"No, Laurie," Galen said, casting a frightened look at her twin.

Laura turned on her friend, her green eyes wild, her voice

seething. "I'm not going to kill myself. I just want to sit on your goddamned porch and get some air!"

Galen held up her hands in submission. "Okay." She walked to the bay window across the room.

Laura went to her. "I'm sorry. It's just—hard."

Galen nodded but did not meet her gaze.

Laura went to the office door. Jake was there, as if rooted to the spot. "Do you mind?"

He stepped aside but followed her.

She stopped short. "Leave me alone."

Jake shrugged, sweeping his hair behind his broad shoulders. "It's my house too, you know."

Laura made a gesture of disgust. "Whatever."

Outside, she sat on one of the cane-bottomed chairs she and Galen had refinished in January. Jake gave her some privacy by going down to the front lawn to sit on the painted wood bench built around a towering oak.

Her heart shattered into even smaller fragments when she recognized it as the sapling that Star had planted the day after she'd first traveled back in time. She'd watched Jason and Corby construct the bench around the tree a day or two later. She and Star had a grand time laughing and taunting the men for building such a big seat around such a tiny tree. The men teased back.

"When we're all dead and buried, this little bitty tree will be ready to bust out of this circle and I'll be looking down through those pearly gates and laughing so hard it'll knock you cackling hens out of your halos."

"Or make you drop your pitchforks," Jason added.

Laura peered up at the sky, focusing on the golden rays poking between two fluffy white clouds. When she was small she'd called those angel clouds and insisted that the rays were sunbeams reflecting off the angels' halos.

There were two rays, reflections of the two people she loved most—Corby and Sabrina.

Her eyes misted and she wiped them with her fingers while on the lawn Jake began to play his flute. It was a tune she recognized, one Corby and Jason also played. It was a traditional prayer melody honoring the sacred mystery of life and the wonder of Mother Earth and all her life-forms.

Laura looked at the sunbeams again. "I'm so sorry, Corby," she whispered, putting her feet on the porch railing as she often did, tipping the chair back slightly, unaware that Galen had waxed the porch. Laura yelped as the chair slid, toppling her backward.

The back of her head hit the floorboards and the sunbeams disappeared into nothingness.

Chapter 60

"JASON'S MOTHER WILL be keeping the children, Rosa,
but I would appreciate you staying here while I'm gone."

The housekeeper wrung her hands. "I wish you wouldn't,
Miss Star. It's dangerous for you to go chasing after the
posse. The mister won't be happy."

Star tucked her bone-handled knife into the shaft of her
high leather boot. "I have to go, Rosa." She twisted her long
hair into a braid. "I'm the one who picked that woman to
look after Sabrina."

"I still can't believe it. She was always so nice and helpful, and Sabrina loves her so."

Star's cinnamon eyes were fierce. "Even poisonous creatures sport pretty colors."

A loud thud outside startled the women.

A rush of adrenaline dislodged the throbbing in the back of
Laura's head when she felt the cold edge of a knife press
against her throat and heard the familiar husky voice of Star
McNamara Hillhouse.

"Where is she?"

Laura opened her eyes, meeting Star's sharp look with

one of her own. "I'm not sure, but I didn't take her." She refused to wince as the knife pricked her skin.

"Then how do you know what I'm talking about?"

"I can't explain if you cut my throat."

Star pulled her knife back a few inches. "Get up." She kept the Bowie pointed at Laura's jugular. "I warned you from the start and you lied to my face. Was it money? Get Sabrina back and I'll give you all I have."

Laura did not flinch when the knife touched her again. "I never lied to anyone. I did not kidnap Sabrina."

Star flicked her wrist, breaking the skin of Laura's neck. "You forget I have Indian blood. Would you like to see how we savages make people talk?"

With a lightning move, Laura disarmed Star, knocking her to the ground. "I can play that game too, but we don't have time. I love Sabrina and I intend to find her before it's too late, but I can't do it alone. It's still Tuesday, isn't it?"

"Yes," Star snapped.

"We need to find her soon. We need to find her before three o'clock tomorrow."

"Three?"

Laura shivered. The time simply popped into her head, but she knew that Sabrina would not be alive after that. "Do you know where Gox Creek is?"

"There is no such place."

Laura stared at her. "How can there not be? I read it in your newspaper. It said that Sabrina would be found in a gully Wednesday afternoon, five miles past Gox Creek."

Star reached for her knife. "You name a time with a location that doesn't exist, and you expect me to go merrily along? How stupid do you think I am? Who's your ringleader? Abel Potts?"

"Potts probably wrote that article. Maybe he goofed."

Star's expression remained firm. "Fox Creek," she said quietly. "Potts is always hitting the wrong keys on our typing machine." She stared at Laura. "I've known Potts for eight years, but if he is in any way involved I want to know now."

"I doubt that he is, but we don't have time to argue. I'd go alone, but I don't know this area. Please show me where to go."

Star spoke to her housekeeper, her stormy eyes never leaving Laura's face. "Rosa, please go into my office. In the bottom left drawer of my desk Jason has a spare set of wrist shackles. Bring them here for me."

Laura helped Star to her feet and then submitted, allowing Star to shove her ahead as they went to the barn to ready the horses.

Star watched impassively as Laura struggled to mount the black gelding, though she did reach over to hand her the reins.

"Let's get going. We can get halfway there by nightfall."

Chapter 61

THE POSSE STOPPED once it became too dark to make out the abductor's trail.

"I feel for that boy," Elan Hillhouse said, as he looked at his nephew, seated far from them.

"We all feel it, Pa," his second son, Jacob, said.

Dr. McNamara swirled the last of his coffee in the tin cup he held in both hands. "Do you have any idea who might be behind this?"

Jason shook his head. "It could be anybody he arrested or their kin out for revenge. He mentioned having some trouble in Fort Smith a while back. Hell, it could even be someone who's after me and mistook Sabrina for one of my girls. If only there was something more to go on, some way to narrow it down."

Corby crushed his cigarette beneath the heel of his boot and quickly scanned the group of men clustered around the low fire, talking among themselves. It rankled, knowing they were probably talking about him, calling him every kind of fool imaginable for being taken in by a pretty face.

If Laura really was from New York, then she must be one of those stage actresses. She had to be to come off so sincere, right down to the schoolgirl blushes.

How could she have been so damned convincing? How could he have been so damned stupid? Reluctantly, he joined the others when Jason called to him.

"I can't shake the feeling that we're missing something," Jason said to him. "Has there been any unusual trouble or strangers hanging around town?"

Corby shrugged his bowed shoulders. "There didn't seem to be since that incident on the train, but then again, my mind hasn't been on business where it belonged."

Corby hated the way his companions averted their eyes, but then Adam Ofuhoma's expression turned from one of pity to realization. "Did anybody notice the ugly cuss who passed through town a couple of days back? I've seen him here and there on the outskirts of town. Even thought I saw him over in McAlester when I took the missus for our anniversary."

Adam looked away from Corby. "When he was in town the other day I saw him say something to Miss Laura. They didn't seem too friendly, but—"

The other deputy broke in. "I think I know who you mean. I caught him poking around the caves 'bout three miles east of the sheriff's place. He was a ugly cuss, a big son of a buck. Had some nasty pockmarks all over his face."

"That's the one."

Corby walked away as the men began speculating on the stranger's involvement, for at the mention of the facial scars a face emerged from the depths of his memory.

The face Corby remembered didn't belong to a big son of a buck but to an adolescent boy who worked for Owen Webster.

Running into Web after all these years couldn't have been coincidence. The business on the train must have been staged to throw him off, keep him looking outside, when all the while the trouble was right under his own nose, lying in his own bed.

Laura must be Webster's whore.

The thought raised the bile in Corby's throat, but it made perfect sense. She had a passing resemblance to Lorena.

Forcing away the pain of betrayal and the burning anger, he concentrated on the next move.

The bastard who took Sabrina would head south to Texas, to Web's ranch, and so would he.

Corby looked back toward the fire. This was his fight. He'd go it alone.

And a small part of him hoped Laura had the good sense to hightail it away once the killing started.

The women sat silently in front of their small campfire, sharing the provisions Star had brought from home, while in the surrounding woods the night creatures stirred, announcing their presence. The owl's baleful shriek mingled with crickets' chirps and toads' croaking.

Laura rubbed the back of her neck, the heavy iron handcuffs off for the moment. Having to wear them was both infuriating and humiliating, but if that was what it took to have Star and her tracking ability on her side, then so be it. She chewed the last of the beef jerky Star had given her, then glanced down at her watch. This was about the time she would usually be finishing the Toddy Toad story. "Ribbet, ribbet, Nancy Newt, it's time for good little toadies to close their eyes," she whispered.

Star suppressed a sad smile as she put the remaining jerky away. "Sabrina loves that story. It makes her so mad that no one can do the voices the way you do."

Laura wiped a tear from the corner of her eye. "We had fun making it up. She colored the pictures so well for such a little thing." Casting her eyes heavenward, Laura repeated the prayer that had been running through her mind all afternoon. *Please keep her safe. Let me find her in time.*

"How many are involved? Who put you up to this?"

Laura turned her attention back to Star. "I don't know. I really don't." She paused. "I don't expect you to believe me, but the truth is that I honestly did appear here out of nowhere. Actually, I came from the year 1999."

It did not surprise her when Star picked up the Colt revolver she'd placed on the ground by her side.

"Where did you manage to hide your time machine? I

wonder if it looks like the one I imagined when I read Mr. Wells's novel."

Rolling her eyes, Laura suppressed her anger, knowing that it would only make things worse. "I know it's crazy, but it's the truth. I came from New York to help my friends Galen and Jake Hillhouse restore their ancestral home—your house. We were using an old family album as a reference. I saw Corby's picture, I became fascinated with him. I think maybe I was sent to help him become close to Sabrina and that Fate or whatever is responsible sent me back to save him and Sabrina."

"Save Corby?"

Since she'd already "stepped in it," Laura decided that she might as well get it all out. "I met a woman in Oklahoma City who was doing work for the historical society. She sent me copies of two newspaper articles that you'll print in a few days. The first said Sabrina's body will be found by Jason and Corby at three o'clock tomorrow and the second said that Corby would commit suicide after the funeral."

Star thought a moment, then lowered her gun. She stood, brushed off the seat of her jeans, and came forward to re-shackle Laura's hands.

Laura submitted. "I know it's crazy, but it's the truth."

"I think Corby might do himself in, if anything happened to Sabrina. We worried about him after Daisy died." She put the provisions back in her saddlebags. "Did you say these supposed future articles I'd publish came from a historical society?"

Laura exhaled a weary sigh. "Yes. They came from the newspaper department of the Oklahoma Historical Society."

Star came forward. "That's odd, because yesterday afternoon, I received a letter requesting that I donate copies of the *Sentinel* to the archives they're assembling." She paused, then unrolled her blanket and Laura's on their respective sides of the fire. "Your future friends, their names are Galen and Jacob?"

"Yes, but Jacob likes to be called Jake. Why?"

"Is this Galen a woman or a man?"

"A woman."

"Does she look like my Nita May, as Nita might look when she's an adult?"

Laura's skin prickled. "I never thought about it, but I suppose. She certainly has her outspokenness."

Star remained silent, then motioned for Laura to lie down before doing the same herself.

"I had the most remarkable dream on New Year's Eve," Star said quietly. "I was startled awake by a blast of cold air. The balcony doors in my bedroom were open. I wanted to get up to close them, but I couldn't. It was as if I was paralyzed. I saw a woman standing on the balcony. She spoke to someone named Jake, commented on how exceptionally bright the stars seemed."

Star paused. "The next thing I knew, it was morning. I told Jason, but he laughed, told me it was punishment for drinking so much of the champagne my uncle Pat smuggled from Boston."

"Then you believe me."

"No," Star said. "We'd better get some sleep. Tomorrow will be a long day."

Laura snuggled down as best she could, turning on her side away from Star. She looked up at the sky, picturing Sabrina's beautiful face. "Good night, sweetie, wherever you are." She pictured Corby next. "I miss you, Corby. I love you."

"You say something, Jace?" Corby asked over his shoulder.

"No. It must have been an animal or something."

"I guess."

Corby stared off at the night sky again, angry that he could not banish Laura from his mind.

His blood boiled to think of her curled up next to old man Webster the way she'd been with him, her small breasts pushing against his back, her silky feminine curls brushing his rear, her hand clasped in his.

The thought of her with another man at all made him furious.

But most of all it hurt.

Chapter 62

IT WAS STILL dark when Laura woke and prepared for the day with a modified version of her t'ai chi routine. The weight and awkwardness of the iron wrist shackles melted away as she cleared her mind and focused her energy on Sabrina, asking her to be brave and patient.

By the time Laura was through, Star had awakened as well. She combed through her hair with her fingers, then rebraided it before adding more wood to the fire to warm a tin of water for tea. She freed Laura before going off to relieve her bladder.

"Why did you uncuff me?" Laura asked, filling a small metal cup for Star.

Star shrugged, offering Laura some of the herbal tea mixture she'd brought from home. "It seems the right thing to do for now."

Laura stirred her tea with her index finger and watched the sky brighten. She took stock of their surroundings, wishing she knew exactly where they were, where they should go. "Coming from Warburton, five miles past Fox Creek would be, what, west?"

"Unless you take it to mean five miles past where the creek empties into the Kiamachi River. Then it's south."

Laura sipped her tea, barely tasting it. "How should we choose which direction to go—flip a coin?" She dropped her cup, scrambled to her feet.

"Hold it," Star said, aiming the Colt revolver she'd tucked into her belt. "Move another muscle and I shoot."

Laura shook her head, her hands out at her sides. "You don't understand. I just remembered something. I can prove what I said about being from the 1990s. Just let me get something out of my pocket. Please."

Star motioned with the gun. "Go ahead."

Laura took out the handful of change and few bills she'd stuck in her jeans at Galen's and dropped them on the ground.

Star glanced at the objects but did not lower her guard. "Sit, and keep your hands where I can see them."

"Wait. I have something in my back pocket too." She took out her driver's license and ATM card, dropping them on the ground. "The money, the cards. That proves I'm telling the truth."

Star studied the items, her eyes darting back to Laura at intervals. "This proves nothing. I imagine that in New York they have advanced printing equipment, that someone is experimenting with various types of celluloid. My husband is commissioned as a United States deputy marshal. We know all about the ingenuity of counterfeiters and other criminals."

Laura groaned. "Then don't believe me. Decide on a direction so we can get going and find Sabrina."

"West. South." Star shook her head. A wry smile curved her mouth as she gestured toward Laura's belongings. "The way they fell resembles an arrow. It's pointing south. Do you believe in omens?"

Laura swallowed hard. "Unless you have a better suggestion, I guess a long shot is better than no shot at all."

They headed south, and Star dismounted within the hour to examine a bush. "This was damaged within the past thirty-six hours or so." She went ahead a few yards, examining the ground and vegetation along the way. She came back, remounted her mare.

"The trail veers off to the left up past that group of oaks. Whoever's been through here didn't take the trouble to cover their passing." She paused, giving Laura a critical look. "Either they think they won't be followed this far out or they're making it easy for someone to find them."

Laura hit Star with a critical look of her own. "For the last time—I don't know who took Sabrina or why. If the trail is easy to follow it's not for my benefit. For all we know, we're following an innocent traveler or someone who's gotten themselves lost."

Star's reaction was nil. "Let's keep moving."

Laura looked at her watch. It was six-thirty. They had less than half a day to find Sabrina.

Jason swore under his breath when he caught sight of his brother approaching from the opposite direction he'd taken to find Corby. He looked to his right, waiting for his father, then to the left for Quinn and the deputies to arrive. He checked his pocket watch. They'd wasted two hours of daylight traveling in circles.

Jacob Hillhouse removed his hat and wiped the sweat from his brow with the back of his hand. "You taught Corby too well, Pa."

"I didn't teach him to cover his trail. Your uncle Tate did that." Elan Hillhouse's black eyes widened. "Tate hated me following him when we were young. His favorite trick was to lead in every direction except the one he was headed."

Jason quickly surveyed their positions. "South." He swore out loud. "There could be a gang of them. It must have something to do with that train business. He knows who they are and where they're going. Why didn't he just tell us? If Laura is involved, it's not like he's the first man ever to be taken in by a conniving woman."

Corby stopped only because his horse hadn't rested since he'd set out. He checked the surrounding brush. That bastard's trail headed right where he knew it would—south to the Kiamachi, then down to Paris, Texas, and the Webster ranch.

Again, Corby wondered how long it had been planned and why he'd been too stupid to see it coming. He felt like a total jackass now for pouring his heart out to Laura about Web and Lorena. He was angry with himself for never listening to Mariah Nitakechi.

She'd been right all along about Laura Bennett. Hell, he should have married Mariah long ago. She would never lie to his face. She'd be a faithful wife, a decent mother. She would never break Sabrina's heart with false kindness or insinuate herself into the family as though she cared for the entire clan.

Not wanting his emotions to break free, Corby splashed his face with water from his canteen. He resaddled Taima, then checked the time. It was a little past eleven. He was closing in. He could feel it.

The more Laura tried not to look at her watch, the more compelled she felt to do so. The time seemed to fly by once they reached Fox Creek and followed it to its end, traveling over narrow, long-forgotten paths, through scraggly brush and close-growing trees. It was one-thirty by the time they forded the Kiamachi River.

Five miles to go. Surely they would make it in time to save Sabrina.

Laura said a quick prayer. If her intuition was right, Sabrina and her father would be reunited by dark. But then, she'd never been intuitive before and wondered why she was putting faith in it now.

Because faith is all that's left.

Laura tried to stretch in the saddle, her neck and shoulders tight and achy from the lengthy ride. Her rear was uncomfortable as well, and she had to force away the torrid memory of the night after another long ride, the ride she and Corby took the day after Jason's birthday party, the day he'd asked her to marry him.

Laura took a deep breath. Surely Corby didn't really believe she was involved in this kidnapping plot. Did their time together mean nothing to him? Didn't the emotional dragons they'd conquered together prove how much she cared, how deeply she loved and trusted him?

Silencing the string of unanswerable questions, Laura steeled her nerves and focused on the path ahead. When this hellish ordeal ended, Corby would see the truth. Somehow, some way, she would regain his trust.

It was two-fifteen when the smell of cooked meat drifted through the air. Star motioned for Laura to dismount and continue on foot. They passed close to a gully and Laura felt a wave of nausea.

This was the gully mentioned in the news article. The one where Sabrina's body was to be dumped.

She and Star looked at one another, then held their breath before peering over the rim. There was nothing at the bottom but some decaying foliage and the sun-bleached bones of some long dead animal. They breathed a collective sigh of relief before continuing along the trail in the direction Star indicated.

Soon Laura felt the kind of sick feeling that signaled something bad, and she placed her hand on Star's shoulder to stop her. "Stay here or head back and try to find Corby and Jason."

Fear, then anger, leapt into Star's eyes before she jerked away. "Having second thoughts? Were you sent to kidnap me too?"

"No, but you have a husband and children who need you. I can go alone. I can handle myself. Just point me in the right direction."

Star dismissed the idea with a defiant shake of her head and drew the Colt from her belt. "I started this nightmare by accepting you into my house. I intend to see it through."

Laura lifted her hands in submission. "Whatever."

Star made Laura lead the way. Laura took a peek at her watch. It was a few minutes before two-thirty.

Time was almost up.

Chapter 63

OWEN WEBSTER TOOK a long sip of Tennessee whiskey from his hip flask, disregarding the thirsty looks of his two hired guns, Barker and Yancy, and choosing instead to center his attention on the Hillhouse whelp.

He took another drink and considered what to do with her. He could have her killed now and left to rot. He could stick around a little longer and wait for that red-skinned sonofabitch to show up and watch the girl die, or he could take the girl back to Texas and keep her.

She was young, but she could work around the ranch and he could start breaking her in the way he had Lorena.

Webster's mouth twisted before he took another long sip of liquor. That last idea was full of possibilities. Maybe he'd get ahold of Hillhouse and keep him penned up until the day came to break the girl in good. Then he'd make Hillhouse watch—and maybe he'd even let the ranch hands have a go.

Yeah, that sounded real good.

He stuck the flask in his hip pocket and walked over to the little Indian, touching her plump chest with one dirty, calloused finger. She was warm and soft, just the way his Lorena had been, and she looked up at him with those same scared doe eyes.

Damn, but she reminded him of his own baby girl.

"I-I hafta pee."

Damn. She even sounded like her.

"Take her, Clint."

"What?"

Webster fixed Barker with a stare. "You heard me. Take her into the bushes. I don't want to smell her piss."

When Barker seemed about to refuse, Webster gave him the look that had been cowing him since boyhood.

He grabbed the girl by the arm, jerking her to her feet, ignoring her cry of pain. "Shut up. Come on and don't piss yer pants."

It was twenty minutes before three.

Laura's breath caught in her throat the instant she saw the man with the pockmarked face dragging Sabrina through the brush. Sabrina tripped over an exposed root and fell. The man yanked her up and her bladder let loose, some of the urine splashing the man's already filthy boot.

His face turned scarlet. He pulled back his hamlike fist. "You little—"

Laura sprang out of her hiding place, and leveled him with a single kick.

She used Sabrina's torn pinafore to wipe the urine off her legs as the girl clung to her neck, whimpering.

"Sssh, sweetie. Please be quiet."

Sabrina cried out when another man appeared, his revolver drawn. Laura cursed herself for being caught unaware.

"Don't bother," he said, looking at the Colt Laura had set on the ground. He took the gun, then nudged his companion with his foot. "You all right?"

Barker grumbled as he came to, and Laura regretted not being in better shape, not causing internal injury.

The man lunged toward Sabrina. "You pissed on me, squaw!"

Laura clasped the shrieking Sabrina to her, a string of expletives falling from her lips.

"What's going on?" another male voice boomed from the other side of the bushes.

"We got us a visitor," Yancy shouted back. He poked

Laura with his gun. "We found us a real pretty lady with a real dirty mouth."

Sandwiched between the men, Laura carried Sabrina, wishing now that she hadn't used Jake's knockout hold on Star to keep her from harm. She shielded Sabrina's face as the man in back shoved them through the jagged bushes. Rubbing her own stinging eyes, she looked about, trying to decide how to get Sabrina under cover before attempting to disarm the men. There would be no half kicks or pulled punches this time.

Clint Barker shoved Laura. "This here is Hillhouse's woman, Web. Screws better than a ten-dollar whore." Laura spat on him, and he laughed when a gust of wind deflected it from her target. "Indian-lovin' bitch."

Owen Webster's alcohol-clouded mind saw the blond hair pulled back, the contempt for Barker and his words; he saw her again in his mind as he'd seen her a decade ago. Then she'd been wearing a simple dress, not a man's pants and shirt, but the scene was the same. Barker's words were the same, the look she gave him the same.

Older, a bit thinner, she was the same as his Lorena.

He stared in disbelief as she hugged the little Indian girl to her breast when Barker made a grab for her—as any mother would.

"Keep your filthy hands off my baby!"

Webster's mind spun. She was Hillhouse's woman. Her child was Hillhouse's whelp. The blond hair, those big green eyes. "Lorena?" he asked in a harsh whisper. "Is that you, baby girl?"

Laura licked her dry lips. "Yes, Papa."

"Aw, that ain't—"

"Papa," Laura interrupted. "Why did you do this? Don't you love me anymore, Papa?"

Webster's puffy eyes misted. "I love you, 'Rena."

"Web, that ain't—"

"Shut up, Clint!" Webster stepped closer to the woman who looked like his dead daughter. "The fall. I buried you."

"I forgive you, Papa," Laura said, using the exact inflection and words that Corby had when repeating Lorena's dying words. She felt a mixture of relief and fear when the drunken rancher's eyes glazed over. She reached a hand out to him. "I'm here for you, Papa. I missed you."

Corby's stomach churned when he came upon the grotesque scene. He swallowed the sour taste in his mouth and tried not to hear Laura tell Webster how eager she was to get back to the ranch and take care of him again. Laura didn't matter to him anymore. What mattered was getting his daughter back unharmed.

He would do it whatever the cost.

From the corner of her eye, Laura caught the sun glinting off the reddish highlights of Star's hair, and she was glad to realize that she wasn't adept at Jake's move after all.

She looked back at Webster, who was ordering her onto his horse. "I'm coming, Papa, but I want it to be us alone," she said, moving toward a large, flat rock fronting the bushes where Star was hiding.

She set Sabrina down and whispered to her, "Stay quiet, sweetie. Aunt Star is hiding back there and she'll get you as soon as I take the bad men away. Do you understand?"

Sabrina nodded, tears running down her cheeks. She sniffled when Laura pried her arms from her neck.

"Come on, girl!"

Laura looked over her shoulder, giving Webster her best false smile. "Let me say good-bye, Papa. Please?"

"Hurry up, then."

Laura hugged and kissed Sabrina, struggling to keep her own tears in check. "I love you, sweetie. Aunt Star will take you to your daddy real soon."

"Pa?"

"Yes. Aunt Star is hiding. She'll take you to him. Sssh, now. Be still."

"Pa!" Sabrina cried, pointing over Laura's shoulder.

Star used the diversion of Corby's appearance to pull Sabrina into hiding, and Laura inched closer to the hired gunmen, ordering herself not to see the blinding hatred Corby was directing at her.

"She's mine now, Indian, so get your red ass outta here."

"You're not taking my daughter, Web. She had nothing to do with Lorena dying."

Laura gasped as she saw Webster's eyes clear. "Corby, no!"

Webster shook his head, seeing Laura for the stranger she was. "Kill the bitch!"

Chapter 64

Corby's shot caught Yancy as he fired, sending his bullet wide.

Clint Barker fired, hitting Corby high in the left shoulder. Corby shot back but only managed to hit the gunman in the thigh before falling to his knees.

Barker aimed again, but Laura landed a karate punch that snapped his neck.

She rushed to Corby's side.

"Get Sabrina. I'm all right."

Owen Webster advanced, both of his guns drawn. Laura took a step back toward Corby.

"I shoulda done this a long time ago." Webster cocked the pistols, squeezed the triggers, and crumpled in the same instant, Star's Bowie knife embedded in his back.

Corby felt one bullet whiz past his head and assumed that the other went wide as well until Laura gasped, collapsing in front of him. He could do nothing but stare at the bright-red blood seeping through the back of her flannel shirt, obliterating the lined pattern.

She'd placed herself in the path of the bullet meant for him.

"Corby! Tend to Sabrina!"

The sharpness of Star's tone jarred him out of his self-imposed trance. He picked up his sobbing daughter and held her close, stroking her dark hair. "Sssh, sweetie. You're safe now," he said, using Laura's term of endearment, his voice unsure, his eyes riveted on Star, who was tearing off her own shirt and pressing it to Laura's back.

"It's bad. She needs a doctor."

"Quinn is riding with the posse. They might be on their way." His voice faltered as he stared at the blood. There was so much blood. Laura was so small. Did she have enough blood left to keep her alive? He continued to stare in shocked silence until Star told him to retrieve her saddlebag.

She dressed the gunshot wound as best she could, then tended to Corby's shoulder. She had just set off to look for the posse when they came upon her.

She was cuffing up the sleeves of the shirt her husband had given her to cover her camisole as they stood off to the side, watching Dr. McNamara remove the bullet from Laura's back.

"It was incredible," Star told Jason. "She seemed to have the old man convinced she was his dead daughter, and I think she might have led them away from Sabrina if—" She broke off as Corby's haunted eyes impaled her.

"Finish it," he said. "She might have led them away if it wasn't for me."

Star averted her eyes and Corby hugged Sabrina close, her sobs subsiding at last. He handed her to Jason when the doctor called him over.

"It missed her heart and lungs, but she's lost a lot of blood and the chance of infection is high. We need to get her into a bed and get medicine in her."

"We passed a farm a long ways back," one of Corby's deputies said.

"A mail train makes an afternoon stop about three miles southeast of here. I can try to head it off and have it wait."

"Maybe we should try the farm," Star said, taking Sabrina from her husband.

"Home would be best," Quinn said.

Elan Hillhouse placed a comforting hand on his nephew's back. "You decide, Corby. She'd want you to."

Corby vacillated between love and hate, compassion and revenge. She'd lied to him from the start, used him body and soul. She'd stepped in front of the bullet meant for him.

"I want to take her home," he said quietly, waiting for negative responses that never came.

Jason mounted his gray and took off toward the mail stop.

One of the deputies approached Quinn. "You want me to head for that homestead and borrow a wagon?"

"Trees are too close for a wagon," Jacob pointed out.

Dr. McNamara thought a moment. "We'll make a travois, or lay her across a saddle and hope for the best."

"What if I hold her?" Corby asked, knowing that the other alternatives would only aggravate Laura's injuries. "If I ride and hold Laurie on my lap, will it help?"

"It certainly can't hurt, and you would be able to apply pressure to the wound, but you also have your own to contend with."

Elan offered to carry Laura, as did Jacob and the deputies, but Corby refused. "I'll do it. I owe her that much."

Although it took every ounce of willpower he possessed to keep his left arm around Laura, he held fast, firmly pressing the bandages against her wound. He felt the warm dampness of her blood and hoped her shirt was just wet from before and not from more blood seeping out.

Laura's head rested against his good shoulder, and he rubbed his cheek against the silky softness of her hair, his mind filling with an endless stream of visions. He prayed for her to survive, partly so he would be spared having another woman's death on his conscience but mostly because he had to know why she'd professed a love that didn't exist in her heart.

It was hard to believe that the physical pleasure they'd shared had been an act on Laura's part, but he knew it was more than a possibility. And yet he couldn't deny the feel of her arousal when they coupled, the way she trembled at his every touch, the loving expression in her eyes when they woke.

He felt more confused than ever.

"I'll get you home, little one," he whispered. "Just hang on."

A rider came alongside. Corby looked up.

"You want me to take over?"

"No, Uncle Elan, but thanks for the offer. Where's 'Brina?"

"She was getting tired, so Star took her. She makes a better pillow."

Corby nodded, managing a halfhearted smile. Laura had been a damned fine pillow for him often enough.

Laura was still alive when they reached the McNamara house, where Quinn kept a second office. They didn't know how long she would remain that way.

Chapter 65

"WE'VE BEEN TOGETHER ten years, Jake. Don't shut me out now. If you don't want to come back, tell me."

"I have personal business here, Steven. I'll come back to L.A. when I'm damned good and ready!"

Standing in the entrance hall, just outside her office, Galen Hillhouse smirked as her brother slammed down the cordless phone receiver. "Still trouble in Paradise, eh?" Her smirk disappeared when Jake's wrathful gaze impaled her. "I'm sorry, okay? Your lifestyle is your business."

Galen returned to her office and turned back to the budget she'd been trying to finish for days. She looked up when her brother spoke.

"I didn't mean to give you the attitude," he said, dropping down onto the old leather sofa to the left of the desk.

"Is the trouble between you and Steve over Laurie? It seemed to start when she came here."

Jake ran his hands through his long hair, then stretched out. "I don't even know anymore, I love her, but not that way," He sat up, shifted uncomfortably, then began to pace like a caged cougar. "This whole thing is so weird. One minute she was on the porch, the next she was gone."

He stopped, his eyes lingering on the college graduation

photo on Galen's desk. He picked it up, touching his finger to Laura's smiling face. "I feel like she needs me. I wish we knew what happened to her. Do you think that friend of hers can dig up any more old papers?"

Galen shrugged, then rooted around on her desk, searching for the pages the photographer had faxed from Oklahoma City. "Here's her num—" She sucked in her breath. Her hand began to tremble.

"What is it?" Jake asked, reaching for the fax.

Galen handed it to him, then began searching for the second one.

"Geez," Jake said, reading to himself.

Sabrina Hillhouse, four-year-old daughter of Sheriff Corby Hillhouse, was rescued yesterday by a search party headed by her father. She was unharmed, her abductors killed. Sheriff Hillhouse sustained a minor gunshot wound to the shoulder. Injured in the fray was Laura Bennett of New York. The former housekeeper of Sheriff Hillhouse sustained a serious wound. It is still not known how Miss Bennett was involved with the kidnapping of Sabrina Hillhouse, though reliable witnesses say that she was instrumental in little Sabrina's being unharmed. Dr. Quinn McNamara has offered little hope for Miss Bennett's recovery.

"What does this mean?" Jake asked, his hand now trembling.

"Like I know? Look at this." Galen handed over the second fax, the one that originally told of Corby Hillhouse's suicide.

"This one is dated a week from now," Jake said. "Oh, Geez, Sis." He dropped the fax as though it was a deadly snake, his eyes unable to look away from the last sentence.

Miss Bennett died early yesterday evening of injuries sustained during the kidnapping and rescue of Sabrina Hillhouse.

"Drive me to the cemetery, Sis. I have to see it for myself."

Galen jumped out from behind her desk, grabbing his arm with both hands. "No. We can't."

"Why? She died."

Galen struggled to find the words. "I don't know why, but we can't." She paused, her fingers nervously raking through her short hair. "Laurie said she could save Sabrina because she hadn't been killed yet in that time. This didn't happen yet. Laurie is still alive. If we believe that, I think we can change it."

Jake shook his head. "I know what you're trying to say, but come on. Do you have a magic wand to get us there?"

"No," Galen said softly. "But maybe you do. Laurie once told me that when you guys do that meditation thing you feel like you're in another world. Maybe that's how she did it."

Jake picked up the graduation photo again. "What have we got to lose? We have seven days, right?"

Chapter 66

CORBY SHOVED HIS hands deep into the pockets of his denims, loose now because of his lack of appetite. He watched intently as Dr. McNamara examined Laura and administered a glass dropperful of an herbal tincture to help ward off infection.

"Is she going to wake up, Quinn? It's been five days," Corby's voice was strained to the limit, a shadow of his former rich baritone.

Dr. McNamara put away his stethoscope. "Comas are unpredictable." He put his hand on Corby's shoulder. "I won't lie to you, son. The longer she remains unconscious, the worse her chances of a recovery become. I'm sorry."

"I know you've done all you can," Corby replied, gazing down at Laura's beautiful, impassive face while the emptiness within him grew. There was so much unfinished between them. It couldn't end this way.

"Why don't you come to the kitchen for something to eat?"

Corby shook his head. "No, thanks. I have to pick 'Brina up from Jace's."

* * *

The house was lifeless without Laura, though Corby did the best he could to keep the informal schedule she'd had Sabrina follow. He tried his hand at making oatmeal cookies, without much success, but Sabrina didn't seem to mind. It broke his heart to hear her talk about how much better they'd be when Laurie came home.

"Will she wake up tomorrow, Pa?"

"I don't know, darlin'. The doctor says we have to wait and see."

"Is Laurie gonna be my ma when she wakes up? Are we gonna marry her?"

Corby got up from the kitchen table and cleared away the cookie crumbs and milk glass. "It's bedtime for you. I'll read you your story."

As she had every night since they'd returned, Sabrina showed her disapproval as soon as Corby finished reading. "You do it bad, Pa. Laurie does it better. You can't make the nanimals talk right. Nobody can. Nobody but Laurie. I miss her."

Corby hugged his daughter, rocked her lightly in the maple chair. "I know you miss her. I do too."

Chapter 67

JAKE MASSAGED HIS pounding temples and looked up at his sister, his face drawn, his eyes showing unspoken pain. "It's like I'm *this* close, but then it's gone." He rubbed his head again. "I thought for sure it would work out here, since this is the last place we were together."

An idea tried to creep into Galen's mind but disappeared before she could seize it. She sagged back against the porch railing. She looked at her watch, then rubbed away the gooseflesh that appeared every time she did so. "We only have one more day. What should we do?"

"I wish I knew. I'm going to run over to that old house again, the one where the sheriff found her. It was Corby's house, right? She'd probably be there."

"I guess. I doubt they had an intensive-care unit or even a real hospital."

Jake stood up. Galen grabbed his arm. "She'd be in a hospital or the next best thing. They had a doctor. Our great-great-grandfather."

Jake shook his head. "I can't imagine how that knowledge helps," he snapped. "There aren't any buildings in town older than World War I. You're talking—what, the 1890s? Wherever his office was doesn't exist."

"There has to be something. Let me call around to the relatives. Maybe they can give us a clue."

"They'll give us a one-way ticket to a rubber room."

"Just like the one we almost gave Laurie?"

Chapter 68

"IT'S A MATTER of time now," Quinn McNamara said, removing his stethoscope from his ears. He touched Corby's shoulder. "Her pulse is weaker, her breathing shallower."

Corby nodded. "Could you do me a favor?"

"Of course."

"Would you send word to Adam that I won't be in today? Maybe you could send word to Star and Jace. I'd kind of like to have someone else here. For Sabrina. It's going to be hard on her."

Quinn patted Corby's shoulder. "It will be hard on all of us. Whatever Laura is or was, she touched us all in some way."

Corby looked away, blinking several times.

Quinn walked to the treatment room door, stopping when Corby called to him.

"Do you think she knows I'm here? Do you think she can feel it if I hold her or hear me if I talk to her?"

"I really don't know."

The faint glimmer in Corby's eyes died. "It was a fool question."

Quinn stepped back across the room. "Not at all. Tell me, do you remember when Jason almost died of pneumonia, the year he and Star first got together?" Corby nodded. Quinn continued, "I've always felt that Star's staying by his side played a vital part in his recovery, that he sensed her presence even though he was unable to respond. That's not to say that Laura is recovering, but . . ."

"I understand," Corby said. "I just wondered."

Chapter 69

GALEN MADE FACES at the telephone receiver. "Mrs. Harjo, I assure you that I'm not kidding. Your house was originally built by one of my ancestors and—no, there's no treasure buried in the walls. My brother and I are doing research— Yes, I did do a stint on CNN. Thank you. About the house—"

Pausing, she looked at Jake. "My brother? His name is Jake. Yes, he's the one with the hair and the motorcycle. Married? Not as such, no."

Galen batted Jake's hand away as he tried to get her attention. "Really? Well, I'm sure he'd love to meet your niece. Can we do it this evening? How soon? Half an hour? Super. We'll be there with bells on."

Hanging up the phone, Galen rested her head on the desktop, looking up only when Jake grabbed a handful of her hair and made her.

"What have you done?"

"I've gotten us access to the inner sanctum, you bloody dolt."

Jake frowned, rubbing his temples. "You know what I mean," he said sharply.

Galen stood, giving him an apologetic look. "Apparently the old gal has an unmarried niece who has come to visit."

"No. Uh—it's not happening in this lifetime."

Galen came around the desk to face him, her hands on her slim hips. "You're an actor. Fake it."

He shook his head. "I'm a stuntman. There's a difference."

"Laurie's life is more important than your heterosexual comfort zone, little brother."

Jake looked down at his twin, but he did not argue.

Laura usually hated these dreams in which she was flying, but now it was different. Now she felt as free as an eagle as she soared above the unspoiled mountains outside Warburton.

Suddenly she realized she *was* an eagle, soaring through the deep blue skies of southeastern Oklahoma. From her vantage point she spied deer grazing in a clearing, a coyote stalking an unsuspecting wild turkey a short distance away. On the edge of a pristine lake a beaver gnawed a branch, and a lone bear cub meandered by for a drink of water.

It was magic and serene and hers to enjoy forever. A golden ray of sunshine enveloped her just then, and she wanted to catch the rising wind and soar toward the light. She let the wind catch her wings, but then her keen eagle's eyes caught something more interesting down below.

Jake Hillhouse sat cross-legged atop a jagged outcropping of rock, his strong, tapered hands resting lightly on his knees, his long black hair hanging loose past his shoulders.

Laura swooped down unbeknownst to her friend and perched on the rock next to him. She called his name. It came out like a screech.

Jake's eyes snapped open. He'd done it. He'd gotten outside himself. He looked at the surreal bird with the piercing green eyes.

"Laurie? Is that you?"

The eagle shrieked, then became a blur, a mist that slowly took human form.

"Why are you here?" Laura asked. "I don't think you belong here."

"Neither do you. I've come to help you get back to Corby."

Laura cocked her head to the side. Corby? The name seemed familiar, but . . . "I don't understand." She looked up. The sun seemed brighter, and it beckoned to something inside her. She raised her arms.

Jake dove at Laura, knocking her backward. "No! You can't go to the light. You'll die if you do."

She fought, getting the upper hand more than once. "Let me go. I have to go!"

"No! Think of Corby and Sabrina. Think of your little girl!"

"Sabrina?" Laura stopped struggling. She lay very still as human memory came back to her. And the pain.

There was so much pain.

"I can't go there. I don't belong there."

"You do," Jake said, helping her sit up. "You said so. You said you were never happier than you were with Corby and Sabrina. Your family."

Laura looked up. The light was calling her.

A silver fox ambled by and sat next to her. It shifted and blurred, becoming her grandfather. "You have to choose, Laurie. Choose your place. With Jake or me."

"There's another choice," Jake said. "There's Corby."

"But he doesn't want me . . ."

Without warning, music came from everywhere and nowhere, echoing on the breeze, grazing the mountaintops, rustling the leafy branches and thick pine boughs.

It was the sweetest sound Laura had ever heard, and it lifted her and transported her with its own swift wings. Higher and higher, faster and faster, she flew through the clear blue sky, tumbling and turning, spinning and soaring until the music ended as suddenly as it had commenced.

And she fell.

Chapter 70

CORBY SAT ON the bed, cradling Laura in his arms, listening to the soothing strains of flute music coming through the open window. It was Jason, playing as he sat out on the rear porch with Star. They'd come, along with Uncle Elan and Aunt Martha, cousin Jacob and his wife, Talulah.

Looking down at Laura's still face, Corby told himself, as he had over the course of the past hour, that it was time to let go, but he couldn't. Too much remained unsaid, too many questions remained unanswered. And although he knew that these unspoken words and unanswerable questions would torment him until his dying day, he simply couldn't walk away from her.

He couldn't because despite everything, she'd believed in him as no one else ever had. She believed he could overcome the guilt of the deaths of his wives and show his daughter how much he loved her. She'd believed he was a good man and father, and she'd made him believe it too.

Corby felt the pulse in Laura's neck. It was so weak, the end was so near. He held her tighter, stroking her honey-gold hair, tracing her delicate cheekbones, the gently tilted nose, the full mouth. She'd betrayed him in the worst way possible, and he knew there were a great many people who thought him the biggest fool ever born to stay with her like this, but he didn't care.

"Good-bye, little one," he said softly before covering her mouth with his for one final kiss.

Laura hit bottom.

It hurt everywhere imaginable and in places she never knew existed. She felt weighted down, as if she were in a coat of fleshy cement. She hated it. She wanted to be free. She wanted to be an eagle. She wanted to soar back toward the pretty rays of the sun . . .

The heaviness began to lessen and the pain subsided long enough for her to feel—pleasure?

It was definitely pleasure and it made her so very warm all over. It made her skin ripple and her heart beat faster.

More. She needed more.

Fighting the lingering weight and discomfort, she forced her body to move.

Corby felt the sting of tears forming behind his closed eyelids, and he imagined that Laura was returning his farewell kiss. He began to pull away, afraid that to continue would sweep him into madness.

It wasn't until he felt the tug of fingers tangling themselves in his hair that he realized this was no hallucination.

He drew back, easing her onto the pillows, joyous at the signs of life on her face, the strength of her pulse. He rushed to the sickroom door. "Quinn, she's awake!"

He hurried back to the bed and stroked Laura's cheek. It warmed beneath his fingers, flushing ever so slightly. "Look at me, little one. Please."

With great effort, Laura raised her eyelids, waiting for the world to pull in and out of focus in super slow motion like some weird B movie. At last her vision cleared, and she saw the most incredible eyes. "Corby?"

"I'm here, Laurie," he said, taking her hand.

Dr. McNamara came in, and Corby smiled at his family, clustered in the doorway. They did not smile back.

Chapter 71

ALTHOUGH SHE FELT worse than she had her first week in rehab, Laura submitted to Dr. McNamara's thorough examination, after which he allowed the Hillhouse family to visit briefly. Corby showed them out, then returned to the treatment room. Laura shifted uncomfortably into a sitting position.

"Don't move. Your back hasn't really had a chance to heal," Corby said.

"I'll live," Laura muttered. "Can't say your relatives are too thrilled by that occurrence, though."

"I don't think it's personal," Corby told her as he sat on the edge of the bed. "I told them everything, about Lorena and Web. I even told them where I was the day Daisy died."

"How did Talulah handle the news?"

"The way you'd expect, Daisy being her baby sister and all." He paused. "The others aren't thinking too highly of me either."

The searing pain in Laura's back was nothing compared to the pain she felt upon seeing the sadness in Corby's eyes. She took his hand, comforted when he closed his fingers around hers. "You didn't need to tell them about you and Mariah."

"I should have done it long ago. It's not right to keep secrets from those you love. I learned that the hard way."

Laura detested the silence that followed, the words he left unsaid.

"Well, I'd better head on home. Ned Cassidy's missus came out to the house to stay with Sabrina."

"Is she all right?" Laura asked quickly, gripping his hand. "She wasn't hurt at all, was she?"

Corby shook his head. "Some scrapes, a few bruises. She was awfully jumpy at first, but she seems to have settled down since last week."

"I was out of it for a whole week? How time flies when you're having fun," Laura said, not even bothering to attempt a smile.

Corby started to pull his hand away. She let him.

"Do you think I could see her?" Laura asked. "Just for a minute, just so I know that she's really safe and sound?"

Corby nodded. "She's always asking about you. She's all mad at me because I braid her pigtails crooked and because the cookies I made her came out like rocks. I won't even tell you how she gets when I try to read her Toddy Toad story." Taking a deep breath, he stood up. "I'd better go and let you get some rest."

He bent down, intending to give her a light kiss on the cheek, but Laura tangled her fingers into his hair, urging his mouth to hers. When their lips touched, it was as it always was between them, the passion igniting at once, driving him on. His mouth molded to hers, his tongue sank inside. She kissed him back, fiercely, it seemed, and he wound his arms around her, needing the feel of warm curves to ease the dark chill filling him during these long, trying days.

He wanted to stay like this forever, to go even further, all the while knowing it was impossible. Grudgingly he ended the kiss, smoothing her hair back from her forehead, letting his fingers glide over the peachy softness of her cheek. "You rest now."

She grabbed his hand one last time. "I love you."

Corby nodded, then left without another word.

Sniffling, Laura closed her eyes, the closing of the

wooden door sounding like the closing of a coffin lid. *Why didn't you let me go with Grandpa, Jake? I don't think I want to be here anymore.*

Over the course of the next few days, Laura tried to negate the wary look that came into Corby's eyes when he didn't realize she was watching him, the subtle changes in body language that contradicted his sociable words.

"The flowers are from 'Brina," he said one evening, depositing a "bouquet" of wilted wildflowers in the untouched water glass on Laura's dinner tray. He sat on the chair next to the bed, playfully picking a corner off the piece of cherry pie that Laura had failed to sample.

"She can't wait for you to come home. She's been badgering Star to teach her how to nurse you back to health." He chuckled. "She spends all her spare time practicing on me. I've been bandaged so many times I'm starting to feel like one of those Egyptian mummies."

Laura's smile was strained. "She told me about that when Star brought her to visit this morning."

As it did with each visit, an awkward silence descended. Corby shifted on his chair. "You feeling all right?"

"I'm okay." Laura paused and looked into his eyes—which he could not keep upon hers for more than a few seconds. "Quinn said I'm well enough to leave if I want to."

Again the silence. The averted eyes.

Laura stroked his scratchy cheek with her fingertips. "We need to clear the air."

Corby took hold of her hand. "Webster's dead. We'll put it behind us—"

Yanking her hand away, Laura gave him a harsh look. "I had nothing to do with Webster, and if you loved me you'd know it. You would know that I would never, ever hurt Sabrina or put her in danger. If you loved me you'd know that I could never use you."

She paused. Corby remained silent.

"Please look at me," she said. He did, his eyes emotionless. "I know the circumstantial evidence is not in my favor, but I have never lied to you. I can look you in the eye right

now and tell you that I had nothing to do with Webster. I
came from the year 1999. I don't know how or why. I think
I was destined to help you and Sabrina become close and to
save her from coming to harm, but I don't know for sure."

She reached for his hand. He let her take it, but did not
clasp hers in return. "I'm telling the truth. You see that, don't
you?"

Corby pulled his hand away, shifted his gaze. "I'm sorry."

"So am I."

The silence was long, the faint ticking of the bedside
clock sounding to Laura like the last nails being pounded in
the coffin.

"Maybe you should go."

Corby did not look at her until he reached the door. "Remember, this was your idea. I was willing to give it another
chance."

Laura offered no reply, needing to marshal her strength
to contain the onslaught of tears trying to form. She set her
dinner tray on the chair and curled into the fetal position,
staring at the flickering shadows cast by the brass lamp that
was mounted to the wall behind the bed.

She must be out of her mind to turn Corby away. It was
pure insanity to think he would actually believe she was some
mystic time traveler without proof. Even with the proof of her
money, driver's license, and bank card Star hadn't believed
her. The circumstantial evidence made the most sense—even
to her.

"I'm doing the right thing," she thought aloud in a vain attempt to drown out the deafening sound of her heart ripping
itself to shreds. "It will be all right in the end. Love will con-
quer all, just like it did in all my favorite books . . ."

Laura choked back her tears.

Love had nothing to do with it because in the end Corby's
doubt would remain. If she did as he suggested and admitted to her "mistake," the doubt would lie dormant beneath
the surface, festering, growing stronger as time passed. Suspicion would worm its way between them as well, and
Corby would eventually question her every move, begin
looking over his shoulder for the next betrayal.

It was better this way.

It was better to end it now before doubt and suspicion buried the love and happiness they'd shared, making him forget it had ever existed at all.

It was definitely better this way.

It was.

Chapter 72

CORBY STOOD NEAR the front window of his office, staring across the street at Cassidy's mercantile, where Laura had gotten a job two weeks ago.

Two weeks.

It felt like a lifetime.

A lifetime of sleepless nights, miserable days. A lifetime of half-eaten meals, most of them practically shoved down his throat by the unmarried ladies of the town. He might have been able to stomach some of it were it not for the fear of choking on all the invisible strings baked in.

He yearned for real food, the kind Laura made, the things no one else could master or come close to duplicating—the tacos and burritos, the bacon cheeseburgers and chili dogs, and, of course, the pizza with extra sauce . . .

Damn it all to hell and back. She belonged at home, not across the street, laughing and joking as she rang up the sales of the great many male customers that Ned's merchandise was attracting lately. Male customers who always took an extra second to slick back their hair and wipe the grime off their boots before stepping through the mercantile's door. The door with the little brass bell attached that had started ringing louder than the church bell did on Sundays.

Corby was wondering if Choctaw law permitted the arrest and long detention of female store clerks for disturbing the peace with noisy brass bells when his deputy Clay Alton came in to start the evening shift.

Clay laughed quietly to himself as he put down the parcel he carried, a square bundle wrapped in brown paper and tied with string. "If Cassidy has any sense, he'll make Miss Laura a partner. Man, that woman has a golden tongue when it comes to sellin'. I only went in to buy a new collar for your cousin Drew's wedding, and I come out with a whole new shirt, a hat, and a pair of boots on order."

The deputy chuckled again, ignorant of Corby's growing discontent. "That pretty little lady sure does know how to sweet-talk a man—" Clay's words froze as a growl rumbled up from Corby's chest. "I didn't mean nothin', Corb."

"I'm heading home," Corby replied through clenched teeth, trying to contain his jealous rage. Laura had a golden tongue all right, but selling shirts and hats was not what he remembered it for.

Laura's pleasant expression evaporated as soon as the door closed behind her latest customer. She went outside to sweep the wooden sidewalk. She stopped abruptly when Corby exited his office, bigger and sexier than ever, swinging up onto his gelding's back with that feline grace. She exhaled a long, weary sigh when he raced past like a man with a mission.

Or a heavy date, her jealous side offered.

No. Corby did not have a date. He was going to pick up Sabrina from Jason's, then spend a quiet evening at home. Alone.

It was pure coincidence that Mariah Nitakechi had come into the store yesterday morning to buy a bottle of perfume. A little bottle of perfume and two pairs of black silk stockings. Silk stockings that cost too much to keep on hand and had to be ordered through one of Mr. Cassidy's competitors. A competitor who just happened to cater to South McAlester's largest brothel.

No. Corby was not sleeping with Mariah again. He

wouldn't. She was a shrew of the highest order, a conniving wench if there ever was one, and Corby had given her her walking papers long ago.

Just the way you gave him his walking papers?

Trying not to feel the burning pang that gripped her, Laura reentered the store and began to alphabetize a row of patent medicine bottles at the far end of the glass-topped counter, telling herself for the millionth time that she had done the right thing by breaking up with Corby. If he thought she was a liar and traitor, then she was better off without him.

She was.

Really.

Mercifully, the bell over the front door jangled, tearing Laura's thoughts away from herself. Star walked in, swinging her mesh handbag.

"Get those dollar signs out of your eyes, Mr. Cassidy, and cut Laura loose for today. We have choir practice before dinner."

Laura shook her head. "I don't think I should. So much has happened since you first asked me to sing at the wedding with you. I doubt I'll be very welcomed."

Star dismissed this with a wave of her hand. "You received an invitation, didn't you?"

That had surprised Laura. "I figured it was a mistake."

"It wasn't. For whatever wrongs you may have done, there was a lot of good. You have the courage to stay here and face us every day. The least we can do is be Christian enough to give you a second chance."

Laura hung up her white apron. "Most of you, anyway."

"Thanks, Mariah. It was a fine meal you made us," Corby said after emptying the tub of Sabrina's bathwater. "And it was real nice of you to help 'Brina wash her hair and all. As soon as she finishes getting dressed, we'll ride you back to town."

"The pleasure was all mine." Mariah smiled her sweetest smile. "You can forget about escorting me home. That little angel of yours went right to sleep."

"She did? That's strange. I've had a devil of a time getting her to fall asleep unless I sit beside her."

"I suppose it takes a woman's touch to get through to her."

"I suppose. Didn't she ask you to read her storybook at least once?"

"No," Mariah said simply, omitting the fact that Sabrina wouldn't let her so much as breathe on the dog-eared thing. "She put on her nightgown and climbed right into bed."

Corby's brow creased. "I can't let you ride back to town in the dark by yourself. I guess you'll have to stay in the spare bedroom. The bed's unmade, but there are clean linens in the bureau."

Mariah smiled a sultry smile and ran her hands over the front of Corby's vest. "You want to help me make the bed?"

Clearing his throat, Corby backed way. "Actually, I was on my way out to the porch to have a smoke. Good night."

"Good night," Mariah crooned, kissing him innocently on the cheek.

Corby inhaled her perfume. It was the same scent Laura wore.

The fresh air and solitude of swaying in the porch swing coupled with Mariah's rich dinner soon made Corby drowsy. He snuffed out his cigarette not long after lighting it and went to his room.

He was dreaming of Laura, as he did every night, only this time it was more vivid, so vivid he could feel her, smell her. "I missed you. I want you so bad."

"I know," she whispered against his bare chest, laving hot, wet kisses along his torso, her hands making quick work of his underdrawers.

He kept his eyes closed, inhaling deeply of her flowery woman's scent as she eased herself down on his shaft, their moans combining as they joined. He reached out to cup her breasts. Her large, heavy breasts.

Mariah gasped when Corby went limp within her. She pulled his hand between her legs.

"No!" he said, squirming out from under her. He grabbed the sheet to wipe her wetness from him, stepping quickly into his pants, breathing deep to swallow the sick tide sweeping over him. He lit the oil lamp. "What do you think you're doing?"

"What you need. What we both need." She knelt and made a grab for his fly. "I'll beg you if you want me to. Is that what she does? I'll do anything she does. I'll do it better. I am better." Mariah clambered off the bed and looked deeply into his eyes.

"I know how lonely you are. I can feel it coming out of you, Corby. I love you. I always have. You don't have to love me. Just let me make you feel better. Let me give you the attention you need."

Corby's resolve wavered, as it had once before. Maybe. Just maybe she could fill in part of the lonely chasm that had taken the place of his soul. Maybe just this once. Just for a little while . . .

"Pa!"

Mariah groaned. "She'll go back to sleep."

"Pa, please!"

Sabrina's frightened voice doused him like an icy shower. "She had a bad dream. You get dressed. We'll take you home."

Laura was walking, with no destination in mind, when Corby's deputy passed by on his nightly rounds. He escorted her home, reading her the riot act in a gentlemanly fashion.

"I heard all about you and the Japanese kicking and such, but you're still a lady and ladies don't go traipsing about in dark, dangerous places."

Laura nodded, stopping in front of the mercantile as Clay told her a risqué joke that put a new spin on the farmer's daughter and the traveling salesman. Her laughter ceased the moment she caught sight of Corby escorting Mariah up the steps of the boardinghouse.

She saw Sabrina seated in the buggy, Corby's gelding tied behind, but her brain would register only what her broken heart wanted it to. Mariah Nitakechi wrapping herself around Corby like the snake she was.

Laura forced her eyes away and shook the hand of the middle-aged deputy. "Thank you for seeing me home."

"My pleasure, ma'am." He tipped his gray hat, turned, then stepped back. "Miss Laura?" He removed his hat, ran his hand through his graying hair. "I know I've been sort of seeing someone, but if you'll be at the wedding this Saturday, I was wondering if you might save a dance for me."

She glanced toward the boardinghouse. Corby was watching. Laura gave the deputy her best smile. "Of course I'll save you a dance. Let's make it two." She kissed his stubbled cheek. "Thank you for walking me home."

Invisible creatures loped through Laura's stomach as the large Hillhouse clan began filling the church on Saturday morning. The invisible creatures ran full speed when Elan and Martha entered, leading their branch of the family. Jason came in with Star and the children. They were followed by Jason's youngest brother, Lucas, and his fiancée, then by Peter, Jacob, their wives and children. Finally Corby entered, leading Sabrina by the hand. They were alone.

Laura breathed a quiet sigh of relief, which Star misinterpreted when she took her seat with the choir.

"The sheer number of Hillhouses is overwhelming, isn't it? There's something a bit unnatural about how the men all have that god-awful grin, though."

"It's something, all right," Laura answered, trying not to notice how Jason flashed that sexy grin at Star the way Corby used to do to her.

She scanned the last of the arriving wedding guests, checking to see if Mariah was slinking in among them. Star tapped her arm, and she looked where she indicated.

Sabrina waved, and she waved back. Corby looked, his chocolate eyes capturing her for one hopeful moment, before he turned his attention elsewhere as if she was someone he didn't know.

Corby tapped his aunt on the shoulder and asked to borrow the small mirror she carried in her handbag. He needed to check his reflection, afraid that the corruption of his encounter with Mariah showed, like in the story Laurie once told him about, *The Picture of Dorian Gray*. There were no physical signs, but he still couldn't bring himself to look Laura in the eye.

Jealousy overshadowed Corby's feelings of remorse following the wedding service as he watched Laura walking a few feet ahead of him in the line to greet the newly married couple. She was surrounded by his unmarried male cousins.

How could she not be, standing as she was with a smile as bright as the noonday sun that highlighted her upswept hair? A man would have to be dead and buried not to notice how those pretty green eyes of hers were accented by the green fabric of her dress, a dress whose bodice clung to her shapely frame.

A man would have to be positively harebrained to let such a beautiful, courageous woman slip through his fingers.

Harebrained or hurt past the point of loving, Corby's cynical side pointed out, as he watched Laura stroll over to the social hall as though she hadn't a care in the world.

Chapter 73

Anxious to get away from the reception, Laura volunteered to assist those preparing the food.

"Heavenly" was the only way to describe how it felt to be in this bustling kitchen watching a huge blue-speckled pot of potatoes boil. Oh, the steam rising from the water was sending wisps of her hair into a frizzing fit, but at least here in front of the potatoes she didn't have to smile and keep up a false front. She leaned closer to the steel range, hoping the steam would ease the ache in her jaws, wondering—as she had all morning—how she'd ever managed to keep smiling all those miserable years in L.A.

Of course, as bad as those times were, they couldn't compare to the misery she'd been living with these past two weeks. It was easy now to think she would never really smile again. However, she had no trouble breaking into a smile an hour later when she returned to the reception area to help set up the buffet tables. There, across the wooden floor, was Corby, teaching Sabrina the two-step, just as he'd taught her an eternity ago.

The happiness on Corby's and Sabrina's faces lifted her own lagging spirits, but her smile soon fell away as a fresh wound rent her inside. The bride and groom "cut in," and the sight of Corby with the bride in his arms was almost too much to bear. This should be their wedding. She should be the one in the lacy white gown . . .

"Hey, now, I thought you women only cried during the ceremony," Elan Hillhouse quipped. He took a crisp white handkerchief from his coat pocket and handed it to Laura. "You'd best wipe those tears quick before all the women join in and we get flooded out the door."

Laura dabbed at her eyes and returned the handkerchief, forcing yet another false smile. "If you're hungry, you'll have to wait. The bride and groom go first."

"I can wait. I just came over to have a look-see and to tell you to stop fretting. My nephew may be as bullheaded as they come, but he's no fool. You took a bullet for him. He won't forget that."

Laura rearranged the pastries on the tray in front of her. "It really doesn't matter. The problem between Corby and me is more complicated than you can imagine."

"I suppose you mean your time-shifting."

Elan's matter-of-fact statement made Laura crumble one of the dainty tea cakes. She brushed the crumbs from the tray, looking to see if anyone had overheard. Apparently no one had, for which she was thankful.

She came around the table. "You know?"

Elan placed her arm through his and led her to a quieter corner. "Jace and Star told me about it after you were shot. They weren't tellin' tales, they just wanted my opinion."

"Do you think I'm crazy or lying? I think the 'lyings' are in the lead, with Corby tipping the scales."

Elan grinned that Hillhouse grin. She wanted to cry.

"Like I said, my nephew is more mulish than the animals out at my farm."

"And you?"

"Well," he said thoughtfully, hooking his thumbs in his vest pockets. "That stuff you had in your pockets was odd, but since I didn't come and go with you I can't say for certain." He paused when Laura sagged back against the wall. "I didn't say I don't believe you." He laughed when she perked up.

"My house doesn't have electric lights or a telephone, but it doesn't make them any less real, now does it? And I get the feeling you wouldn't keep yourself so down in the mouth with that story if all you had to do was tell Corby you were involved with those no-goods and ask him to forgive you."

Laura nodded. "I considered doing that. Maybe I should, just to end it so we can start over."

"But you won't and you know it," Elan said, handing her the handkerchief again.

"I won't admit to a crime I didn't commit, even if it means losing him."

"Corby'll come around sooner or later."

"I hope so," Laura said, her eyes seeking out Corby, who was across the hall speaking to some of his relatives—quite content to be without her, from the looks of it.

She was watching him.

Every quivering nerve in Corby's body sensed it, every inch of his skin felt as though her hands were upon him. He glanced over his shoulder to confirm his intuition, and when he saw that pink blush creep into her pale cheeks he had to look away, for his member began to respond as it always did. He was thankful when his cousin grabbed his arm.

"Come on. They're lining up for the food."

Despite the protesting grumble of his stomach, Corby stepped out of the buffet line when Laura took her place to help serve. He wanted her so bad it hurt, and although he was trying to fight it, the sight of her doling out gravy and biscuits damn near made him swoon, especially when he saw his cousin Jason dab a bit of gravy on Star's cheek, then lean over to kiss it off.

Corby went outside and found a shady spot to compose himself. Why was Laura doing this to him? Why was he letting her? Didn't she see he could forgive her mistake of being involved with Web? It was hard for a woman alone in these parts. She'd needed a man's protection, and that came with a price, but she'd absolved herself in the end, so why did she insist on her innocence? Why did she continue to cling to that crazy time-traveling nonsense? The truth might be shameful, but it was the truth. Anyone could see that.

Corby's attention was drawn to the sound of his daughter's excited voice.

"Pa! Help me 'fore I drop it!"

Corby got up and took the heavy food dish from Sabrina. "Why did they give you all this? You can't eat it."

Sabrina plopped down to the grass. "Laurie said you look scrawny. She said to bring this and sit here till you eat it all gone like I ate my sammich." She looked back toward the side door of the social hall and waved.

Corby's heart lurched when Laura waved back. She needed to fix herself a plate because she was looking scrawny too. Corby stared down at the things she'd chosen for him. His favorite foods.

"Eat, Pa, so I can go play."

He set the plate on the ground. "You go play—we'll be leaving soon."

"You hafta eat it all gone. I promised Laurie." Sabrina handed her father the piece of chicken.

He took a bite. "You still love Laurie, don't you?"

"Yep. That bad man wanted to hurt me, but she wouldn't let him." Sabrina gave her father a critical look. "I want her to be my ma. You promised you were gonna marry us to her and I could wear a fancy dress."

"Sabrina, sometimes things happen that we don't expect and make it hard to keep a promise."

Sabrina tossed her braids over her shoulders. "I want Laurie to be my ma. Don't you marry us to that boarding-house lady. She's mean."

The corners of Corby's mouth rose a fraction. It would be easy to imagine that Laura was Sabrina's mother, for their eyes shared the same irate gleam at the mention of Mariah.

"I'm not going to marry Mrs. Nitakechi."

"Good. She's mean an' she can'ts do magic like Laurie." Sabrina's brow crinkled. "Pa, how come Laurie did magic for Martha Jane, but not me?"

A chill ran down Corby's spine, but he dismissed it. "You go play."

Sabrina stayed put, her lower lip protruding in a pout. "Why didn't Laurie do magic for me? I wanna see her distapeer too."

It took a moment for the words to slip past Corby's sadness. "What did you say?"

"I wanna see Laurie do magic."

Corby held his impatience in check. "What else, 'Brina? Did you say Laurie disappeared?"

Sabrina pouted again. "Yep. Martha Jane said she saw it when she was hiding at Uncle Jace's birfday. Jimmy was countin' and me an' Nita May—"

"Tell me what Martha Jane saw," Corby interrupted, not wanting her to lose her original train of thought. "Tell me, darlin'. It's important."

"I don't wanna," Sabrina said, pulling her hands away.

Corby lifted her to his lap, wondering where she came by her stubbornness. "Please tell me, Sabrina."

"Nope. I don't wanna."

Chapter 74

CORBY TOOK SEVERAL steadying breaths. "You don't have to tell me now. Go and play. I promise I'll eat."

As Sabrina scampered away, her words lingered in Corby's confused mind.

Why didn't Laurie do magic for me? I wanna see her distapeer too.

Corby's suspicious nature fought hard to keep him from finding Laura, holding her and never letting go. He couldn't believe her fantastic story had been true all along, the answer so simple his daughter would never think to question it.

It was a little too simple.

Sabrina adored Laura and would happily go along with anything she deemed a game. Jace's girl was the same—quiet, more a follower than a leader. It was quite convenient that Laura's "magic" hadn't happened in front of the older twin, Nita, who'd been speaking her mind since she'd formed her first word, or in front of Jacob's boys, who were too old to be coerced into anything.

Another comment came back to haunt Corby, the comment his deputy made just the other day.

That pretty little lady sure does know how to sweet-talk...

Yes, she did. She could undoubtedly talk the world's best snake oil salesman into selling his prized rattler. It would be nothing to get an innocent child to believe in such fancy.

Corby wrestled with the anger, remembering how upset Laura had been at the party. She'd been terrified that she'd "gone home." Such fear couldn't be acted, could it?

Was it truly possible that she'd traveled through time? Did his New Year's Eve wish help to make it happen?

No, it was not possible. Wishes did not come true. People did not travel through time upon getting bumps on the head.

"Sheriff?"

Corby looked up. He stood, leaving his food to the gathering ants. "What do you want, Potts?"

The reporter fiddled with his striped bow tie, checked his pocket watch. Looked at his shoes.

"Do you want something or not?"

Potts cleared his throat. "There's been something on my mind, and I'd like to set it straight."

Corby waited. Potts fidgeted. "I am not in the mood for games, Abel. If you have something to say, say it."

Potts took a step back. "I'm the Concerned Citizen. The one who wrote you that letter when Miss Bennett started working for you." He shrank back again when Corby tensed. "It was Mariah's idea. I just went along with it . . . I'm sorry."

Corby let the reporter rush away and found himself more than willing to believe Laura's crazy tale.

"No cutting in. Get your own woman," Jason Hillhouse said when Corby tapped him on the shoulder.

"I want to, but I need your help."

Jason and Star followed Corby out of the social hall as he explained what Sabrina and Potts had said. When he finished, Star's eyes opened wide.

"Now it makes sense," she said to Jason. "Do you remember what your mother told us?"

Jason looked to Corby. "Martha Jane kept breaking into

tears when we were all gone. She told my parents she was afraid we'd all be 'magicked away' like Sabrina and Laura. We didn't think anything of it."

"Where's Laura?" Star asked.

"I didn't see her. I wanted to find out what you thought first."

"You find her," Jason said. "We'll round up Martha Jane and meet you over in the church. It's quieter there, and Martha will be less skittish."

Corby couldn't find Laura in the social hall, the kitchen, or anywhere on the church grounds, and with the excitement of the wedding reception, no one had taken notice of her leaving.

Assuming she'd left by conventional means.

His eyes fixed upon the wooden cross attached to the church roof, Corby prayed it wasn't too late, that Laura was still in Warburton. Perhaps Jace and Star had found her. He died a little inside when he found only Star, alone with her daughter. Jason came in the side door. He was alone.

Jason gave Corby a sympathetic look, then picked up his daughter. "Tell Uncle Corby what you told us."

The child's lip quivered, and she buried her face in her father's shoulder. "I'm afraid. I told 'Brina and she got 'magicked away' too."

Corby felt his insides twist, certain that the lawman in him had been correct all along. Laura could be worse than he imagined, threatening innocent children.

Jason gently lifted Martha Jane's head. "You're safe, sweetheart. No one will hurt you if you tell. Bad men took Sabrina. There was no magic."

Martha looked to her mother for confirmation. "Tell us again, honey."

Martha Jane looked at Corby, then back to her father. "We was playin' upstairs like you told us to. Nita was countin' and me and Jimmy and Sabrina hided. I hided by the steps and I heard you and Mama laughing in the kitchen and I looked through the posts and saw Laurie. She was smiling and she kind of fell and hit her head but she didn't say 'ouch,' she just distapeered."

"What else, honey?" Star prodded.

"You an' Daddy came out of the kitchen hugging and kissing and then Laurie undistapeered. She was crying."

"Martha Jane," Corby said softly. "Did Laurie tell you to say that? Did she tell you you'd get 'magicked away' like Sabrina if you didn't tell us this?"

The girl shook her head. "I saw it. Nita May says I'm a fibber, but I'm not. I don't fib."

Jason kissed her forehead. "We know you don't, sweetheart. I'll take you out to play."

Star spoke to Corby once they left. "She's telling the truth, Corby. As incredible as it is, she saw Laura disappear and reappear."

Anguish buckled Corby's knees. He sank onto the nearest pew. Star laid her hand on his shoulder, and he took from his jacket the heavily creased letter he'd been carrying since Star had delivered it to him. He read it for the thousandth time, understanding it for the first time. "Why was I such a damned fool?"

"We all made the same mistake. I thought that money she had with 1998 on it was counterfeit."

Corby shook his head. "It was up to me to believe her. As close as we were, the things we shared. After everything, I still couldn't believe her, but I believed that she was in with Web. I almost killed her that day. If she hadn't been holding on to Sabrina . . ."

"Stop blaming yourself. Sabrina is safe and Laura is alive. She'll understand. You can start over."

"But what if it's too late? What if whatever brought her here took her back? No one saw her go . . ." He couldn't finish his sentence or acknowledge the tiny doubt buried far inside himself.

Chapter 75

LAURA ROCKED BACK and forth on the edge of the brass bed, hugging Corby's pillow to her chest. She closed her eyes and inhaled his scent. It was useless to expect a miracle. No matter what Elan Hillhouse said, Corby would never believe the truth. The cold, cold look he'd given her when she sent the food plate over proved there was no hope. She'd seen the dish on the ground. He hadn't touched it. Probably thought she'd tried to poison him.

She looked at her watch. She had a little time left to sit here and remember. She remembered the smell of him, the way he would tell her the day's town gossip, the feel of his big body next to her at night, within her . . .

This was masochism, pure and simple, and yet Laura remained where she was, storing up the memories to take with her to California. She'd decided late last night that if she and Corby did not resolve things today she would head out to her "future" birthplace and start a new life on her own.

The world was hers for the taking. She could work hard, buy up prime real estate long before it became prime real estate. Maybe she'd even get into show biz in a few years, once Hollywood began to take root. She could hobnob with the greats—Pickford, Fairbanks, Chaplin. She could party with the great Barrymore. He'd been one handsome guy. He couldn't compare to Corby, but . . .

This new life would be good. She would be able to do a lot of good. She could set up a trust fund for Matthew Hillhouse to pass on to his future grandchildren. She would do the same for Sabrina, even any other children that Corby might have . . .

Sniffling, she looked down at her watch again. Five more minutes, then she'd head back to town to catch that train.

Chapter 76

CORBY STOPPED HIS gelding at the cutoff to Sam Choate's shack. He was certainly in no hurry to go home and rest, as Star had suggested after they'd scoured the town looking for Laura. He couldn't rest at home, anyway. He needed a bottle of rotgut liquor to dull the painful memories. That wasn't such a bad idea, considering that Sabrina was staying with Star and Jace tonight.

He'd pay a visit to old Sam. He'd get stinking drunk, then tomorrow he'd start looking for another place to live. Maybe he'd build a new house near where he'd grown up. There were painful memories there, too, but at least he'd been able to put those behind him.

With Laura's help, his heart reminded him.

Corby looked at the road to Sam's, knowing full well he wouldn't go there to get drunk. He was paid to stop the sale and consumption of that swill. Besides, he didn't really want to leave the house his cousin had given him—Laura was still there. He felt her every time he walked in the door. He needed to feel that now and always.

Chapter 77

GET A MOVE *on, girl,* Laura told her traitorous body as the minute hand on her watch clicked to the two and her legs failed to lift her to a standing position. She looked in the bureau mirror. "Corby doesn't want you."

She stood up so fast she almost fell.

Impulsively, she took the pillow from Corby's side of the bed and stuffed it into her new valise, then removed her engagement ring and laid it in the pillow's place. She checked Sabrina's room one last time to make sure she hadn't forgotten to leave the gift. She'd made two cloth dolls. They were Toddy the Toad and Nancy the Newt, all dressed in the wedding finery she'd made from scraps of fabric and lace Mr. Cassidy had given her.

"I'll miss you, sweetie. Please don't forget me," she whispered, blowing a kiss into the room. She headed to the door.

Corby came through the woods at the rear of the house, then went directly to the barn. He watered and fed Taima. Three steps from the barn door he stopped. He wasn't in the mood to go in the house just yet. He'd stay out here. Maybe take a nap in the hayloft.

Then again, a nice hot bath might be good.

* * *

Angry with himself for ruining his own happiness, Corby shoved the kitchen door hard, freezing in shock when it hit something on the other side, something that cried out in pain.

He pulled the door toward him, freezing again when he saw Laura, her hands clutching her nose, blood trickling between her fingers. A reddish-purple mark was forming on her forehead, and then it began to disappear.

She began to disappear.

"Nooo!"

Refusing to let it end this way, Corby lunged forward, grabbed Laura by the shoulders, and crushed her to his chest just as visions of a dilapidated house and drunken teenagers came into view.

Chapter 78

FOR THE SECOND time that day, Corby felt his knees weaken, and he scooped Laura up and carried her to the sofa. He set her down, then knelt on the floor beside her

And finally he believed. Totally, every sliver of doubt gone forever.

He took his handkerchief from his jacket and wiped the blood from Laura's face, relieved that her nose was not broken. He kissed the tip of her nose, her bruised forehead, and her sweet, sweet mouth.

She began to regain consciousness, responding to the press of his mouth by parting her lips, inviting his tongue inside, welcoming him home.

Corby pulled back and watched her eyes flutter open as they had the day he'd found her. She smiled that same fanciful smile and it took his breath away, like before.

"Even in my dreams you have those bedroom eyes."

"It's no dream, little one," Corby assured her, smoothing back wisps of hair from her face. "This is no dream."

Laura blinked. She sat up. "I'm sorry. I—"

"No," Corby said, stopping her. He held fast to her hands, made her sit. He sat beside her. "I'm never letting you go again."

"But—"

"But nothing. I believe you, Laurie. I believe that you really came from another time."

Laura yanked her hands away. "You're just saying that."

"No." He cupped her face in his hands, his thumbs stroking her cheeks. Her skin flushed, grew warm. "I truly believe you."

Laura pulled away again. She stood up, shot him a suspicious look. "Why now?"

"Sabrina told me Martha Jane saw it happen at Jason's party. I asked Martha—"

"Tomorrow you'll start wondering if I told her to make it up. You might even think I told Sabrina to get Martha to lie or I'd have her kidnapped again."

Corby winced, then stood to face her. "This morning that might have been the case." Laura turned away, and he gently took hold of her shoulders, held her in place. "I know that you've been telling the truth because *I* saw it happen. I went with you, just now. The door hit you, you started to fade away, and I grabbed you and went too."

Laura began to tremble and he held her close. "It was so strange. It was dark, then bright, and I saw colors like a fireworks show. I think we were in this room, but it was different. There was no furniture and the air smelled funny. I think I saw someone in the corner and through the window I saw this *thing* in the sky. It was like a machine and it was flying, but it looked like a tadpole with a big head and a tail . . ."

Laura pulled back. "It was a helicopter. I heard it. They fly over on their way to the hospital sometimes."

She drowned herself in Corby's kiss, her blood igniting as his hands deftly opened her dress, unfastened the ribbons and tiny buttons securing her camisole and petticoat. She blushed when she finally stood before him in the sheer white bra and panties she'd put on that last day at Galen's. She loved the way Corby's eyes roamed over the white silk stockings and green satin garters she'd gotten from the mercantile.

"These are new . . ." Her words turned to a soft moan as Corby knelt before her, his hands running up her thighs to remove the stockings. He peeled them off along with her shoes, gliding his rough hands over her legs, hips, and rear.

"You don't know how many times I stopped myself from coming over to Cassidy's and doing this very thing."

"About as many times as I wanted to come to the jail, I suppose." Heat rushed to her cheeks when Corby grinned at her. The heat shot lower when he tickled her navel with his tongue.

"Don't," she said weakly, taking half a step back when he moved lower. "I want you. All of you."

Corby scooped her up and strode to the bedroom, setting her down, letting her bare hip rub against his hardness as he lowered her to the feather mattress. He stripped off his clothes and stretched out beside her.

His hands were everywhere, his lips close behind, shooting shivers and sparks through her like never before. His mouth moved from her wrist to her arm to her shoulder, her neck. He traced the wire securing her small pearl earrings with the tip of his tongue, making her squirm. He stroked her hip with his fingers, turning her onto her side to face him. "Having you back is like having my own little piece of heaven."

The hunger in his eyes nipped at her. The wild beat of his heart called to her like a savage love song, and she had to possess what she'd been starving for these long, torturous weeks. Methodically, Laura moved over him with her hands, her breasts, her own desire building as he writhed beneath her, murmuring her name.

She couldn't get enough of his body and would have been content to touch and taste until the end of time, but Corby had other ideas. He pulled her atop him until her dewy feminine curls brushed his shaft.

"Love me, Laurie."

"Always," she promised, straddling him, sighing when he thrust up into her hot depths, filling her, making her feel whole for the first time since she'd come back.

The pleasure exploded so quickly and with such force it clouded her vision and Laura feared she might be slipping back in time again, but Corby's heavy breathing and moan when his own climax came told her that she was still here, right where she belonged, right where she'd always wanted to be.

Weaving her fingers in his hair she struggled to catch her breath, listening to the frantic beating of Corby's heart as she lay crumpled against his chest. He began to wriggle his hips and she laughed lightly. "Sorry, Sheriff. I don't think I have the strength just yet."

"Me neither, but there's something poking my backside."

Laura moved off him so he could turn over and retrieve the offending object.

"What have we here?" he asked, holding up the engagement ring.

"I left it in place of your pillow. I thought if you found someone . . ."

"I found someone," he said, sliding the ring back onto her finger. He kissed her softly, then stroked the side of her face. "I hate to be unromantic, but I am so hungry I could eat an entire side of beef. I haven't had a decent meal in I don't know how long."

Laura laughed and ruffled his hair. "The one drawback about this time is that you can't pick up the phone and call the pizza-delivery guy."

"You can order *that* from the telephone?" Corby teased. As he hoped, Laura blushed.

"Homemade is always better," she admitted.

Corby cradled her in his arms. "We can get cleaned up and go back to the party."

Laura gave him a skeptical look. "I think the reception is over by now."

"You've never been to a Hillhouse wedding. The diehards will be there until midnight. Star and Jason's lasted two full days."

Laura laughed. Then Corby took hold of her left hand and peered deeply into her eyes, making her forget everything.

"Will you marry me, Laura Bennett?"

Laura hesitated until a tiny voice inside confirmed what her heart told her. She'd gotten her wish and she wouldn't ever be pulled away again. "I'll marry you as soon as we can arrange it."

Corby let out a whoop. "Then let's start the arranging."

Laura didn't realize he meant that literally until he began looking for Rev. Graves as soon as they reached the church.

"Reverend, over here!"

Laura held on to Corby with both hands. "You can't ask him to marry us now. What will your cousin say if we horn in on his wedding day?"

There was a wicked glint in Corby's eyes. "Drew won't say anything unless he wants to spend his wedding night in a lonely jail cell."

Laura gasped. "Corby Hillhouse, you wouldn't dare!"

"I would," he said seriously, bound and determined to show the world that Laura was his.

Forever.

Epilogue

GALEN HILLHOUSE GAVE the balding banker a stern look. "Don't keep us in suspense. If you have something for us, fork it over."

"Wait a minute," Jake said, holding up his hand. "I want to hear the story first."

The banker cleaned his wire-framed glasses as he spoke. "In a nutshell, more than sixty years ago one of your ancestors left a package in a safe-deposit box in a bank that this bank later acquired. She stipulated that the contents be delivered to a Galen and Jake Hillhouse of Warburton today, New Year's Eve, and that you look at the contents of the box before nightfall." He paused to replace his glasses. "It was an unusual request, to be sure, but since a sizable monetary deposit was left, we were quite happy to comply."

He removed an envelope from his top desk drawer. "This document was left as well. It simply states that for keeping the contents of the box and delivering it at the specified time, the bank becomes the sole owner of the initial monetary deposit and the accumulated interest and you, of course, receive the contents of the safety-deposit box."

The twins read and signed the agreement, then were presented with a simple walnut box. "I assure you that the contents have never been tampered with. As you can see, the original wax seal where the top and bottom of the box meet is still intact." He took a small brass key from the breast pocket of his suit and handed it to Galen. "Would you like me to leave while you open it?"

"Yes."

"No," Jake said, taking the box from his perturbed sister. "I want to open it at home." He stood and thanked the bank president, then left, refusing to let Galen so much as touch the box until they were back in the office at the B&B.

Galen held up the key. "Give me the bleeding box. We might be sitting on the Hillhouse family jewels. They could be worth a fortune!"

Jake set the box on the desk and let her unlock it as he took her letter opener and ran it around the wax seal. He sat on the edge of the antique desk, watching in amusement as his eager sister closed her eyes and gingerly touched the lid she'd been so anxious to get at.

"I don't think it's a bomb."

Galen stuck out her tongue. "I covered the IRA for five years, remember?" She lifted the lid. Inside was a photograph album similar to their great-grandmother's album, except this one was of hand-tooled leather, not velvet. Jake stood beside her to get a better view.

Inside, over the first photo, was a letter addressed to them.

Dear Galen and Jake,

It all began with New Year's Eve wishes and a Hillhouse family album, so it's only right that it come full circle. I've been saving these to "share" with you and I hope you like them.

Thank you for helping make my wishes come true and a special thanks to you, Jake, for being there

*when I needed you most. I'll never forget you. I love
you.*

*I don't want to miss out on any of this wonderful
life, so I'll stop here. Take care and think of me sometimes.*

Love,
Laurie
Important P.S.
*If you guys have any wishes of your own, wish them
on the brightest star you see as the clock strikes mid-
night tonight, because whatever you wish for will
come true.*
Believe me. I know.

The Hillhouse twins were smiling contentedly after they
looked through Laura's album. She and Corby had a son in
May 1900. They'd named him Tate, after Corby's father,
and given him the middle names of Jacob and Alexander.
The photos showed Corby and Laura always smiling as their
children grew up with Galen and Jake's grandfather in the
opening decades of the twentieth century.

Galen closed the album, resting her hand on the cover. "I
feel better. I was a little freaked when we couldn't find any
more newspaper stories at the historical society. I'm glad
Laurie found that happily-ever-after she always wanted."

"I guess so," Jake agreed.

"Do you think it's true? That business about wishing on
the star?"

Jake shrugged. "I don't know, but after all that's happened, I'm ready to believe anything."

Galen nodded, her thoughts drifting off.

If you enjoyed *Timeless Wish*
you won't want to miss
Firebird
The stunning new novel from
Janice Graham

Coming in August from Berkley Books

One

So far as we know, no modern poet has written of the Flint Hills, which is surprising since they are perfectly attuned to his lyre. In their physical characteristics they reflect want and despair. A line of low-flung hills stretching from the Osage Nation on the south to the Kaw River on the north, they present a pinched and frowning face to those who gaze on them. Their verbiage is scant. Jagged rocks rise everywhere to their surface. The Flint Hills never laugh. In the early spring, when the sparse grass first turns to green upon them, they smile saltily and sardonically. But as spring turns to summer, they grow sullen again and hopeless.

Death is no stranger to them.

—JAY E. HOUSE
Philadelphia Public Ledger (1931)

Ethan Brown was in love with the Flint Hills. His father had been a railroad man, not a rancher, but you would have thought he had been born into a dynasty of men connected to this land, the way he loved it. He loved it the way certain peoples love their homeland, with a spiritual dimension, like the Jews love Jerusalem and the Irish their Emerald Isle. He had never loved a woman quite like this, but that was about to change.

He was, at this very moment, ruminating on the idea of marriage as he sat in the passenger seat of the sheriff's car, staring gloomily at the bloodied, mangled carcass of a calf lying in the headlights in the middle of the road. Ethan's long, muscular legs were thrust under the dashboard and his hat brushed the roof every time he turned his head, but Clay's car was a lot warmer than Ethan's truck, which took forever to heat up. Ethan poured a cup of coffee from a scratched metal thermos his father had carried on the Santa Fe line on cold October nights like this, and passed it to the sheriff.

"Thanks."

"You bet."

They looked over the dashboard at the calf; there was nowhere else to look.

"I had to shoot her. She was still breathin'," said Clay apologetically.

"You did the right thing."

"I don't like to put down other men's animals, but she was sufferin'."

Ethan tried to shake his head, but his hat caught. "Nobody's gonna blame you. Tom'll be grateful to you."

"I sure appreciate your comin' out here in the middle of the night. I can't leave this mess out here. Just beggin' for another accident."

"The guy wasn't hurt?"

"Naw. He was a little shook up, but he had a big four-wheeler, comin' back from a huntin' trip. Just a little fender damage."

She was a small calf, but it took the two men some mighty effort to heave her stiff carcass into the back of Ethan's truck. Then Clay picked up his markers and flares, and the two men headed home along the county road that wound through the prairie.

As Ethan drove along, his eyes fell on the bright pink hair clip on the dashboard. He had taken it out of Katie Anne's hair the night before, when she had climbed on top of him. He remembered the way her hair had looked when it fell around her face, the way it smelled, the way it curled softly over her naked shoulders. He began thinking about her again and forgot about the dead animal in the bed of the truck behind him.

As he turned off on the road toward the Mackey ranch, Ethan noticed the sky was beginning to lighten. He had hoped he would be able to go back to bed, to draw his long, tired body up next to Katie Anne's, but there wouldn't be time now. He might as well stir up some eggs and make another pot of coffee because as soon as day broke he would have to be out on the range, looking for the downed fence. There was no way of telling where the calf had gotten loose; there were thousands of miles of fence. Thousands of miles.

Ethan Brown had met Katherine Anne Mackey when his father was dying of cancer, which was also the year he turned forty. Katie Anne was twenty-seven—old enough to keep him interested and young enough to keep him entertained. She was the kind of girl Ethan had always avoided when he was younger; she was certainly nothing like Paula, his first wife. Katie Anne got rowdy, told dirty jokes, and wore sexy underwear. She lived in the guest house on her father's ranch, a beautiful limestone structure with wood-burning fireplaces built against the south slope of one of the highest hills in western Chase County. Tom Mackey, her father, was a fifth-generation rancher whose ancestors had been among the first to raise cattle in the Flint Hills. Tom owned about half the Flint Hills, give or take a few hundred thousand acres, and, rumor had it, about half the state of Oklahoma, and he knew everything there was to know about cattle ranching.

Ethan had found himself drawn to Katie Anne's place; it was like a smaller version of the home he had always dreamed of building in the hills, and he would tear over there in his truck from his law office, his heart full of aching, and then Katie Anne would entertain him with her quick wit and her stock of cold beer and her soft, sexy body, and he would leave in the morning thinking how marvelous she was, with his heart still full and aching.

All that year Ethan had felt a terrible cloud over his head, a psychic weight that at times seemed tangible; he even quit wearing the cross and Saint Christopher's medal his mother had given him when he went away to college his freshman year, as though shedding the gold around his neck might lessen his spiritual burden. If Ethan had dared to examine his conscience honestly he might have eventually come to understand the nature of his malaise, but Katie Anne had come along, and the relief she brought enabled him to skim over the top of those painful months.

Once every two weeks he would visit his father in Abilene; always, on the drive back home, he felt that troubling sensation grow like the cancer that was consuming his father. On several occasions he tried to speak about it to Katie Anne; he ventured very tentatively into these intimate waters with her, for she seemed to dislike all talk about things sad and depressing. He yearned to confess his despair, to understand it and define it, and maybe ease a little the terrible anguish in his heart. But when he would broach the subject, when he would finally begin to say the things that meant something to him, Katie Anne would grow terribly distracted. In the middle of his sentence she would stand up and ask him if he wanted another beer. "I'm still listening," she would toss at him sweetly. Or she would decide to clear the table at that moment. Or set the alarm clock. Mostly, it was her eyes. Ethan was very good at reading eyes. He often wished he weren't. He noticed an immediate change in her eyes, the way they glazed over, pulled her just out of range of hearing as soon as he brought up the subject of his father.

Occasionally, when Ethan would come over straight from a visit to Abilene, she would politely ask about the old man, and Ethan would respond with a terse comment such as, "Well, he's pretty grumpy," or "He's feeling a little better." But she didn't want to hear any more than that, so after a while he quit trying to talk about it. Ethan didn't like Katie Anne very much when her eyes began to dance away from him, when she fidgeted and thought about other things and pretended to be listening, although her eyes didn't pretend very well. And Ethan wanted very much to like Katie Anne. There was so much about her he did like.

Katie Anne, like her father, was devoted to the animals and the prairie lands that sustained them. Her knowledge of ranching almost equaled his. The Mackeys were an intelligent, educated family, and occasionally, on a quiet evening in her parents' company when the talk turned to more controversial issues such as public access to the Flint Hills or environmentalism, she would surprise Ethan with her perspicacity. These occasional glimpses of a critical edge to her mind, albeit all too infrequent, led him to believe there was another side to her nature that could, with time and the right influence, be brought out and nurtured. Right away Ethan recognized her remarkable gift for remaining touchingly feminine and yet very much at ease around the crude, coarse men who populated her world. She was the first ranch hand he had ever watched castrate a young bull wearing pale pink nail polish.

So that summer, while his father lay dying, Ethan and Katie Anne talked about ranching, about the cattle, about the land; they talked about country music, about the new truck Ethan was going to buy. They drank a lot of beer and barbecued a lot of streaks with their friends, and Ethan even got used to watching her dance with other guys at the South Forty, where they spent a lot of time on weekends. Ethan hated to dance, but Katie Ann danced with a sexual energy he had never seen in a woman. She loved to be watched. And she was good. There wasn't a step she didn't know or a partner she couldn't keep up with. So Ethan would sit and drink with his buddies while Katie Anne danced, and the guys would talk about what a goddamn lucky son of a bitch he was.

Then his father died, and although Ethan was with him in those final hours, even though he'd held the old man's hand and cradled his mother's head against his strong chest while she grieved, there nevertheless lingered in Ethan's mind a sense of things unresolved, and Katie Anne, guilty by association, somehow figured into it all.

Three years had passed since then, and everyone just assumed they would be married. Several times Katie Anne had casually proposed dates to him, none of which Ethan had taken seriously. As of yet there was no formal engagement, but Ethan was making his plans. Assiduously, carefully, very cautiously, the way he proceeded in law, he was building the life he had always dreamed of. He had never moved from the rather inconvenient third-floor attic office in the old Salmon P. Chase House that he had leased upon his arrival in Cottonwood Falls, fresh on the heels of his divorce, but this was no indication of his success. His had grown to a shamefully lucrative practice. Chase Countians loved Ethan Brown, not only for his impressive academic credentials and his faultless knowledge of the law, but because he was a man of conscience. He was also a man's man, a strong man with callused hands and strong legs that gripped the flanks of a horse with authority.

Now, at last, his dreams were coming true. From the earnings of his law practice he had purchased his land and was building his house. In a few years he would be able to buy a small herd. It was time to get married.

Two

Ethan pulled the string of barbed wire tight and looped it around the stake he had just pounded back into the ground. It was a windy day and the loose end of wire whipped wildly in his hand. It smacked him across the cheek near his eye and he flinched. He caught the loose end with a gloved hand and finished nailing it down, then he removed his glove and wiped away the warm blood that trickled down his face.

As he untied his horse and swung up into the saddle he thought he caught a whiff of fire. He lifted his head into the wind and sniffed the air, his nostrils twitching like sensitive radar seeking out an intruder. But he couldn't find the smell again. It was gone as quickly as it had come. Perhaps he had only imagined it.

He dug his heels into the horse's ribs and took off at a trot, following the fence as it curved over the hills.

This was not the burning season, and yet the hills seemed to be aflame in their burnished October garb. The copper-colored grasses, short after a long summer's grazing, stood out sharply against the fiercely blue sky. They reminded Ethan of the short-cropped head of a red-haired boy on his first day back at school, all trim and clean and embarrassed.

From the other side of the fence, down the hill toward the highway, came a bleating sound. *Not another one*, he thought. It was past two in the afternoon, and he had a desk piled with work waiting for him in town, but he turned his horse around and rode her up to the top of the hill, where he could see down into the valley below.

He had forgotten all about Emma Fergusen's funeral until that moment when he looked down on the Old Cemetery, an outcropping of modest tombstones circumscribed by a rusty chain-link fence. It stood out in the middle of nowhere; the only access was a narrow blacktop county road. But this afternoon the side of the road was lined with trucks and cars, and the old graves were obscured by mourners of the newly dead. The service was over. As he watched, the cemetery emptied, and within a few minutes there were only the black limousine from the mortuary and a little girl holding the hand of a woman in black who stood looking down into the open grave. Ethan had meant to attend the funeral. He was handling Emma Fergusen's estate and her will was sitting on top of a pile of folders in his office. But the dead calf had seized his attention. The loss, about $500, was Tom Mackey's, but it was all the same to Ethan. Tom Mackey was like a father to him.

Ethan shifted his gaze from the mourners and scanned the narrow stretch of bottomland. He saw the heifer standing in a little tree-shaded gully just below the cemetery. To reach her he would have to jump the fence or ride two miles to the next gate. He guided the mare back down the hill and stopped to study the ground to determine the best place to jump. The fence wasn't high, but the ground was treacherous. Hidden underneath the smooth russet-colored bed of grass lay rock outcroppings and potholes: burrows, dens, things that could splinter a horse's leg like a matchstick, all of them obscured by the deceptive harmony of waving grasses. Ethan found a spot that looked safe but he got down off his horse and walked the approach, just to make sure. He spread apart the barbed wire and slipped through to check out the other side. When he got back up on his horse he glanced down at the cemetery again. He had hoped the woman and child would be gone, but they were still standing by the grave. *That would be Emma's daughter*, he thought in passing. *And her granddaughter*. Ethan's heartbeat quickened but he didn't give himself time to fret. He settled his mind and whispered to his horse, then he kicked her flanks hard, and within a few seconds he felt her pull her forelegs underneath and with a mighty surge of strength from her powerful hind legs sail into the air.

The woman looked up just as the horse appeared in the sky and she gasped. It seemed frozen there in space for the longest time, a black, deep-chested horse outlined against the blue sky, and then hooves hit the ground with a thud, and the horse and rider thundered down the slope of the hill.

"Maman!" cried the child in awe. *"Tu as vu ça?"*

The woman was still staring, speechless, when she heard her father call from the limousine.

"Annette!"

She turned around.

"You can come back another time," her father called in a pinched voice.

Annette took one last look at her mother's grave and knew she would never come back. She held out her hand to her daughter and they walked together to the limousine.

TIME PASSAGES

Our Town

...where love is always right around the corner!

▪ ▪